Critical acclaim for
BAND OF BROTHERS

"It's . . . a first-rate thriller. Ernest K. Gann has simply moved his reminiscences, and his heroes, to the derring-do days of the first transport pilots in the Far East." —*Newsday*

"The pacing of the book . . . the building of suspense, the releases, the rebuilding . . . is expertly done." —*Boston Herald Advertiser*

"A thriller from cover to cover! Gann's ability to tell a story about planes and pilots and flying is unsurpassed. *Band of Brothers* is one you won't want to miss!" —*Aviation Book Club*

"Throughout the story is a nostalgic yearning for those good old days before jet flight when flying was less electronic and more of an adventure, when the toast of the Royal Air Force was 'May the skin of your ass never cover the head of a banjo!'

"For anyone interested in fliers and flying, *Band of Brothers* is a must. As a matter of fact, even if you aren't particularly hooked on the subject, it is still a good novel with interesting characters set against a colorful scene as well as the magnificent panorama of the skies. Unlike his beleaguered man from Manila, Ernie Gann will not let you down in a rice paddy."
—*San Francisco Chronicle & Examiner*

Ernest K. Gann's new mystery thriller!

BAND OF BROTHERS brilliantly captures the excitement and exhilaration of jet-age adventure . . . of the chivalry that exists among men only in the face of danger.

When Alexander Malloy—a legend among pilots since the days of barnstorming and stunt-flying—is blamed for the disastrous Boeing 727 crash en route from Manila to Taiwan, the aviation world is shocked.

Only one man, Lewis Horn, an old flying buddy, is convinced that Chinese officials are engaged in a cover-up. Regardless of the consequences, he resolves to rescue Malloy from prison in Taipei.

For the mission Horn recruits four more pilots . . . to form the **BAND OF BROTHERS!**

By Ernest K. Gann

Band of Brothers

Ernest K. Gann

BALLANTINE BOOKS • NEW YORK

Library of Congress Catalog Card Number: 73-11828

SBN 345-24250-5-150

This edition published by arrangement with Simon and Schuster

First Printing: October, 1974

PRINTED IN CANADA

BALLANTINE BOOKS
A Division of Random House, Inc.
201 East 50th Street, New York, N.Y. 10022
Simultaneously published by
Ballantine Books, Ltd., Toronto Canada

ACKNOWLEDGING . . .

In general the events in this book are fictional. So are the characters.

If both elements ring true, then much of that atmosphere is due to the patient tolerance of my many friends in the profession.

Old comrade Tom Boyd eased the way from the beginning. Then there was René Lim Robertson, and various of her relations, who so long ago revealed to me certain faults and attributes of the Oriental mind and way.

At what was once the most famous aerodrome in the world, a place called Croydon, a fine gathering of English air nobility was arranged by BOAC's T. E. Scott-Chard. Included were Captains A. L. Wilcockson (OBE), Ronald Ballantine, and G. H. Easton. Before and after that gathering there was always the superb inspiration of my friend Captain O. P. Jones (OBE).

And also in England I am indebted to Hugh Field and Ann Tilbury of the magazine *Flight,* and to Jack Nelson Sullivan for research.

In France there was that devoted historian Henri Beaubois, and those Air France stalwarts Commandant Jean Dabry and George Libert. Their warmth and dedication to my curiosity quite removed the stains left by the officiousness of their mother airline.

In Belgium there was the energetic André Seydel to display Sabena; Alfred van Hoorebeck, the historian, to set me straight on details; and the very formidable Pilote de Ligne George Jaspis, whose high spirits lofted me into previously unknown skies.

In Germany Horst Burgsmüller of Lufthansa persuaded two very fine airmen that my project was worth their time and attention. They were the famous Captain Rudolph Mayr, whose career since a very young man has been soaked in adventure. There was also his frequent comrade Franz Preuschoff, whose devotion to accuracy as an aviation historian now equals his former dedication as a flight engineer.

The ground, water, and sky of Holland have long been familiar to me and so have the aerial affairs of KLM. I salute the memory of my friendship with the late Captain William van Veenendaal, who so vividly represented that peculiar dignity which KLM pilots once carried over half the world. And my flying comrade Major General Alfred Kalberer (Ret.), who once flew for KLM, deserves my everlasting thanks for his continuous sympathy and cornucopia of information.

Many other "pilots of the line" have contributed both knowingly and unwittingly to this work. Captain Ed Mack Miller arranged for me to "fly" the pertinent approach in a 727 simulator. Captain Jack Leffler of United was always willing to dig up oddments of detail which otherwise could not have been included. There was Captain Bob Heard of Northwest and Captains Van Ausdell and Schreffler of TWA. And Senior Test Pilot Donald Knutson of Boeing, who first checked the manuscript.

Herewith my gratitude to a whole tribe of airmen all over the world who have troubled to confide in me and who I know are generous enough to forgive if I have not separately called their names.

Ernest K. Gan
San Juan Island

May it be granted to thee to alight upon the waters of the beautiful west and to sail to thy place . . .

—from an Egyptian manuscript, 1500 B.C.

May the skin of your ass never cover the head of a banjo!

—old RAF toast

FOR THE INFORMATION OF THE AUTHORITIES

QUALIFICATIONS:

CAPT. WILLIAM OLIVER CHATSWORTH, OBE (British Passport)

BORN: Beckenham, Kent, England. RESIDES: Didcot, Berks
EDUCATED: Beckenham Grammar School
EMPLOYMENT: Pilot Imperial Airways (later BOAC) 1932–present
SERVICE AND LICENSE: North Atlantic, Continental, Middle East, and Far East routes. Currently qualified on Canadian CL 44, Comet 4, Boeing 707. Master Pilot. Special assignments include Royal Aircraft establishment, Farnsborough. Total: 32,000 flight hours

CAPT. JAN ANTON VAN GROOTES (Dutch Passport)

BORN: Vlaardingen, Holland. RESIDES: The Hague
EMPLOYMENT: Command Pilot KLM (Koninklijke Luchtvaart Maatschappij)
SERVICE: European–East Indies route. North Atlantic. Member KLM Technical Research Bureau. Total: 24,000 flight hours
LANGUAGES: Dutch, French, German, English

CAPT. ÉTIENNE DIDEROT (French Passport)

BORN: Marseilles, France. RESIDES: Brussels, Belgium

EDUCATION, Primary and Secondary: Brazzaville, Congo. University Toulouse

EMPLOYMENT: Sabena Airlines. Qualified Europe and East Africa routes all current equipment. Presently flying Boeing 707s Brussels–Johannesburg. Total: 10,000 flight hours (approx.)

CAPT. KARL WILLIE MOLLER (West German Passport)

BORN: Zeppelinheim, Germany.   RESIDES: Frankfurt

EMPLOYMENT: Lufthansa Airlines. Senior Pilot. Currently qualified on Boeing 707 and 727. North and South Atlantic routes. Europe and South America. Total flight hours: 18,000 +

CAPT. LEWIS HORN (U.S.A. Passport)

BORN: St. Paul, Minnesota.   RESIDES: Manhasset, New York

EDUCATION: University of Minnesota

EMPLOYMENT: Trans-Atlantic Airways. License ATR 366311. Currently qualified on Douglas DC-8, Boeing 720 b, Boeing 727. North Atlantic and Caribbean routes. Total flight hours: 11,000 +

Our desire is to cooperate fully with the officials involved. Further details will be made available if required.

1

Mr. Wellington Kee was very proud of his status as one of the senior controllers at Taipei International Airport. He was also pleased with his salary, which was a great deal more than most Chinese were able to capture during these discouraging times when the aging Chiang was still rating about reconquering mainland China. All thinking people knew this was political nonsense, but they knew better than to say so if they worked for the government.

Mr. Wellington Kee was a small round man with a face like an overripe apple. He was bald and meticulous of manner. His command of English, the international language of aviation, plus a favorable word from a distant relative in the Executive Yuan, accounted for his original hiring by the Civil Aeronautics Administration of the Chinese Republic.

Now on this humid October night Wellington Kee made a loud sucking noise as he sipped at the teacup he had placed beside his microphone. He sucked and watched the occasional spewings against the tower windows of rain which gathered into rivulets and distorted the view beyond. On clearer nights he normally enjoyed a sweeping view from his 110-foot-high perch. Beyond the perimeter and runway lights lay the city of Taipei itself, glittering in the night with promises of easily imaginable delights. At his back there was a considerable area of unlighted shadow, which would be the Keelung River and the hills to the north. Across the river and a considerable distance to the west he could see the pagodalike Grand Hotel, which was built on the side of a hill. Sometimes the hotel appeared to

1

hang from the heavens in more ways than one, for government employees of Wellington Kee's civil status could only speculate upon the extravagant entertainments which must take place within such a splendid building. Only tourists and very great officials could afford to be at ease within its rather complex and expensive environs.

Air traffic had been sparse this night, and the lack of activity had brought a nearly overwhelming sense of ennui upon Wellington Kee. There had been one flight earlier in the evening from Hong Kong, one from Guam, and two more within the past hour from Tokyo. Now until the end of his shift only one flight was scheduled. That would be Far Eastern's flight three coming north from Manila, and Wellington Kee could hardly wait for a hand-off from Approach Control once the aircraft had arrived within the control area.

Even as he yawned and stretched his arms as high above his head as he could reach and then stood on tiptoe for as long as his balance held, he heard Approach Control acknowledging flight three's arrival over Taoyuan at eleven thousand feet. That would be over a navigational aid about twenty miles southwest of the airport. As he listened to the flat tones of the squawk box reciting flight three's clearance for descent, Kee continued to stretch and calculated he had approximately five minutes before his part in the routine performance.

Every man of technical status in government service had an assistant, and Wellington Kee had two. Now he nodded to the white shirts that marked their location in the gloom of the darkened tower and said in his thick Fukien dialect, "Bring up the approach lights and give me a ceiling and visibility estimate. I want you to reach your estimates individually."

While he waited for their judgments, which he expected to find in at least small error (otherwise why was he in charge?), he made a considerable business of tapping the glass face of the altimeter on the console before him and reading the barometric pressure.

He sucked again at his teacup while he listened to the squawk box. He was pleased to compare his own slightly accented English with that of the approach controller, and he judged his own diction definitely superior. He heard the approach controller clear Far Eastern flight three for an automatic direction finder approach to Taipei Airport and he heard the customary advice to call Taipei tower upon passing the outer marker. He listened to the acknowledgments and clearance repetitions transmitted by flight three and decided his own English was better than that of the first officer or the flight engineer, whichever was doing the talking. The captain of course would be an American, as were all Far Eastern's, and his voice would be easily recognizable.

Wellington Kee listened more attentively while flight three reported approaching the outer marker and requested a change to tower frequency. When it was granted he put down his cup and addressed the microphone. He waited patiently. No aircraft would have to wait for a reply from Taipei tower if Kee was on duty.

"Taipei tower. . . . Far Eastern three."

"Roger, Far Eastern three," Wellington Kee said carefully. "Continue approach to runway ten. Wind zero eight zero at ten knots. Altimeter two nine five five. Report approach lights in sight."

Flight three acknowledged the advice and silence once more enwrapped the darkened tower. Kee broke it with a final slurp at his tea. Then his assistants said they were ready with their weather observations—ceiling overcast three thousand with lower scattered clouds one thousand. Light to moderate rain with visibility two to three miles. Kee grunted his approval. Their conclusions were comfortably close to his own.

Kee waited and still there was only silence. He squirmed in his chair and heard it scrape against the cement floor. He watched the anemometer climb to fifteen knots and then subside. It brought a soft yet audible lashing of raindrops against the windows.

Kee noted it was near the end of his shift, and he was momentarily annoyed that his relief had not as yet appeared. Or perhaps he was waiting in the darkness behind him?

He turned to look at the doorway. It was not only securely locked at all times but guarded by a soldier on the outside, as was every other vital facility about the airport. For, Kee reminded himself wistfully, his country was more than technically at war with Mao's communist bandits and apparently would be forever.

Disappointed at the lack of activity in the vicinity of the door, he looked out toward the west, where he now might reasonably expect to find the running lights of Far Eastern three. Had they ignored his request to report the runway approach lights in sight? If so he would consider filing a report against the American captain. Almost at once he decided against such action, since it would involve a great deal of paperwork. There was no other traffic, so the American captain could hardly be accused of creating a dangerous situation.

Once more he studied the windows to the west and saw only rain dribbling across a black sky. He turned to the white shirt on his right. "What time did you record our last transmission?"

"Eight nineteen."

Four minutes had gone by since then. Certainly flight three must have passed the outer marker? Kee cleared his throat and pressed his microphone button.

"Far Eastern three . . . Taipei tower. Have you passed the outer marker?"

Silence. Kee frowned. There was a faint note of annoyance in his voice when he spoke again. "Far Eastern three? Do you have the runway lights in sight? Say your position."

Silence.

"Far Eastern three . . . Taipei tower. If you read me show a light."

Kee decided that the Boeing must have experienced total radio failure. Given all the back-ups and redundancies in a jet airliner's electrical system, it was a situation that simply could not happen.

He pressed the switch on the squawk box and addressed his colleague in Approach Control. "Have you had any contact with Far Eastern's flight three since the hand-off?"

"Negative."

"Thanks. Please check Center and see if they've heard anything."

"Will do."

Wellington Kee was becoming increasingly uneasy.

This sort of thing had never happened before. Airliners just didn't vanish in the night—especially on final approach.

"Far Eastern flight three. Do you read Taipei tower on one one eight decimal one?"

He continued calling and searching the sky for four additional minutes. Quite to his surprise he found that his heart was beating with ever-increasing tempo, and the tea he had consumed had transformed itself into a flood of perspiration.

Wellington Kee rose to take a final look into the western darkness and, seeing nothing, leaned down until his wet face was close to the squawk box. He pressed the switch reluctantly.

"Tower here. I think we have a serious problem."

Y. K. Tien enjoyed several blood connections within the government. He had two cousins in the Legislative Yuan, an uncle in Customs, and another uncle in the Ministry of Communications who had been particularly helpful. It was thanks to him that Y. K. Tien had been appointed official photographer to the Ministry, a job not overly demanding and thus well suited to Tien's mild character. He sat for days, sometimes for more than a week, without any demand being made for his services, but the possibility that he might be considered a drone had never troubled him. There were countless people employed within the various government offices who did nothing at all.

Tien was a small man with a potbelly which projected forward and hung down from his waistline like a marsupial pouch. When he was required to perform, he normally photographed the installation of new transformers, downed power lines, new type insulators or telephonic equipment, and sometimes special circuitry for techinical reference and study. His photographs were usually in focus but not much more, since he had little interest in his profession.

Like so many Chinese, Tien was a realist and, recognizing his limitations, was content to enjoy the vicarious thrills he found in the creations of others. Perhaps that is why he was an avid philatelist and longed for a small store of his own where he could deal in beautiful stamps.

There was considerable appreciation of all beautiful things locked in Tien's most inner being, and he was deeply distressed at the ugly task assigned him on an otherwise lovely morning. He had been roused from his slumbers long before dawn and transported by government car to the plateau which rose west of the city. Arriving just as the sun was melting away the mist which lay over a rice paddy, he was directed to photograph everything within range of his lens.

The perimeter of the paddy was lined with peasants who stood and pointed and squatted and spit and groaned and fell silent as they watched the revelations of disaster. Soldiers were everywhere, and it seemed to Tien they interfered more than helped with the removal of bodies from the wreckage which rested in the shallow water of the paddy.

At first Tien's task was not too unbearable, although he disliked removing his shoes and rolling up his pants so he could wade through the muck and photograph the aircraft's tail section, which lay some distance from the main wreckage.

The tall tail rose at an angle toward the clear blue sky, and Tien saw how the tip of it glistened in the first of the sun. One of the men probing about its conical base recognized him and insisted he photograph the black box which he held in his muddy hands. Tien learned he was a technician from the Aeronautics Administration, and he said the box was a recorder which contained the last communications between the aircraft and the ground in addition to whatever orders or comments the crew might have exchanged. They agreed it was a marvelous device, and Tien's mannerisms as he set about photographing the box suggested his own very important connection with it. Since he assumed all of the crew were dead, it suddenly occurred to him that the image of the black box he saw on the camera's ground glass had an eerie quality. And why not? Within that small receptacle were stored forever the voices of men who would never be heard again. He photographed it first as found, with muddy exterior, and then again after the technician had cleaned it.

Next Tien sloshed across the paddy and photographed the main wreckage from several angles. He was relieved that the firemen and military rescue teams who disappeared and reappeared within the great broken shell of metal did not find anything while his lens was pointed in their direction.

Finally he crossed the paddy to the opposite side, where he photographed a piece of wing and a single engine which had somehow broken away and was buried partway in the surrounding dike. It was here that he was discovered by his supervisor, who told him to come at once to the dike on the opposite side. It was extremely important, he declared, and there must be no delay.

Tien suspected the origin of his supervisor's demand and did his best to comply. Holding his camera high lest he splash it with water, he tried to set a fast pace across the paddy. But it was like moving in a dream, so as he approached the dike and saw what he knew he would see, he moved ever more slowly. Even the angry urgings of his supervisor echoing clearly across the water failed to increase his pace.

Tien shut one eye and hid his other behind the camera's viewfinder. He tried to think of the images he observed on the ground glass as remote things, not parts of humans like himself who only a few hours before had various functions to perform. Under the direction of his supervisor he focused on nakedness askew, and ruptured spleens, and smashed heads in want of a body. These things, buzzing with flies, were arranged all along the length of the dike like broken toys on a shelf, and even as he worked Tien saw the rescue teams were bringing more.

By the time he was finished the sun was searing hot, and Tien was trembling so much that in order to avoid a fuzzy negative he was obliged to greatly increase the shutter speed of his camera. His supervisor, whose dedication to the gruesome task seemed to magnify when they were joined by an Army officer, kept fanning the flies away from each object and cautioning Tien repeatedly of the necessity for clarity and detail.

Finally they were done, and as he put away his camera Tien ventured to inquire if anyone had survived the crash.

"Yes. All but one of the crew."

"No others?"

"Yes. But how many I cannot say. They were taken away first to the hospitals."

His chief then said that if Tien was sure he had photographed everything he could go.

Tien turned his back on the scene and half ran to the end of the dike. Once there, he paused in the shade of a group of trees and tried to vomit. But he had not eaten since the evening before and his efforts produced only a dry hacking. Bending over, he stared at the dark blotches his spittle had made upon the ocher earth, and suddenly he wanted nothing more of his life than to hear the birds in the trees above him.

October 15, 1963

CIVIL AERONAUTICS ADMINISTRATION
MINISTRY OF COMMUNICATIONS

ACCIDENT
FAR EASTERN AIRWAYS BOEING 727

CONFIDENTIAL   (Translation)

1. Prior to accident aircraft was certified airworthy. See log, documents, and overhaul data, 1963.

2. Weather analysis: Temperature, atmospheric pressure, and wind velocity at time of crash would dismiss any possibility of violent turbulence or other harmful meteorological phenomena. Thus accident not caused by weather factors.

See pertinent meteorology data October 5–7, 1963.

3. Two hours before and after subject accident a total of five aircraft landed at Taipei International Airport. Thus accident not due to any failure in instrument landing system.

See traffic record, Customs and Immigration forms, October 5, 1963, 1900–2300 hrs.

4. According to voice recordings, normal contacts were maintained between aircraft and Air Traffic Control. No errors were made. Thus accident not due to any fault of ATC personnel.

See pertinent recording tapes #607–42, 607–43, 1900–2300 hrs., October 5, 1963.

5. CONCLUSION: Captain Alexander Malloy, American citizen (Work Permit #87426), was in com-

mand of the flight. Captain Malloy did misjudge his approach to the outer marker and ignored available radio navigational aids. His approach to Taipei Airport was much below the required altitude and the aircraft struck the ground approximately 12 miles southwest of the runway. The accident was therefore due to pilot negligence.

DISTRIBUTION:
AACL: MGDR (via President)
SAP
SAFE
AVP
FILE (4)
CB

The apartment on the Ile de la Cité was so old the parquet floors rose and fell as if under the influence of a distant ocean, but the commanding view across the Seine toward the Left Bank made such a residence nearly priceless to those who still valued Old World Charm combined with a chic address.

Each time he flew to Paris and found an excuse to visit his friends, Captain Lew Horn made a secret wager with himself that the fragile *ascenseur* which hoisted him from ground level to the apartment would refuse its duty. Smiling fondly upon its antiquity, he often wondered if his 180 pounds plus suitcase and flight kit would not exceed its gross take-off capability.

He moved with great natural dignity, and yet any suggestion of the pompous was instantly denied by the wry amusement in his eyes. His features were devoid of excess flesh, hard-cut, and reflecting about the set of his mouth a life of special responsibility. His eyebrows, heavy twin hedges flecked with gray, plainly signaled his enjoyment of challenge.

At present Captain Horn was a very unhappy man. A divorce, he had recently discovered, was a far more traumatic experience than he had ever imagined. To his friends Geoff and Dorothy, who owned the apartment, he explained, "This is not one of my regular Paris flights. The line has given me a leave, so if you don't object, I may stay more than a night or two. Barbara and I have decided to part company while we are still friends. I suppose it was my fault because I have been away so much and there were no children to hold us together."

It was typical of Geoff and Dorothy, he thought, that they would at first make no further inquiries. Instead they had inaugurated a tour of the Parisian galleries, for they knew that if there was one thing other than flying itself capable of recharging Horn's spirits, it was painting. He could become utterly lost in a good exhibition, and his own skyscapes in oil and watercolor revealed a surprising sensitivity.

"It is something I'm saving for my retirement instead of money," he had told them quietly. "I intend to become a painter, clumsy as my present work may be."

"At least you have twenty years to improve," Geoff had once commented after studying several of his North Atlantic skies.

"How do you know he won't someday hang in the Louvre?" Dorothy had asked.

"Because there isn't a tree in the whole complex big enough for the job. Thank God he doesn't fly like he paints."

These, Horn had decided, were the kind of friends he needed when what had been the good life suddenly spun out of control. Had it been only a week since Brewster had summoned him to the office from which he directed the overseas flight operations of his airline?

Brewster had closed the door, offered a cigar which was refused, and assumed his confidential pilot-to-pilot pose. "Have a good trip?"

"Thunderstorms all around Paris. Once we cleared them, fine weather all the way. The winds forecast was wrong as usual, so we were ten minutes late."

"Don't try to snow me. You were lost," Brewster stated with a half smile.

"How did you know?"

"I know innumerable things. They include such information as your taking three of your stewardesses for a midnight swim in the fountain beneath the Eiffel Tower. The gendarmes' report is even more explicit than the photo stories in *Figaro* and the *Paris-Soir*." Brewster held up a paper and shook it as if it was contaminated. "Our people in advertising spend hundreds of thousands every year to assure the traveling public our captains are supercautious, square-jawed, eagle-eyed father images. You don't make it any easier for them."

Horn wanted to say he regretted the incident. It had been a hot and muggy night, the plaza beneath the tower was deserted, and only one of the stewardesses had disrobed completely. He decided to remain silent out of deference to his superior.

Brewster was a man pushing sixty very hard, one of the real old-timers from Douglas DC-2 days when the whole line cheered if all fourteen seats in one airplane were booked. His battered face betrayed every minute of a very hard life aloft as well as on the ground, and his always melancholy eyes seemed perpetually yearning for a return of more exciting times. Horn was convinced that soon he would accept a retirement gift watch from the company and would then, like a very old elephant, just go away to a remote place and die. Watching his tormented eyes that afternoon, Horn realized that he loved the man, as did most of Brewster's captains. He knew no hours, his job was his life, and Horn thought he must be very lonely.

"As if your recent Parisian caper were not enough," Brewster intoned, "I am adding to your remarkable file this further report." He held up another paper. "It states that on a routine test flight exactly ten days ago you executed a slow roll in the Boeing 727 which this company entrusted to your tender mercies."

"It was an impulse. I asked the crew if they minded and they said go right ahead. We made sure everything was tied down—"

"Thumbing through your file, I am impressed by what is *not* included. I am personally aware that you have received two speeding tickets within the past few months and that you drove a formula one racing car at Mineola during the June Rally and furthermore won with an average speed of one hundred and thirty-four point five miles per hour. When your victory was announced over the public address system and in the newspapers, you were identified as a captain of this line. I again wonder how the image of a staid, reliable aircraft commander suffered in our customers' eyes."

"Would it have been better if I had come in last?"

Brewster ignored him as he ruffled through additional papers. "You own an aerobatic airplane, and on April tenth last year received a citation from the FAA for performing aerobatics at an illegal altitude in the vicinity of Farmingdale, Long Island. The altitude was stated as fifty feet. Three years ago while you were still flying first officer you were involved in a sordid tavern brawl which resulted in injury to an unidentified man."

"He was drunk and threw a glass of beer in my wife's face. What would you have done?"

Brewster doubled his frecked fists and placed them deliberately on the file before him. "What am I going to do with you, Horn? As a pilot, I am willing to concede you have class. You pass your flight checks with grades no one can match. But you're a goddamned maverick and the days for mavericks in this business are long gone. There is no room for your kind in a modern airline. And another thing —" Brewster relaxed his fists and an unusual softness came to his eyes—"it is one of those things so far not in your file."

Horn sensed his discomfort when he said, "I understand you and Barbara are having a problem."

"Is there a married couple that doesn't?"

"You know as well as I do that a man with emotional problems has no business flying a hundred and eighty passengers across the ocean or anywhere else for that matter."

"I keep my ground life and my flying life separated."

"Nonsense. Certain things just won't stay on the ground. They haunt a man no matter where he is. I don't like it and the company doesn't like it, and because I don't want a hassle with your union I am going to make a mandatory suggestion upon which I expect you to act as the sensible man I wish you were."

"I can't decide if you're going for my throat or my groin."

Suddenly Horn remembered a memo which had been part of the company's recent paper blizzard. It was, he decided, beautiful evidence of the company's indifference to the flight records of those pioneers who had flown through the early days and made the aviation industry a safe nest for vice presidents.

". . . regarding the company presentation of retirement watches. It should be distinctly understood that the gift is *only* of the Accutron astronaut watch itself. If you wish a medallion the cost is $13.00, and pilots must make their own arrangements for engraving."

"Why don't you take a trip?" Brewster was saying.

"I'm sleepy. I've been up all night herding a flying machine across the ocean. With three round trips to Paris I've done enough traveling for this month."

"Go to some place off our routes. There's always South America."

"I hate South America."

"How about South Africa? You can get an interline pass. It will cost you only a few dollars."

"I don't like apartheid."

"Jesus, you're hard to please. How about Scandinavia?"

"I've spent so much time in the Tivoli Gardens I feel like one of the performers. The Danes and the Norwegians are fine people, but I can't stand the arrogance of the Swedes."

"You're a bigot."

"Granted. Now can I go home and get some sleep?"

"You haven't got a home to go to and you know it. In my desk there is a carbon of a company pass you signed, which proves that Barbara has gone to Mexico City. Make it easy for me, will you? How about two months fishing in New Zealand? An old chum of mine is still flying down there and he knows where—"

"Make what easy for you?"

Brewster poked a heavy finger at Horn, aiming it at the end of his nose. "Captain Horn, I am trying to notify you as gently as your hard head permits that you are taking a two-month voluntary leave of absence whether you want to or not."

Thanks."

"When you return we will hope that your personal troubles will have subsided and will no longer threaten even potential distraction. Do you want me to put it into a memo for you?"

"No. I have received the message."

"I had hoped you would see things my way."

Now, studying the mauve morning light which splayed upon the rooftops of Paris, Horn wondered if he dared attempt to capture it on paper. He had brought his watercolors along, hoping they would lure his thoughts away from Barbara and his own failures in her behalf. The plan so far had not worked.

"I can't seem to develop much enthusiasm for anything," he had told Geoff.

"Don't let all those things her lawyer says depress you. It's routine to label you as cruel and inhuman."

Reading the interlocutory decree, Dorothy quoted, "It says here you are fiscally irresponsible?"

"That refers to my paying fifteen thousand dollars for an aerobatic airplane."

"Don't you get enough flying?"

"That little airplane seems to bleed off some of the orneriness in me. Barbara thought I should use the money to buy more life insurance."

"What's this reference in paragraph six about being *indolent?*"

"That refers to my sleeping during the daytime. Our Paris flights take off from New York at night. I like to take a long nap before departure."

"Your metabolisms were ill matched," Dorothy said as she lifted page after page of the legal brief. "And what's this about being antisocial? Did you beat her?"

"Every time one of her family dropped by for a visit, I hid all the whiskey except for about two inches in one bottle. I have never seen people who could put away so much when the price was right."

"And mental harassment?"

"We took a trip to Honolulu. We were going to bed after a party and she came out of the bathroom with her face packed in some kind of cosmetic mud she had bought over there. I didn't really mean it quite the way it sounded when I told her she looked like a pig at a luau, but it didn't go over very well."

During the ensuing silence Geoff made an elaborate show of replenishing his brandy.

"And then, of course, there is Orville Wright. Barbara hated him on sight."

Geoff wanted to know what the Wright brothers had to do with his marital difficulties. He was under the impression they were gone to a pioneers' reward.

"Orville Wright is my mynah bird. I had a charter flight to India about a year ago and picked him up then. We seem to understand each other. There were times when Barbara complained I talked more to Orville than I did to her."

"Maybe you had more in common," Dorothy said.

"Now, now," Geoff reprimanded gently.

The next morning Horn decided that Brewster had been right. He was finding it difficult to think about anything except divorce.

He heard Rosalie the Spanish maid call softly to him, and he turned to see his breakfast set upon a small table opposite the fireplace. She smiled and held out a copy of the Paris *Herald*. As he sat down she poured his tea and lifted a silver cover to display two warm brioches. At least, he thought, although he had sometimes forgotten to pick up the little things in Paris that Barbara invariably wanted, he had always remembered Rosalie's requests from the opposite side of the ocean. She was passionately fond of American country music, preferably if some wandering cowboy was looking for a full belly and a place to tie his horse. Horn had often wondered what visions her mind constructed while she listened to the twanging voices in a language she could not understand. Was there some secret communication between the lonely of all nations?

He opened the paper and spread it beside his plate. He instantly recognized a familiar face staring defiantly from the front page. He caught his breath as he read the caption beneath the photograph: AIRLINE CAPTAIN TO CHINESE PRISON.

The story filed in Taipei told in frustrating generalities how Captain Alex Malloy had been in command of a Far Eastern jet which "fell out of the sky" on approaching Taipei Airport. Fourteen passengers including one crew member had been killed and forty-six injured. Captain Malloy had been charged with "criminal negligence" by the Chinese. He was now awaiting sentence in a Taipei hospital where he was recovering from minor injuries.

Horn shook his head in disbelief and quickly reread the story. Even as he did so visions of his boyhood competed with the sketchy details for his attention.

The first time he had seen Alex Malloy he had been only eight years old. Now on a Paris morning with his untouched breakfast before him it seemed he could once again hear Malloy's basso profundo voice dominating the rest of the church choir, and even more vividly he remembered that unforgettable moment when he had been introduced to the man who had flown longer than Horn had yet lived.

When Alex Malloy had taken his hand and squeezed it firmly, both a permanent hero and his own career had been born. For the time had been 1931, a vintage year for aeronautical swashbuckling, and Malloy was then employed by the newly formed Northwest Airlines flying the mails and occasional passengers between St. Paul and Chicago. Horn had heard of Malloy's comrades, a lusty, recalcitrant lot. Flying for the several infant airlines, they established their own legends and stylishly filled the empty niche left by Pony Express riders.

By his tenth birthday Horn could recite the names of all the fliers whose names, like Lindbergh's, sparkled temporarily in the skies, some fakers, some dreamers, and some who were only desperate for fame. There were Coste and Bellonte, the Frenchmen who flew the Atlantic; and Kingsford-Smith, the Australian who flew the Pacific. There were many women who also sought fame in a dangerous fashion—Phoebe Omlie, Louise Thaden, Elsie MacKay, Blanche Noyes, Maryse Bastil, and Madeline Charnaux of France and Elly Beinhorn and Hanna Reitsch of Germany—names made by their owners and collected by young Lewis Horn as his playmates collected stamps.

He had also collected photographs of the aircraft flown by Alex Malloy and his kind: the Lairds and Boeing Monomails; the Swallows, which were wholly unsuited to Varney's western mountain routes; the Travel-Airs, which were not much better; and the tri-motor Fords which simultaneously tested a man's patience and muscles. The fortunate pilots on TAT (Transcontinental Air Transport) flew the sleek Northrop Alphas, which were long ahead of their day, while the less blessed American Airways pilots flew Pitcairns and Stinsons and Fairchilds.

Horn smiled when he remembered how he had so often aimed his bicycle toward the Mississippi River bank which had become St. Paul's airport. If he was lucky he might find Alex Malloy, who always seemed to have time for schoolboys.

"Hey, stork legs! *You* again? Sit down. We'll hangar-fly a while."

Then Malloy would tell of his life aloft. For young Horn, listening to his voice was like actually sweating or freezing in an open cockpit, and there were moments when he thought he could hear the full-throated sound of a Liberty engine. His eager mind absorbed every detail of troubled flights when awkward combinations of weather or mechanical failures caused Alex and his comrades to abandon their craft and take to their parachutes. He learned that such drastic methods were not normal and, unless the situation was obviously hopeless, were considered bad manners. He learned the terminology of flight along with special profanities, and one magic afternoon Malloy had clamped an oversize helmet on his head and taken him aloft in a Laird Speedwing. Afterward there was never any question as to what Horn would do with his life.

Horn read the story once again, seeking a few clues which might better explain what had happened. "*Criminal negligence?*" It was preposterous. No pilot in the history of aviation had ever been so charged. Since every pilot was himself sitting in the front of the aircraft, such an accusation assumed he was suicidal or hopelessly out of his wits.

Horn was very aware that his was still an extraordinarily proud profession—a throwback if only because so few were drawn to it by money alone. Men like Alex Malloy had long ago established certain traditions, and a man who habitually betrayed them did not last very long. A careless pilot, an exhibitionist, a man who drank late and addressed himself to the task next morning, or even a man who momentarily lost controls of his thinking in a tight spot soon found himself ostracized and eventually nudged or pushed into another way of life.

Horn had little sympathy for the minority who exploited the sky as a tradesman does his shop. It saddened him to watch such individuals make a landing which they managed with barely passable skill. Once the engines were shut down the same type would invariably walk away without so much as a backward glance at the great bird which had allowed him to accomplish a minor miracle.

"The bastard is more interested in his golf game than he is in passing a good flight check," Brewster would complain. "He flies like a zombie."

Men of Brewster's era and Alex Malloy's—men who had begun their careers in frail craft of wood, wire, and fabric and continued straight on through to jets—were easily incensed at latecomers who took flying for granted. They would say, "When handling an aircraft, caress it, don't rape it!" Yet as electronics and computers took over, their words were less heeded; and the very young men, blinded by ever-increasing complication, were also troubled because they could not understand how there could be a sentimental relationship between man and machine.

Certainly, Horn thought, Alex Malloy would be the last man flying to be negligent. And "criminal negligence" was in this case accusing him of mass murder. What had really happened?

Geoff had already gone to the office and Dorothy, who avoided breakfast, was still in their bedroom.

As he strode to the telephone, Horn became increasingly determined. Since his promotion to captain, word had passed from one crew member to another: ". . . If Horn's face begins to look like it belongs on Mount Rushmore, beware. You've just done something very wrong."

During a recent transatlantic flight a new and overbold crew member had relayed the comment to Horn. Without troubling to smile, Horn had said, "A man named Malloy once told me I was not in command of an aircraft to win a popularity contest. The less I allow you to get away with up here the better captain you'll make someday. If you allow yourself to make little errors, sooner or later you'll start making big ones, which may lead to your killing some people—including yourself."

Waiting for Geoff to come to the telephone, Horn reflected that it had been two years since he had heard from Alex Malloy—a brief letter telling of his marriage to a Chinese girl named, incongruously, *Sylvia*.

"Geoff? I have a problem. I want to call Taipei, New York, and maybe London, Frankfurt, and Amsterdam on your phone."

"I should have known better than to let you in the house."

"How do I pay you?"

"Madame and I accept money of any kind, even a check with the name Horn on it."

"It might bounce. Barbara and I had a joint account and I have no way of knowing what she has been doing to it the last few weeks."

"Charge it to therapy."

"A friend of mine is in deep trouble—"

"Good. That's what you need."

He placed the first call to the operations manager of Far Eastern Airways in Taipei, and while he waited for the connection he made a list of several names. They were all men he knew had flown with Alex Malloy at one time or another. The four prefixed by crosses would be his first choices—Diderot of Air France, Moller of Lufthansa, Chatsworth of BOAC, and van Grootes of KLM.

He left the telephone and began to pace between the windows overlooking a Paris he no longer saw and the table where his breakfast had turned cold. As he thought about Alex Malloy and rapidly refined his plan, he rejoiced in the sensation of once again being his own man.

2

Aviation news, regardless of its reliability, can travel around the world in less than twenty-four hours. What happened in Bangkok at midnight may be recounted by a crew member in Tokyo the following morning, or in Athens, or Cairo. Rumors fly with very nearly the speed of a jet transport; thus when the Chinese civil court moved in on Malloy's disaster, innumerable reports began circulating among international crews.

It was said that the accident investigation had been rigged. Word was passed that the hearing court displayed a total lack of comprehension when the vital technical points of the accident were introduced. Malloy was already in prison. In spite of his injuries he had been forced to stand throughout his trial. The Chinese prosecutor repeatedly held gory photographs of the crash victims before his eyes. There was even one wild rumor that Malloy had been summarily shot.

As the telephone tolls mounted, Horn managed a wry smile when he realized that with his interline reduction he could have flown to Taipei for less.

Dorothy arranged an appointment with a French lawyer who had lived in Taiwan. Horn was astounded to learn that juries did not exist, and while a defendant was not officially held to be guilty until proven innocent, in practice the mood of the court often was the converse. A procurator argued the case for the court and the defendant was usually required to stand throughout. Three judges reached a verdict after hearing the evidence provided by both the procurator and the defense lawyer. If found guilty, appeals were possible, but almost never successful.

Horn found his total effort both discouraging and inspiring. And, he thought, a lesson in the humanities.

A pilot in Kansas City had been particularly outspoken. "I'm not surprised Malloy is in a jam. I always did think he'd kill a lot of people someday. It was only a question of where and when. Alex is one of those pig-headed old-timers who still flies by the seat of his pants. They should have jerked his license long ago."

After this rebuff Horn made a local call to a man who flew for Air France. Alex had given him his original checkout in Boeing 707s.

"Of course . . . Malloy. I was very fond of him, yes. But I do not think it is any business of mine, you understand? Bad luck, yes. But I suppose it was inevitable, yes?" He refused to say why he thought a disaster inevitable, and the conversation came to nothing.

Or had it? Horn wondered. If his plan were to have any substance, then only the bare truths counted. Those who joined him must sift every factor whether based on grudge or not.

He finally got through to Taipei. Sheldon Spencer, Far Eastern Airways' operations manager, was cold and uncommunicative. He refused to state any opinion on the crash except to say it had been thoroughly investigated by the Chinese Civil Aeronautics Administration. Their findings had confirmed that nothing had been wrong with the aircraft itself. Pressed for his estimate of the "criminal negligence" charge, he stated that the judges were still deliberating and a verdict would soon be announced. The conversation was terminated so abruptly Horn was left staring at the dead instrument in his hand.

An unexpected reaction came from Brewster in New York.

"I've known that wonderful old bastard for years. He was flying Fords out of Chicago while I was pushing Fokkers out of Memphis to Dallas. Good pilot but always in some kind of trouble, which is why he has had so many jobs. Hell, Alex and I and a few other hard-nosed characters founded the Airline Pilots Association. Finally brought in Behncke to run it for us. Almost got fired myself for messing in that. If you take my advice you'll steer clear of this thing. Go to the Riviera and start a new life. There's something called the Club Méditerranée—"

Horn told him how much Alex had done for him—as his first teacher, his first captain and mentor. "I feel I owe him for the best part of my life," he insisted.

"Better just write him a letter and say you're sorry."

"Boss, that doesn't sound like you. I need all the help I can get. Why don't you level with me?"

"Okay. You asked for it. Your airline and mine is presently negotiating with the Chinese government for landing rights in Taiwan. It is a very ticklish business, and the outcome is entirely dependent on the whims of Chiang's government officials—"

"What the hell has all that got to do with Alex Malloy?"

"Maybe nothing. But instinct tells me the Chinese would not smile upon a company that encourages one of its pilots to meddle in their affairs. If we failed to get the rights, well . . ."

"I see."

"Alex will survive. He's a tough customer. You may not, as far as this airline is concerned. Do you read me?"

"Loud and clear."

"Then make your next call to the Club Méditerranée. They have a place in Corsica with a fine beach."

That same day Horn contacted Diderot of Air France, who had flown with Alex Malloy in Constellations just after World War Two. Alex had then been serving as a Lockheed check pilot, helping rusty French Crews get back into the transatlantic business.

Diderot had sounded honestly concerned while he excused himself from active participation. "I have been retired for three years now, so I do not think my opinions would be too valuable. They have—how do you say?—snipped my wings. But I have a son, Étienne, who flies for Sabena, and he also greatly admires Alex. I'll give you his number in Brussels. He is very intelligent. Of course, *I* think so."

The call to Captain Étienne Diderot was short and fruitful: "If Alex is in trouble I will go to him anywhere in the world."

Hong Kong was chosen for the rendezvous, and there also would come Willie Moller of Lufthansa, who grunted angrily and said he had read of the affair and had been wondering what he might do to help.

Horn had caught Jan van Grootes at Schiphol Airport, Amsterdam, just before he took his KLM flight to New York.

"In two days when I return I am at your disposal. If the company will not give me a leave I will simply take one."

Horn was very pleased about van Grootes, because he knew Alex as well or better than any of the others. The huge Dutchman would make his delegation seem totally unbiased and professional. Early in his planning Horn had decided not to call on any of his countrymen. They must not seem a group of Americans gathered together in defense of one of their own.

Four days later Horn flew to London, where he boarded a BOAC Boeing bound for Hong Kong. He was very proud and pleased that his seat companion was Captain William Oliver Chatsworth, also of BOAC. He had agreed to join the delegation with one proviso: "The bloody criminal negligence charge reflects on us all. If at all possible we must disprove it. But if Alex is guilty, then we must recognize that fact and be willing to condemn him publicly."

"I can't believe he is guilty," Horn replied.

"Right. I doubt it myself, so let's have a go at it."

Chatsworth was squat of torso, bandy-legged, and he affected a defiantly shaped little goatee in addition to a mustache of Guardsman's proportions. In spite of his overall appearance, which often reminded Horn of a greviously offended rooster, he radiated immense dignity. Having flown with BOAC since the 1930s when it was known as Imperial Airways, Chatsworth was considered a true peer by those not even born when he was flying the British ensign in Handley Page Hannibals and Viscounts to places which could then still be regarded as part of the Empire.

Even in a jet it is a long way out to Hong Kong from London, and it seemed an endless flight to men unaccustomed to riding as passengers. Before they even reached the Middle East Horn had abandoned the novel he had purchased at London Airport. He dozed for a while, then sketched some painting ideas in the blank-paged book he liked to carry in his coat pocket. They were very rough designs, and as long as they remained so—he smiled ruefully —they could safely be considered potential masterpieces. Later in the same sketchbook he found himself setting down a preliminary outline of the delegation's objections.

"First: Determine the true cause of Alex's crash."

He made a question mark after that intention and added. "How do we know that has not already been determined?" Then he made the figure "2" and after it wrote, "Five international captains of the line, highly experienced, different backgrounds and national environments . . . if agree after investigation . . . make great impression . . . unless something kooky? Object—free Alex of *criminal and/or negligence* charge even if pilot error involved? If charge holds, any one of us vulnerable to same after even minor accident. Or dead pilots tell no tales. Contact IFALPA about possible boycott Taiwan?"

After very slowly forming the figure "3" his hand halted. What was the delegation really going to do if it turned out that Alex was guilty? He scribbled a note: "Never forget who organized this expedition. If it fails or someone is hurt don't look in a mirror."

Horn closed his eyes and thought of the very last day in Paris, when he had finally been able to reach Alex's wife. It was strange, he thought, how her voice haunted him. He had barely introduced himself when Sylvia had said, "Of course I know all about you, Lew Horn. Alex has often spoken of you. He will be very thrilled to know you called."

"Called? I'm coming and bringing four more of his friends with me. Something has to be done."

"I must warn you it will be very difficult. Alex is under arrest. Even for me to see him I must have official permission."

"Does he know what went wrong?"

"No. He is very positive all was well when he suddenly flew into the ground."

"Do you think there will be any official objection to our coming?"

"Yes."

"Do you object—or would Alex for some reason?"

"Of course not. But this is a very small country. I suggest you do not state your reason for coming to the immigration officials. Better to say you are simply tourists. I will meet your flight and explain."

"I thought you were Chinese. You sound like an American girl."

"I should. I graduated from Boston University and lived for some time in San Francisco. Be sure to let me know your flight."

Why should the voice of a woman he had never met endure so long after a telephone conversation? There had been a plaintive quality to Sylvia's voice, but he could recall no direct appeal. Had he read something into the conversation which had not been there at all?

He noticed Chatworth's lips were moving rhythmically, although his eyes remained tightly closed.

"What the hell are you chewing?"

"I am rehearsing a speech for my retirement ceremony which takes place July next. I was considering something by Tennyson. How I saw the heavens fill with commerce . . . pilots of the purple twilight dropping down with costly bales—British pilots, of course. That sort of potage."

"You will then be the ten thousandth pilot who bored those who came to wish him well in his dotage."

"Really? I say, that rhymes. I never realized you had a lighter side. You're such a formidable chap, rather like the Earl of Flint, I should think. I taught him to fly years ago, and I soloed him with misgivings because of his iron conviction that right was might. Once he fixed on an idea, he was worse than a bulldog. He eventually killed himself buzzing his own manor—caught a wingtip on one of the metal storks that decorated his chimneys. From a study of his flight path I am certain he saw the chimney perfectly clearly but he would be damned if he would let it get in his way. He was sort of an English Don Quixote, and I am wondering if you are not presently possessed of the same urges."

"Just what are you getting at?"

"Well, you go storming off into the sunset, lance at the ready, having persuaded us all it is our duty to attack evils which may or may not exist. Has it occurred to you that not one of the four of us has seen or talked to Alex in at least three years? A lot can happen to a man in that time. Depending upon the circumstances, he can go completely to pieces."

"I have faith in Alex. He is the only totally honest man I have ever known—with himself as well as others. He is no ordinary person."

"Granted. He is worth saving if circumstances have not placed him beyond salvage. We could find that to be the situation."

"You are a ray of sunshine today."

"I am simply being realistic. I keep remembering poor Geoffrey de Havilland, who seemed to have been crowned king of his profession because of his wonderful designs—D.H. Fours, Moths, Mosquitoes, Doves—all wonderful aircraft for their time. Then he created his masterpiece, which of course was the Comet. Can you imagine the man responsible for the first jet airliner, can you imagine his discovering that his masterpiece had a fatal flaw?"

Listening to Chatsworth expound on the Comet, Horn understood the personal disaster its failure had meant to every British flying man. It had been more than just an airplane, because it represented the revival of English spirit after the war; and it became a very real challenge to the worldwide leadership of the Americans, who were still flying piston engines.

"We were on our way to rule the skies even as we had once ruled the seas. While the rest of the world still wallowed through the weather at low altitudes, our Comet was breaking all records. Everyone, including the royal family, wanted to fly in the world's only jet transport. Alas . . . came January of fifty-four. Gibson, a man we all trusted implicitly, left Rome on schedule and then—nothing. Pieces of his beautiful Comet were found off the island of Elba. While we were still fussing about trying to determine what had gone wrong, another Comet chartered by South African Airways, left Rome bound for Cairo. There was no distress message, no warning of any sort. It exploded and crashed south of Naples. Both disasters occurred at high altitudes and there was a dismal flap in the press about man venturing further into the earth's envelope than the good Lord intended."

Chatsworth paused and shook his head. "It's hard to believe how only a few years ago we had so much to learn about flying above twenty thousand feet."

Horn glanced at his companion and found him thoughtfully stroking his goatee.

"Someday I'd like to try painting your portrait." Horn was surprised to find himself making such a suggestion, for he had never had any luck with portraits.

"I would pose only if you painted the real Chatsworth. Are you aware that I am really six feet four inches tall and weigh fifteen stone? I am also a talented cellist, a superb chef, and the last of the great lovers. Can you capture all that?"

"Why not? My work has often been compared with Gainsborough's."

They fell silent for a time, each comfortable and pleased with the other's company. The soft whisper of the slipstream against the window had nearly lulled Horn to sleep when he heard Chatsworth saying, "We had to find some way to fly the Comets safely. And we had to hurry because you Americans were already out of the development stage. I think about Sir Geoffrey when I consider the sort of thing we may be getting ourselves in for with Alex. The Comet explosions could not conceivably have been caused by pilot error. Then who or what was the villian? Likewise if Alex was not guilty of personal error, why did he prang into the ground?"

Horn remembered reading of the de Havilland engineers' dogged research during the agonizing period their Comets remained on the ground. Eventually they had lowered a Comet fuselage into a huge water tank and changed the interior pressure continuously to simulate the expansion and contraction it would endure ascending and descending through the earth's lower atmospheres. They had found that it was like bending a tin can continuously back and forth. After the equivalent of nine thousand hours' flying time a fracture appeared near the corner of a window and the riddle was solved.

"I hope," Chatsworth said quietly, "Alex hasn't changed too much. Like de Havilland, he was rather a symbol."

East of Beirut the cabin crew served tea, and Horn noticed how Chatsworth was treated as if he were royalty.

"Tradition," Chatsworth said apologetically. "People go on about pilots who have been with BOAC a long time. I suppose they consider me a contemporary of Alcock and Brown or even Blériot."

"Aren't you?"

"Go to hell."

"While you're basking in attention I will remind you that your goatee wiggles when you eat—out of sync with your chin."

"You colonists should keep a civil tongue in your head and your great bloody elbow off my armrest. Now sit up and enjoy good solid British food."

It was curious, Horn thought, how only a few days ago he had been so absorbed in Barbara and the divorce. Now Alex and his troubles had taken almost complete charge of his mind.

"You knew Alex as well as anyone. What impressed you the most about him? You must have thought a great deal of him to make this trip."

Chatsworth popped a small cake into his mouth and chewed on it thoughtfully. "Are you talking about his flying ability or his personal character?"

"Both. My boss Brewster believes you can't separate the two, and I'm beginning to believe he's right."

"I should say Alex's rather rare devotion to the truth. He was very fierce about it, you know. Gave one of our pilots a dreadful time during the war because he erred—not that he didn't deserve a lashing."

"That quality in Alex might be very important when we start asking questions. What I'm trying to get at is when does the quiet little bank teller decide to embezzle the cash box, or when does the pastor you would never suspect start fondling the little boys?"

"If you're suggesting we examine a highly technical matter on the basis of a man's personal behavior, then you are asking us to solve the human equation. It can't be done."

"We certainly can't ignore the human factor. About a month after I made captain I made a visual approach at Prestwick. It was a rainy night and I was right on the approach path, but when I looked up from my instruments I saw the runway lights and it was obvious I was so high I would overshoot unless I descended immediately. The illusion was so convincing I eased back on the power and shoved the nose down—which might have put us in the ocean a good mile short of the runway. My co-pilot was a born diplomat. He sang out loud and clear, 'Oh, you take the low road and I'll take the high road and I'll be in Scotland afore ye.' "

Horn paused and smiled at the memory. "Suddenly I got the message and pulled up. But I *might not have.* When I returned home from that trip I made a special trip to see the Libbey-Owens glass experts. I learned some surprising things about the refractive index of windshields and the angle of incidence of light. Rain not only reduces vision, the ripples and blurs of accumulating water act as prisms and can make you believe you are higher than you actually are. Speed and rain compound the illusion. Did you know it is possible to observe an apparent horizon as much as twelve hundred feet below the true article?"

"I had no idea the differential could be that great."

"We ran a series of tests and found night rain illusions could deceive the eye as much as two hundred feet for every half mile distant from the source of light. Now suppose Alex thought he saw the lights of Taipei Airport or even some other lights. If the illusion was sufficient, he just might have flown into the ground."

"I shouldn't think Alex would be suckered into such a trap. He may not always have been a paragon of virtue, but he's a wise old bird."

"I thought I was too until that night at Prestwick."

As he attempted to visualize Alex Malloy and his crew on the flight deck during their descent into Taipei, Horn was only vaguely aware of the stewardess who took away his tea tray. She asked Chatsworth if he would come forward to the flight deck. The captain wanted a word about the Guild of Air Pilots and Navigators.

Would you excuse me?" Chatsworth carefully wiped his mustache. "It was my fate to have been one of the founders of our Guild."

"Yes, *sir!* Yes indeed, *sir,*" Horn said, imitating the stewardess.

Chatsworth rose, straightened his tie, then leaned down to Horn. "Envy does not become you."

As Horn watched Chatsworth draw himself up to his full five feet six inches, take a brace, and stride grandly toward the flight deck, he whispered to himself, "Britons, Britons never shall be slaves."

3

In the early mornings the glowering hill which looms directly behind Taipei's Grand Hotel becomes a part of the neo-Ming architecture. The lower slopes of the hill provide a broad stage upon which the hotel, like the fortress of a legendary mandarin, seems to float in mid-air. Except in the typhoon season, Taipei is not subject to high winds, and by early morning the stagnant air has wrapped itself around the hotel. Since even the burning sun frequently fails to dissipate the suffocating mixture of fog and smog which blankets the city, dawn is the time when many citizens indulge their need for physical exercise on the hill behind the hotel.

When Horn awakened he discovered it was only five A.M. local time. He yawned and remembered that he had changed his watch from Paris time just before he had finally turned out the light. He had managed three hours' sleep, which under the circumstances, he reminded himself, was more than he had any right to expect.

Still yawning, he went to the floor-length window and pulled back the curtains. He stood for a moment dazed from lack of sleep, and with his eyes closed he stretched his arms upward. When he opened his eyes he was astounded to find he had an audience. On the grass beneath his window several Chinese men and women were also stretching and bending with catlike grace. Now several had halted their calisthenics and were looking directly at him. The women were chuckling and pointing in his direction and the men were laughing. Suddenly Horn realized that he was stark naked. He immediately retreated from the window. I hope, he thought ruefully, they were only laughing because Orientals so rarely see hair on a man's chest!

As he slipped into a pair of light cotton slacks he noticed the blue-covered report which he had read and reread through most of the night. It had fallen from his hands to the floor when he could no longer keep his eyes open. He picked up the volume which in 120 dreary pages made up the official Chinese CAA version of why Captain Alex Malloy had flown his magnificent aircraft into a rice paddy and instantly transformed it into a mass of flaming junk.

If everything in that report was true, Horn had reluctantly decided, then certainly pilot error was involved, although the charge of "criminal negligence" was still absurd.

Yet there were enough assumptions within those pages and strangely contradictory testimony to justify a more thorough investigation. Why had the Chinese so easily reached a convenient verdict? If it stood, Alex Malloy, the onetime stormy petrel now brought to earth and held captive, was beyond saving.

As he read through the night, Horn had known a distinct sense of exhilaration. The men who had agreed to join him in this far-off land must each feel accused and their own integrity questioned. They had the courage to admit that it might have been any one of them sliding down through the rain on that deceptively tranquil night. They were men with a dedication and therefore complete. They would understand that if Alex even suspected he had made an error there would be no lifting his despair. His act confirmed as stupid or careless in any sense would mean for them all an unforgivable breach of trust.

Except for a sleepy-eyed bellboy, the lobby of the Grand Hotel was deserted. Horn crossed it rapidly, passed through the double glass doors to the portico, and was instantly disappointed. Instead of refreshing crisp morning air the humid atmosphere bore so heavily upon him that he slowed his pace and for a moment considered abandoning his plan to climb the hill behind the hotel. He hesitated, then went on, passing those Chinese on the terrace who had only minutes before laughed at his exposure in the window. Be damned to them and international amity, he thought. Am I supposed to take a bow to make sure they recognize me with my clothes on?

He continued up a terrace and once into the trees entered a park laced with paths and small open recreational areas. As the first sunlight filtered through the trees, he was only vaguely aware of the varied activity he passed at every turn of the path. The hill was alive with people engaged in all manner of recreation. Some were dancing, some were marching about in a semimilitary style, others were playing musical instruments, or at badminton or croquet. One clearing had been taken over by a group of Japanese who were dueling and posturing with Samurai swords. He passed several solemn groups practicing yoga. Horn's own indifference to distraction, he suddenly realized, was quite the equal of theirs.

As he climbed and perspired he thought of what an unexpected shock it had been meeting Alex's wife at the airport. While Diderot had chatted with her in French and Moller in German, he had stood dumbly aside and regarded Sylvia with tactless fervor. The wife of a helpless friend, his finicky conscience kept insisting, did not need any competition from divorcés on the rebound.

She had been waiting just beyond the immigration barriers at the airport and had ever so gently waved her hand and smiled. During the thunder of stamps being applied to his passport he had continued to stare at her until finally he was passed through the barrier.

She had come to him holding out a white-gloved hand. "Welcome to Taipei, Captain Horn. I am Sylvia Malloy and I bring you also warm welcome from Alex."

"It *is* warm," was all he could think to say, and afterward when the others joined them he fumbled every single introduction. It had made little difference. She had seemed removed from the noisy tumult in the terminal, utterly serene in her high-necked jade green gown. Her skin was golden and unblemished by cosmetics except for accents about her eyes, which were a deep umber, lively, and very intelligent. When she led them toward the line of waiting taxis, he had told himself over and over again to stop acting like a damned fool. He had actually resented van Grootes, who had become old-world courtly and had bowed and kissed her hand.

When they arrived at the Grand Hotel, Moller with

his bludgeonlike Teutonic manner had insisted she join them in the bar for a nightcap. Whether she wished it or not, Sylvia automatically became the star attraction, and the bits and pieces of her background only made her more tantalizing.

Father was at one time in the natural camphor oil industry until its collapse because of synthetics. . . . She graduated not only from Boston University, but also from the Sorbonne . . . and two years at the University of Munich. Plays tennis . . . Diderot compliments her on her excellent French . . . Moller the same for her German.

All too soon she had smiled and said, "You must be very tired after your long flight. The best way to express my personal gratitude for coming is to let you rest."

As she rose, five chairs were hastily pushed back. How small and fragile she had appeared surrounded by five men.

"I have received permission from the police for you to visit Alex at five tomorrow afternoon. Meanwhile you will want to study this." She placed a manila envelope on the table and explained that it contained the Chinese CCA report.

Why, Horn wondered the next morning, should the vision of Sylvia persist in intruding upon his concentration? The issue was Alex and nothing else should matter. Why had he crashed into that rice paddy? A believable explanation was certainly not to be found in the dogmatic report which accused Captain Malloy of ignoring signals received from the approach landing system at Taipei Airport and letting down prematurely. The report also claimed the approach systems were functioning normally, as proven by the routine arrival of two airliners within the hour prior to Captain Malloy's disaster and two more airliners within the following three hours. *There,* Horn thought, continuing his climb, was the sticker. Not one of the other crews had reported anything abnormal.

Below the collection of signatures on the last page of the report were several handwritten notes which he assumed must have been added by Sylvia.

For your interest:

1. Two days after this report was approved, wreckage of the 727 was totally demolished and hauled away. Whereabouts unknown.

2. Rice paddy where most of wreckage found originally cleared and replanted 3 days after crash. Local peasants reimbursed for crop loss by government official. (Department unknown.)

3. Sentencing by court scheduled end of next week. Expect guilty verdict. Punishment could run from 5 years to life depending on mood of judges.

4. *Warning.* Do not expect cooperation from Chinese CAA or other government departments. They have reached these conclusions and would lose great face if forced to change same. If you do not understand face, will be glad to explain—no, not glad, but will explain. Sorry. Face is the curse of the Orient.

Horn knew very well what was meant by face, even though an exact definition was almost impossible for the Caucasian mind to appreciate. To Chinese, face was a multitude of factors all linked together to form reputation, yet it was not at all the same as pride in the Occidental sense. A rich man wore fine clothes else he might lose face, a clerk armed his pocket with many pencils to assure face and a bureaucrat assigned as many minions as possible between himself and the public to guarantee face. Even the lowliest of the low who were the gatherers of night soil worried about face.

Below the listed notes a final sentence had been written diagonally across the corner of the page: "If you wish to talk with Leonard Wu the first officer I will try to arrange it. He is being very careful and difficult. As you see, *he has not helped Alex's case.*"

As Horn neared the top of the hill the trees gave way to underbrush and he saw that a high radio tower occupied the summit. For reasons he had never thoroughly understood, views from high places always seemed to clarify his thinking. Now he wanted to explore certain fundamentals before he met with the others. They would have their own ideas, which might be distracting if considered before the known facts were recognized.

What was the true cause of any aircraft accident? Truth was always elusive, and often the most carefully researched reports missed it completely. Only in mathematics was the truth fixed. All else was subject to human interference or interpretation, which immediately meant the denial of truth or at least some bending.

Reason ruled the report on Alex's crash. But it could be a deceitful tool if employed without the senses, and sometimes reason could lie outrageously.

The investigators had very obviously reasoned that because the aircraft had contacted the ground before its appointed moment the culprit *had* to be the pilot. Reason was added to reason when the safe arrival of other aircraft before and after the crash was introduced as a convincing argument. Final reasoning clinched the opinion when the electronic and flight systems in the aircraft were found to be functioning normally, and the testimony of Leonard Wu confirmed that fact. Yes and Alex had also admitted finding no fault with the aircraft or its navigational systems.

Yet the truth was in Alex. He had testified he could not understand why he had suddenly felt the aircraft strike the earth when he should have had more than a thousand feet to spare. And he claimed to be astonished that the crash had occurred nearly thirteen miles from the end of the runway at Taipei.

Alex Malloy did not lie. He was a perfectionist and a prudent believer in his trust. Then how in the name of reason could he have made such a colossal blunder?

Horn was pleased that he had troubled to climb the hill, for the view of the Taipei area was rewarding. Almost directly below, the dun-colored Keelung River snaked its way to the sea; and beyond, to the east, was the Taipei Airport. The city itself, steaming in the caldron of the morning, pressed close upon the airport and covered a broad flat area. All of it was held in the coils of the Hsintien River, which flowed west and then north and then westerly again until it eventually joined the Keelung.

Horn watched as a Douglas DC-8 whined down from the stagnant clouds in the western sky, passed over the Hsintien River and the fringe of the city and then, as if pulled by invisible wires, slid gently down to the airport runway. After a moment he heard the muffled screech of the DC-8's tires, and he thought how the identical sound should have been made by Alex's jet if he had landed safely just a month ago. Even Alex's approach from the west should have been identical, for on the plateau which rose between the Hsintien River and the sea stood the small building in which the "outer marker" was located. Every modern airport had such an electronic navigational aid to serve approaching aircraft as a lighthouse serves ships at sea. Alex had been cleared to that position and, according to the report he had transmitted, was "approaching the outer marker." So he had reached the very mouth of the harbor.

Horn tried to locate the outer marker station visually, but in spite of his elevation he could not distinguish it. Beyond its approximate location, some six miles farther to the southwest, was the place Alex had flown into the ground. Wiping the perspiration from his eyes, Horn resolved to bring a pair of binoculars the next time he climbed the hill.

He glanced at his watch and was surprised to find it was nearly seven o'clock. At once he started descending the winding path, for he had agreed to meet with the others at eight. Before seeing Alex they must have a very clear picture of those last fateful minutes. Each man stood a chance of being magnified, not so much in the rescue of a single comrade, but in a vindication of all they represented.

Halfway down the hill he decided the incongruity of Alex's making such an amateurish mistake might be a positive note. Could something over which he had no control have influenced his decision?

As he emerged from the lower woods and walked rapidly toward the hotel he was satisfied that at last his thoughts had taken a healthier turn.

Horn took a quick shower and was delighted to find himself whistling. He had not felt the urge to whistle for months—not since that certain morning in what now seemed like another life when he had landed at Kennedy International after a routine flight from Paris. It had been a morning of very marginal visibility, but there had been only a ten-minute traffic hold. The instrument approach had gone off smoothly, and he had left the aircraft with a sense of a job well done. He had checked through his company bulletins.

Recently there have been a number of runway excursions during landing rollouts. This is sufficient reason to re-examine our landing techniques, since the same old problems are recurring . . .

Trailing vortex wakes have certain characteristics which a pilot can use in visualizing their location and avoiding it . . .

Recent incidents caused us to review the coordination necessary between Flight Officers and Stewardesses with respect to emergency evacuation of passengers . . .

On your April schedules please note champagne service will be eliminated on PAR-JFK flights 606 and 700 due to inappropriate hours of these flights.

At last, wearying of the paper bombardment which confronted him every time he returned from a trip, he had stuffed an additional handful of bulletins into his flight bag. As always on those early morning arrivals he had yearned for a shower and a bed. He smiled now as he remembered how he had been whistling to keep awake while he waited for the parking lot bus.

A man had come to him out of the morning mist. "Captain Horn?"

"Yes?"

"I have a paper here which will interest you."

"Thanks, no. I've just collected all the papers I need."

"Not like this one." The man had smiled and Horn had automatically accepted the offered envelope.

"Thank you," the man had said and walked away.

As he opened the envelope he had resumed his whistling. When he realized he had just been served with divorce papers he stopped. In spite of the airport din all about him he had stood in his own special silence reading the paper for what had seemed like a very long time.

Now he thought it significant that he once more felt like whistling.

Promptly at eight he crossed the lobby to the portico where they had agreed to meet. Van Grootes was waiting for him. Although his pith helmet had seen better days he wore it with the assurance of an ex-colonial.

Smiling, Horn extended his hand. "Where are the elephants?"

Van Grootes laughed and patted his helmet tenderly. "I haven't had an excuse to wear this Kipling relic since the Japanese ran us out of Java in 'forty-two."

Of all the delegation, Horn decided van Grootes was the most imposing. He was known the world over as one of the "greats" of KLM, which was an airline that commanded respect everywhere. Horn had called him because he knew Alex had spent two years flying for KLM just before World War Two and had been obliged to fly the Java run as van Grootes's co-pilot.

When they had met for the first time in Hong Kong Horn had been ill prepared for the giant who took his hand most gently in his paw.

"I am honored you would include me."

Certainly God had never smiled upon van Grootes's outward appearance. His nose was a great damask carbuncle decorated on both sides with an assortment of wens. A variety of craters rubbled his face until it seemed to have suffered a miniature barrage. His skin was the color of rusted iron and his mouth over large. His massive head was so set on his shoulders it seemed to turn like a tank turret and his heavy-fingered hands would have suited a Dutch sailor before the mast.

After only two days in his company Horn was convinced van Grootes must be one of the most compassionate men he had ever known—and, he suspected, a terribly lonely man.

"Congratulations," van Grootes was saying. "Only an American optimist could have gathered such a crew and made us join hands so soon on the other side of the world. It is like rounding up the inhabitants of a forest and telling them now be nice while we all go to the zoo together."

Diderot, looking as if he were ready for a tennis match, sauntered out from the lobby. He yawned, frowned at his wristwatch, and asked the correct local time.

"You are late," van Grootes grumbled, "but every Frenchman keeps his own time."

Next Chatsworth joined them. "I've just had a chat with a man at our embassy who tells me there is absolutely no hope of our renting a small aircraft to refly Alex's flight path. He kept reminding me these people are still very much at war with the mainland Chinese, as if I didn't know."

A Mercedes taxi pulled beneath the portico and Moller stepped out. He was perspiring heavily. He pointed his half-smoked cigar at the taxi. "I have found the only driver in Taipei who understands my English. I lie a little and say to him I know all about Mercedes and if something breaks I send him the piece he needs. So we have ten per cent from the regular rate."

Horn held a map of the Taipei area before the driver and pointed to the plateau area. Moments later they were careening down the hill from the hotel.

"The chauffeur is crazy," Diderot said languidly. "He will kill us all."

They sped through the city itself, crossed a muddy river, and charged through the narrow streets of several small villages. Finally the road climbed the face of the plateau and became so rough the four men in the back of the taxi clung to one another for support. They laughed nervously until the driver accelerated to even higher speeds. Van Grootes growled, "Tell the son of a bitch to slow down!"

Horn, who sat beside the driver tapped him gently and made a downward motion with his hand. To relieve his own tension he turned back to the others. "There are two peaks in the crash area, both about eight hundred feet high. We should see them now."

They all pretended to search the horizon ahead, but Horn suspected they were really seeking distraction.

Moller said, "Why don't you people use meters? Is crazy, this feet business."

Chatsworth asked Diderot if he knew the Normans had brought the *mille* along with them when they invaded England.

"The *mille* is one thousand Roman military double strides."

Diderot failed to display the slightest interest. His eyes were fixed on the twisting road ahead as he said softly, "We are all going to die."

"A meter is a meter and a kilometer is a kilometer," Moller stated firmly. "You always know where you are."

They passed through several tea farms and came to a region of rice paddies. Finally the driver stopped by a narrow path and pointed to a grove of trees.

Although it had been hot inside the taxi, Horn was unprepared for the sun's assault. It seemed to hammer upon his head, and as they walked along the path the stinking air from the surrounding paddies felt almost solid.

"This must be the right place. There is the bamboo grove. You can see where the landing gear cut through."

When they came to the grove of trees they paused and wiped the sweat from their faces and stared at the rice paddy which stretched before them.

Horn opened the blue-covered investigation report which graphically portrayed the final moments of Alex Malloy's flight. The profile drawing was laid out in scale and illustrated how he had barely missed a factory chimney some half mile to the west. Yes, there was the chimney. Then, still descending, he had skimmed through the tops of a bamboo grove and almost immediately smashed into the rice paddy. In the overview diagram the surrounding dikes all matched, and on the opposite side of the paddy a line of peasants' huts was indicated.

"Everything seems to check," Horn said, "but I can't understand how things could be so thoroughly cleaned up in such a short time."

"There is no indication anything happened here," Diderot agreed. "It is very peaceful."

"And hot," Moller added.

Horn thought the contrast between the two men might never be more marked. Moller was dripping in perspiration and very red in the face. He surveyed the rice paddy with deep suspicion, his considerable jaw was set, and his gray eyes were hard with determination.

Diderot somehow managed to appear cool. He was leaning against a tree and looking off into the distance as if he had little interest in the situation. Occasionally he waved his hand to drive away a fly.

Chatsworth was studying a map. He turned until he faced the Formosa Strait in the distance and then looked back toward the city of Taipei.

"I'd be willing to wager that thirty years ago this sort

of thing wouldn't have happened. The whole approach procedure would have been different. We would have homed
on some kind of a beacon, then turned out over the sea for
let-down without fear of hitting anything. Once we had visibility we would make for the shoreline, find the mouth of
the Tanshui River, and follow it directly to the airport.
Simple as that, and I daresay the entire approach could be
made below one hundred feet if necessary. One sometimes
wonders how much progress we've made."

Moller sneered. "You make such nice slow approaches in your old Short flying boats, but you try that in a jet
you bust your ass. And at night you never fly. This is not
nineteen thirty-five."

Both men were right, Horn thought. Too often the
flying business had been asked to lie down with a lion before all of its teeth were removed. Electronic aids, their
magic hidden within expensive black boxes, almost never
failed. Almost. And when it happened it seemed that their
very perfection had sometimes been the cause of failure in
the human partner. The unfortunate man had trusted implicitly in their capability, and in the process had lost his
own ability to think. The ultimate result was always a melancholy patch of earth with an atmosphere much like this
rice paddy. Every year, somewhere in the world, some
highly expert man made a fatal mistake. The question was
always why. Had the man betrayed the devices at his command, or was it the other way around?

There was always an official answer, because there
had to be one, but they were rarely satisfying. Soon afterward the stories disappeared from the news and the airlines
returned to the comfort of their remarkable passenger-
seat-mile safety statistics. Which was fine, Horn decided,
except for those identified by a negative statistic.

He squinted at the rice paddy baking in the sun and
thought, Maybe here, where the nearly impossible happened and the man responsible is still alive, we may learn
at least one why.

They surveyed the scene in silence until Chatsworth
suggested that since they were unable to refly Malloy's final

approach Horn might try reading the radio contacts aloud.

"I think we might visualize things a bit better. Only the last few contacts are important. Perhaps listening might just spark an idea in one of us."

Horn opened the report and searched for the section which carried the radio contacts.

"Let's take it from the time he was approaching Hsinchu. That's a beacon about thirty-six miles to the southwest of Taipei, about twenty-some miles from here. That's where he entered the control area."

They turned toward the southwest, and as he started to read he saw their eyes turn instinctively toward the sky.

" 'Far Eastern three from Taipei approach. Clearance.' "

" 'Ready to copy.' "

" 'After passing PO descend and maintain five thousand. Cross GM at five thousand.' "

" 'Roger. Understand cross GM five thousand.' "

Horn paused. "PO is the identifier for Hsinchu, and GM is the identifier for Taoyuan, which is the next beacon. Any questions?"

They shook their heads.

"GM is nineteen miles closer to Taipei," Horn said, turning more toward the west. "It should be about five miles from where we stand."

"Only five miles?" Moller asked. "That's a hell of a fast descent if he came down from five thousand and hit this paddy."

"Remember he didn't expect to hit a paddy or anything else," Chatsworth said. He held his own map before him and slipped on his spectacles.

"I'm a bit puzzled," Chatsworth went on, "about his original clearance to the area. It strikes me as odd that a flight from Manila should have been routed all the way round the west coast of Formosa. The east coast is much more direct."

"Maybe they have a traffic problem and it was easier that night to give vectors for final approach?" van Grootes said.

"Apparently they do not give vectors here," Horn said. "Every pilot is on his own."

"Yah." Moller nodded. "That is much better if you don't have trained controllers."

"I prefer to be on my own all the time," Diderot said.

And so, Horn thought, would I if the beehive nature of modern air traffic were not such a factor. Approaching Taipei on instruments is hardly the same as joining the throng around New York, Paris, or London. If the few aircraft using the Taipei airspace on the night of Alex's crash composed the typical traffic, then they hardly needed the complication of radar vectoring from the ground.

"The next call is from the aircraft. Listen. 'Taipei approach . . . Far Eastern three is over GM at five thousand.' Then Taipei approach came back and said, 'Cleared to LK direct for straight-in ADF approach.' "

"ADF approach?" Chatsworth asked.

"That's what the tape said. I don't know why he wasn't cleared for a normal ILS approach."

"We must find out," Moller said. "And by the way, who is doing the talking from the aircraft—Alex or the co-pilot?"

"It doesn't specify. This is just a straight read-out from the tapes. Now we have Alex cleared to LK, which is the identifier for the outer marker beacon. It is located on this plateau about seven miles from where we stand and is six miles from the end of the runway at Taipei."

Chatsworth said, "Obviously Alex thought he was lined up for a normal landing. His undercarriage was down. I think that is very significant."

"I disagree," Diderot said. "Why would he put his gear down when he still had so far to go?"

"But did he know how far he had to go? Does Taipei have a distance measuring system?" van Grootes asked.

"There is no such system," Horn said. "We're getting ahead of ourselves. Bear with me through these radio exchanges and then we'll all understand the sequence of events."

"Right," Chatsworth said firmly and Horn was grateful to him. A supercharged foursome of rugged individuals accustomed to command did not make the most docile audience, he thought. He waited until he was certain of their full attention. The whole solution to the crash might be revealed in the next few flight minutes.

He noticed that the birds twittering in the trees had suddenly become silent as if they too waited for the final exchange between the ground and the ghost of Far Eastern flight three.

"The weather seems reasonable for an ADF approach. Here is the tower giving it to Alex: 'Latest Taipei weather, scattered clouds eight hundred feet, broken two thousand, overcast five thousand. Visibility three miles. Light rain. Altimeter two nine five five.' Flight three acknowledged."

"If the Chinese would let us listen to the voice tape we would know who made the acknowledgement," Moller interrupted.

"What difference does it make?" van Grootes grunted. "Verdammt, Moller. Will you let the man read on?"

"It makes a big difference. Suppose Alex was busy at something we don't know about just at this minute. Suppose he failed to set *his* altimeter because his mind was elsewhere . . . or his fingers turned the setting knob wrong? It could happen."

Since the very early days when a second pilot had been included in the cockpit the theory had been that two men setting two different instruments would not make the identical mistake and the difference would be their warning. Yet it had happened.

"Did anyone check the altimeters after the crash?" Diderot asked.

"According to this report all flight instruments were destroyed."

"I don't believe it."

Moller continued to stare at the sky as he said, "I wonder if something could have happened back in the cabin at just the wrong time. Something the attendants could not handle? Maybe they called Alex about it? Something unusual enough to distract his attention from his altimeter setting or even his altitude?"

Horn closed his eyes momentarily while he tried to remove himself from the rice paddy and visualize Alex's busy flight deck. Certain things are the same in any airliner during final descent. The overhead loudspeakers would be voluble with clearances, and as the aircraft slowed below two hundred and fifty knots the hissing of the slipstream would become softer. It would be hot on the flight deck and the overall smell would have been of shirts in need of changing. Manila was always steaming, and Alex's crew would have exuded that internationally fusty aroma which possesses all crews toward the end of a flight. It was caused, he thought, by a combination of physical inactivity, subconscious anxieties, perpetual indigestion from the sort of food served only at airports, all seasoned with faint emissions of artificial leather, plastic, and overheated ceramics in the electronic systems.

Because he had been in their place so many times Horn could easily picture Alex and Leonard Wu surrounded by a galaxy of individually illuminated dials, toggle switches, buttons, and levers—the devices which caused modern jet aircraft to cost so many millions. Their faces would be faintly illuminated from below, and Tseu, the engineer who was soon to die, would be at his console just behind them. He would be watching his engine instruments or recording the final details of the flight in his log. If he was an old-timer he might also reassure himself that the pilots' two altimeters were set according to the numbers he had heard transmitted from the ground.

On that night there would have been rain hissing along the windshield and probably there would have been minor turbulence as they descended—enough to jostle the whole cramped display. In response the approach charts, which Alex would certainly have clipped to his control yoke, would quiver as if to demand attention.

Horn opened his eyes before his thoughts drifted further. He tapped the report. "The time separations for the next transmissions are approximately one minute apart, so I'll read them straight through." As if he were actually on the flight deck, Horn instinctively lowered the palm of his free hand.

" 'Flaps twenty-five degrees.' Then someone, presumably Leonard Wu, repeats, 'Flaps twenty-five degrees.' "

"Next voice: 'Approaching outer marker!' "

"Who said that?"

"There is no way of telling. This is straight off the aircraft flight recorder. Ten seconds later here's a voice: " 'Gear down' That presumably was Alex's voice, since it was acknowledged immediately by either Leonard Wu or Tseu the engineer. Five seconds later there is a confirming voice: 'Landing gear down and locked.' "

Diderot asked, "How much time has elapsed since they reported approaching the outer marker?"

"Let's see . . . back here? A total of thirty-five seconds. Now stay with me. You're descending on instruments with the outer marker just coming up and everything in landing configuration. You have no idea that in approximately two minutes everything is going to come unglued. All right? Here we go. These are the voices."

Horn waited a moment before he began. He wanted to be sure that his reading was dispassionate.

" 'Check approach clearance.'

" 'Check.'

" 'Airspeed?'

" 'One forty-two . . . one thirty-eight . . . one forty. Right on.'

"Now there is a ten-second pause, then someone says, *'Hey!* What goes on here?'

" 'I have an MDA light! Hold your altitude.'

" 'I see—'

" 'What the—'

" 'Something's wrong.'

" 'Oh, Jesus Christ!' "

Horn lowered the report. In spite of the heat he felt a sudden chill. He saw that the others were staring at the earth beneath their feet as if they were embarrassed.

He heard the birds resume their twittering. Had they actually stopped while the ghost of flight three flew again, or had it just been his imagination?

At last van Grootes broke the stillness. "That was the end of the tape—nothing more?"

Horn shook his head. He had hoped for more reaction from the others. They seemed stunned. At least, he thought, one of them might have queried the statement "I have an MDA light." MDA was the acronym for minimum descent altitude, and each pilot had a light on his instrument panel activated by a radar sensor when that actual height had been reached. It could be preset to any desired minimum altitude, three hundred feet or four hundred feet.

Unlike the pressure altimeter, which gave the height above sea level and was set according to local atmospheric pressure, the MDA light meant exactly what it said. When it came on there was that precise distance between a man's precious rump and the cruel earth. It was never to be denied.

Now with the diagrams in the report compared with reality, Horn decided the sequence of events was all the more mystifying. Certainly Alex had warning he was too low, and he would have recovered if there had been enough time. Before he could correct he had barely missed a chimney, plowed through a grove of bamboo and plunged into this rice paddy.

Van Grootes echoed his thoughts. "I cannot understand why a man of Alex's experience would have let down here. After someone said, 'I have an MDA light,' the next voices sounded surprised. 'Something's wrong.' 'What the —' Then, you might say, astonishment. 'Oh, Jesus Christ!' Was that an oath spoken in anger, or a phrase of discovery . . . or maybe a prayer?"

"What are you getting at?" Moller asked.

"I'm not sure. But this looks and sounds like a mistake no skilled man would make if he were in full possession of his faculties."

"*If,*" Moller growled. "That's what I wonder. I am thinking as we stand here that not one of us would ever make such mistake."

For an instant Horn had trouble holding back his anger. He wanted to ask Moller who the hell he thought he was to be incapable of a mistake. He had implied that Alex was less of a pilot than himself or the others. Worse, he had revived the gnawing question of Alex's possible deterioration. His resentment subsided when he reminded himself how Moller had immediately accepted his invitation to help.

Horn had been standing before the others, facing them with the grove of trees at his back. The path along which they had walked from the road to the rice paddy was also behind him. He started to move, then held his position when Chatsworth spoke very softly.

"Don't look now, but my recent inattention has been caused by some curious activities behind your back. While you were reading two men appeared and held a brief conversation with our taxi driver. My distance vision is still twenty over fifteen, and I assure you they were not peasants. One of them held up a pair of binoculars and gave us rather a good going over." Chatsworth smiled with his eyes. "Have you ever had the feeling you were being followed?"

After a moment he said, "Now you can turn around. They have just walked away."

4

I, H. G. Liang, having heard the evidence presented before me in Taipei District Court on Docket Number 302, do find the following:

1. Captain Alex Malloy, a U.S. citizen residing in Taiwan and holding Chinese CAA Airline Transport License No. 1380, was in command of Far Eastern Airways flight three on the night of October 5, 1963.

2. The said flight did crash, resulting in the death of 14 passengers and injury to 46.

3. I find the defendant, Captain Alex Malloy, guilty as charged.

H. G. Liang
Judge, District Court

Recommended: 10 years P.S. (Penal Servitude). Revocation of license.

It was nearly noon before they arrived back at the Grand Hotel. Horn asked the doorman to translate his questions and the driver's answers. Who were the men who had talked to him at the rice paddy? The driver claimed he had no idea. How did they happen to be there? He did not know. Did one of them have a pair of binoculars? The driver did not know. Were they on foot or did they have a car parked nearby? Finally Horn decided the driver was either monumentally stupid or one of China's finest actors. Either way he was a waste of time.

The uniformed boy behind the reception desk handed him a message with his room key.

"When you return please come to the lower tea room. Downstairs at the end of lobby. I must see you." It was signed "Sylvia."

She was sitting in a fan-backed wicker chair near a window. The brilliant sunlight bounced off a plaster wall outdoors and by some trick of reflection caused her skin to appear softly luminescent, a glowing quality Horn realized he had appreciated in the finest Oriental sculpture. He paused a moment, wanting to prolong his private enjoyment of her simple beauty.

She was looking out the window, her face in serene repose. Horn sidestepped cautiously so that he might view her head from a different angle. You dauber, he thought. If you had not wasted your life flying you might be able to paint that. Now you might be able to suggest the light contrast between the hot wall and the cool of the tea room, but you would never capture the glow of the girl.

A waiter passed between them and his movement caught her eye so that she turned toward Horn. "Hi!"

When he failed to move, her eyes became puzzled. "Are you all right, Captain?"

"Yes." He approached her slowly. "I was just trying to prolong something you wouldn't understand."

"Ah?"

He sat down opposite her and when their eyes met again he sought desperately for some quick distraction. "I was regretting something that could never happen. Very foolish of me."

He saw that she was waiting for more, and he twisted uncomfortably in his chair while he tried to think how he could tell her about his painting without sounding foolish. Where the hell was the waiter? Why didn't he come and interrupt?

"It was hot where we were this morning," Horn said lamely. "I'm thirsty."

His hand signaling finally caught a waiter's attention. Horn ordered a ginger beer, and when the waiter left he saw a smile playing about Sylvia's eyes. She was still waiting for an explanation.

"Well . . . I happened to observe you before you knew I had arrived. I thought with that dress you are wearing—its ultramarine blue, contrast it with the hot light behind you—your face in shadow, a subdued value done just right of course. It should make a great painting."

"Alex told me you painted. And very well. I am not so sure I'd like my face as a subdued value. Couldn't you glamorize me a bit? If you wish I'll even practice looking inscrutable."

"Alex was wrong. I'm not very good. That's what I was regretting—a career that can never be. My business is flying airplanes. I love the job and I'm good at it. That should be enough for one man."

"Why couldn't you become a painter too?"

"Because I was practicing aerobatics and instrument approaches when I might have been practicing line and composition. I admire experts in any profession and have trouble tolerating people who don't know what they are doing. Besides I think forty is a little late to start a new career."

"You should have known my grandfather."

"Was he a painter?"

"No, a liver. Before the war he had a house in Canton, and as a little girl I was taken to see him so that once a year he could poke me in the stomach and pat my behind and tell me how fast I was growing up. He always had at least two concubines, and during one visit I dared to ask him who they were. I was young enough to pretend I didn't know. He said they were his allies, and I asked him allies against what? Age, he said without batting an eye. He explained how the girls changed very rapidly with every passing day while he remained the same if he avoided the mirror. The contrast deceived him into believing time had halted. I remember him saying, 'They are my clock of life. Only when they appear very old to me will I know my own end must be near.' "

Horn chuckled. "Very wise man." It occurred to him that after such a frustrating morning these moments were particularly pleasant.

"Hold old was your grandfather when he died?"

"Oh, he's very much alive! He's outlived at least six concubines that I have known. He's over eighty and lives in Tainan. I still go to see him once a year."

"Is the old rascal still poking you in the stomach?"

She laughed, which pleased him immensely. How many women, he wondered, would manage to laugh when they were so beset with troubles?

"No. Now he reminds me my grandmother's feet were bound and yet she died a happy woman. He says women with too much education are like firecrackers with a lighted fuse. A man never knows if they are going to just fizzle and hiss or explode."

"I have a feeling that meeting your grandfather might be one of the more unforgettable events in my life."

The waiter arrived with his ginger beer. Horn signed the chit, and when he looked up he saw that Sylvia's face had changed completely. He saw only sadness now. She avoided his eyes when she said, "I cannot tell you how relieved I am that you are here. I had almost given up hope."

"Don't." To bolster his own confidence he paused while he half drained his glass. "We'll work this out somehow. We had a good morning."

Good? What had been good about it? They had not discovered one new clue except the possibility that someone might be trailing them. It was really a morning wasted when time was so valuable.

He waited for her to speak. Certainly she had not asked him to come here simply to talk about her grandfather. Yet she remained silent, looking out the window at the bare plaster wall.

"You are practicing being inscrutable," he said gently.

"I was thinking of Alex. And I am very frightened. Twice a week when I am permitted to see Alex I stage a pathetic little matinee for him. I smile very bravely and tell him there is nothing to worry about. I invent rumors I have supposedly heard about how favorably the judges were impressed with his honest testimony. I feel I must do this to save him . . . and myself. We have so much to lose."

She paused and for an instant her eyes sought Horn's. Then she looked away and passed her hand along the ebony sheen of her hair.

"My playacting worked, because I soon realized Alex was putting on his own show from the time I arrived in his room until I left. He laughed almost as vigorously as he always had and sometimes we would read something to each other which amused us both. Or we would talk about how we were going to make a serious effort to improve our tennis once he was well and free. We even drew plans for enlarging our little house in Hishu Lane. It was mutual deceit and it worked excellently, even though I knew he could not drive that horrible night from his thoughts. Then I had to tell him you were coming."

Now Horn found himself wishing he had brought at least one of the others along. He saw only anguish in her dark eyes and he wanted very much to reassure her.

"Alex had always fought his own battles and I believe he had convinced himself that somehow he could win this one. When I told him you were coming with four other friends, he didn't react as I hoped he would. He is in a wheelchair and he took my hand and I could feel him trembling. He said, 'I am afraid. When they see me they are going to ask themselves why they came so far to view my ruins. They might even not recognize me, let alone believe me.'

I told him my grandfather always said a man will travel far to know the truth and that you must be too wise to accept anything else."

"We'll certainly do our best." Horn said, wishing he could come up with a more inspiring comment.

"No matter how Alex behaves when you see him, this will not be an ordinary reunion. He is very much aware that all of you can mentally share that night with him. Meeting you again could be more agonizing for him than his trial."

"I understand. We will be careful."

She hesitated, then looked directly into his eyes. "I hope you realize that if your findings confirm his guilt you may kill your friend."

"I will pass the word."

At once she seemed relieved and he marveled at her ability to transform herself.

"Chinese," she began briskly, "are a family people. We live, prosper, and die in the family, and even a distant relative is accepted as long as he does not offend the family. So I have been this morning to see my sister-in-law."

He thought to ask her if she had a sister exactly like herself and immediately changed his mind. This was no time for whimsy.

"My sister-in-law. is a cousin to Leonard Wu. After I had admired her new baby—frankly I find admiring babies a bore, but this time it had to be done—I begged her to call

Leonard and ask him to see you. At first he refused, but she put the Wu family twist on his arm and explained you meant no harm. He agreed to see one of you alone. I said it would be you."

"When?"

"Tonight at nine. I will take you to his place. He does not want to talk about the crash with anyone, let alone a stranger who is an expert. You had better think of something to fill the silences." She stood up and he rose so rapidly in response he struck the table heavily.

He caught his glass just before it capsized. "Sorry! This seems to be my clumsy day."

They laughed together at his awkwardness. Then she held out her hand. "Thank you for your understanding."

"There are several thousand questions I would like to ask you—"

"I must go to the police now. Your permits to visit Alex are to be ready at one o'clock. They are very punctual. I will return to pick you up at four forty-five. It is only a short way to the sanitarium."

He found himself watching her walk away as if she were a shadow from one of his most pleasant dreams. She seemed to glide rather than walk, her small perfectly proportioned body gracefully outlined beneath the long Chinese dress.

Before their lunch arrived van Grootes excused himself from the table. He explained to the others that the Taiwan heat seemed to have brought on a slight recurrence of his malaria. He would like to lie down.

When he reached his room he removed his shoes and socks and, sighing heavily, lowered his bulk to the bed. A great weariness had come upon him and he knew that it was not altogether the heat or any recurrence of the malaria he had known on KLM's tropical service.

Staring at the huge immobile ceiling fan which presumably would take over if the hotel air conditioning broke down, he again asked himself why he had come to Taipei. Perhaps, he thought, in spite of my size I am a small person within, and am now seeking some kind of retribution for what Alex Malloy once did to me. Do I want to see him humbled at last? Or do I hope to heal that festering wound inflicted so long ago? Now, as the English say, the shoe is on the other foot. Did I forgive him for my injured pride, or did I forgive him because he was right?

When he flew for KLM Malloy had established an uncanny record for being right. Had the law of averages finally caught up with him? Could he, at last, have been so very wrong?

He remembered they had first met when the legendary Albert Plesman of KLM had hired several American pilots because there were simply not enough qualified Dutchmen available. That would have been about 1936? Not one of those Americans had ever learned to pronounce the full name of their new employer correctly: Koninklijke Luchtvaart Maatschappij. Of the Americans, Malloy had certainly been the most controversial if not the most popular. He had often gone out of his way to flaunt his expertise and even show his contempt for the more relaxed Dutch way of flying. In spite of KLM's magnificent safety record, Malloy had insisted the company's veteran pilots were frequently standing into danger. His attitude had not gone down very well with such stalwarts as Geysendorffer, van Veenendaal, Koppen, Frijns, Smirnoff, and Parmentier— or van Grootes for that matter. God damn it, the man had been so *intense!*

Van Grootes closed his eyes. In some ways it seemed like only yesterday since he had taken Alex Malloy on his check flight out to Java. KLM had just acquired DC-3s for the long run and he had been pleased to have a co-pilot who was experienced in the type, although word was already about that this particular American was something of a tiger. It was said that when he had taken the written examination, which after a trip out to Java as co-pilot would qualify him for his own command, Alex had supplied some unorthodox answers. The examination was elaborate and exhausting. Many veteran pilots doubted if they could pass it without reference to manuals. These were not allowed, and the first question alone, which covered seven thousand miles of air routes, was enough to test the mental sharpness of any man.

"Write from memory the highest altitudes in meters *and* feet, the distances, the magnetic courses, and the radio aids between Alexandria, Egypt, and Medan, Sumatra. Next, make a reasonably accurate drawing of every major airdrome along the route, including the bed capacity of the local hostel, fuel available, cargo facilities, local money used with its present exchange rate against the Dutch guilder, and the language used."

Question number two was less a matter of memorization and more revealing of the way an applicant might think. It went something like, "If you took off from Rangoon for Bangkok and arriving there found Bangkok closed because of weather, what would you do? Give courses, distances, and radio aids."

Malloy's answer, written in English, was unmistakable in any language.

"Any pilot who worked for KLM and left Rangoon for Bangkok without enough fuel to return to Rangoon *should be fired*." Now he remembered, Malloy had offered even more than he was asked.

"*However,* in the unlikely circumstance the pilot on his return should find the weather at Rangoon also closed in, a good alternate would be Akyab to the north. It is a small strip, but usable. Located on a peninsula. Operated by missionaries."

Then he had given the number of beds available, the distance from Rangoon, and the course. He had remarked there were no radio aids.

Malloy had passed the exam with one of the highest grades ever recorded. That was the trouble with the man. He was, or had been, so always and infuriatingly right. On the ground he had been easygoing—in the air exactly the opposite. Very well then, how could he have been so incredibly wrong a month ago?

Van Grootes rolled over on his side and stared out the window. The view was mostly of sky and a slant of the hill behind the hotel. A large black bird was thermalling above the slope, circling endlessly against the blue-white sky. It reminded him of the great birds he had watched in India and Java, where the heat had been much the same. He should have known better than to risk a return to the tropics. Too often the heat had brought a recurrence of his malaria. Or was the memory of that time still so strong he had become paranoid on the subject? Or now, lying here, was he only trying to escape from thinking about Malloy and the incident which was really an accident?

According to custom, they had met at the KLM operations office the day before the flight. They had been informed of the general weather trends, which would be updated just before actual take-off. As aircraft commander he had been issued a briefcase in which there were twenty-four different kinds of money, with a small book indicating that day's convertibility into Dutch guilders.

Frightened by the ravings of Hitler, many Jews were emigrating from Europe to Australia. Some chose to go partway with KLM. The aircraft on that flight had been a DC-3, which normally carried twenty-one passengers on the European runs, but only eleven out to Java because of the heavy mail loads.

For the immigrants nine extra canvas seats had been placed in the center aisle, and even before they had taken off from Schiphol van Grootes had done his best to comfort them. His Yiddish was fragmentary, but his German was fluent and he had told them, "Be at peace. You are going to a real promised land, and this half-Jew will see you arrive there safely."

Now he found that many details of that flight were dissolved in the memories of other flights over the same route, yet small and odd things were strangely clear. There was Malloy's complaint about KLM's Wright engines, which he said were ever so much rougher than the Pratt and Whitneys he had been flying in the United States. A Dutch co-pilot would never have offered such a negative opinion of his employer's wisdom. KLM considered the Wrights superior to most European-built engines and they had served very faithfully. Yet in retrospect, Malloy's undiplomatic remarks had been based on undeniable truths.

For flight crews, the first day of an East Indies flight was a long one. Fortunately the Jews had been reassured by their captain. Many went to sleep immediately after their midnight take-off from Amsterdam. They had flown on to Budapest, where three more Jews were boarded, then to Bucharest, and finally after a full day in the air had landed at Athens.

When did we sleep? van Grootes wondered. Eighteen hours on duty, and then the following morning just before dawn the schedule called for a departure to Alexandria. There they had refueled and flown on to Lydda in Palestine, where the passengers had lunch and Malloy had experienced his first taste of Middle Eastern heat.

Van Grootes listened to the soft whirring of the air conditioning vent above his bed and thought how precious such a system might have been in Lydda on that blazing noon when he and his passengers were soaked in their own sweat.

By mid-afternoon of the second day, with the sun on their tail, they had descended upon Baghdad, where the air often simmered at 120 degrees Fahrenheit. The interior of the aircraft was like a caldron. Incredible how the memory retained details and so often lost the big events! Remember telling Malloy that one way to keep from wilting was to think of Imperial Airways and thank God he was not working for them. "You bet your bloody life their asses are hotter than yours!"

Van Grootes closed his eyes and smiled. He had not thought of those times for years. The poor bloody English. He could see them now in their pukka-sahib whites, red-faced and suffering stoically in the heat.

Although they had recently introduced "C" class flying boats on their route to India, the British were still flying the overland desert route in Handley Page Hannibals, really a vast assembly of aircraft parts flying in loose formation at a cruising speed of one hundred miles per hour. With a very limited ceiling, they were obliged to fly low over the desert, no more than two or three hundred feet. The turbulence and heat in those lower depths would try the most hardy adventurer, but then the English, he thought, had somehow developed a special insensitivity to physical discomfort. While KLM would climb to ten or twelve thousand feet and at least enjoy cool temperatures in flight, the Hannibals plodded along just above a ditch which the RAF had cut across the desert as a navigational aid. They invariably arrived in Baghdad hours after KLM. Chatsworth might have been one of those poor fellows. He must ask him.

The Indies flights carried four in the crew—commandant, first officer (or co-pilot), radio operator, and steward. Although he was qualified as a commandant and therefore entitled to wear three bars on his shoulder straps, that first Indies flight for Malloy had been his official introduction to the route itself. Hence he had been obliged to serve as co-pilot. That he might better assimilate its peculiarities, van Grootes had allowed him to do most of the actual flying, although, as always, responsibility for the flight's safety remained with the aircraft commander.

Malloy had demonstrated on the first take-off from Schiphol that his handling of a DC-3 was of the very highest order. Pleasantly relaxed, van Grootes had spent most of the flight in the right-hand seat doing the book work, secretly assessing Malloy as a man and a pilot.

How surprisingly easy it was even now to visualize the other members of the crew! The radio operator was Hofstra, a very quiet near-sighted man from Utrecht. He had formerly been in steamships with Royal Rotterdamscher Lloyd. Weber was the steward. He had also learned his craft in ships.

On the third day the flight continued to Basra on the Euphrates, thence to a place called Jask on the Gulf of Oman, which was nothing more than a sandspit aerodrome twenty feet above the level of the sea. The Persian government had provided a shed for customs and medical inspectors, who seemed to enjoy their reputation as the most hardheaded bureaucrats east of Suez. There was also a canteen for snacks and a few flea-bitten camels for the passengers to photograph at so many rials per pose.

There were occasions at Jask when Imperial Airways would arrive before KLM had finished the formalities and refueling. A Hannibal would come floating in from Karachi westbound, and because of the heat and subsequent discomfort of their passengers in comparison with his own, van Grootes would look the other way and pretend they were not really there. He had never been sure why he had always been so acutely aware of misery in others. It is like a disease, he thought. During the war, although he never had suffered actual privation, he had actually experienced great physical discomfort when he thought of the agonies of others.

Yes, there is something about me that longs for martyrdom, he decided. Or am I just a little crazy, which would explain my telling Lew Horn I would go around the world to help a man who hardly strained himself to help me?

Air France would also drop in to Jask for fuel. Van Grootes smiled as he envisioned the French Detwoitine 338s, an aircraft said to have had a DC-3 for a mother and a Fokker for a father. They were also much slower than KLM Douglases and could not approach their command of altitude.

It had been at Jask while they waited for their official papers to be pounded with the inspectors' stamps that he had asked Malloy what he would do if one of their engines should suddenly quit during take-off.

There was a reason for his question beyond the instinct of self-preservation. He had wanted to learn more of the way Malloy thought. Certainly he could recite the proper "engineout" procedures—full power, gear up, clean airplane, maintain airspeed, determine which engine . . . et cetera. The drill for remaining airborne on one engine was the same for DC-3s wherever in the world they flew. Given a minimum of breaks, he was convinced Malloy could perform a safe return to most aerodromes. But at Jask? The aerodrome was barely acceptable for length. And at these temperatures the performance of any aircraft was severely reduced, even though the altitude was practically sea level.

His own morose contemplation of Jask during previous flights had invariably left him without enthusiasm for the place. How would the American assess the situation?

He could see Malloy now, squinting at the shimmering sea. He had barely glanced at the dazzling expanse of the aerodrome and had answered almost to quickly, "We would go for a swim."

Van Grootes had thought, Excellent! Here is a man who had not tried to impress me with a lot of garbage about how if this were so and that were so then he would solve the problem according to the book. Here was no procedural disciple who placed all his faith in the written manual. Here was a realist. He had been willing to recognize that such a load of fuel and passengers combined with the temperature and length of the aerodrome would demand all the power of *both* engines if he expected to stay in the air.

Was that the moment he had begun to like the American? A cockpit is the proper place for pessimists. The pilot who anticipates the worst and is ready for it rarely encounters it.

Later Malloy had further revealed his style by utilizing what few precautions were available at Jask. When he taxied out he went to the very limit of the aerodrome and even then carefully swung the DC-3's tail around so that it stood between two oil cans marking the perimeter. Thus he troubled to gain an additional hundred feet of take-off run over that available to more casual pilots. He blasted the tail off the ground *before* he released the brakes and, with the DC-3 nearly in flying attitude, eliminated even the minor drag of the tail wheel. The reward for his extra care had been one of the shortest take-offs van Grootes had ever seen. He knew then that Alex Malloy was his kind of pilot. He knew how to minimize the pucker factor.

From Jask they had flown on to Karachi and then eastward through the amber afternoon, holding the hopelessly inaccurate Indian charts on their knees and marking them according to what they observed below. Whole villages and towns were shown incorrectly or not at all, and even valleys, roads, and streams were often so far off accurate position they were more dangerous than useful as navigational aids. Only the railroads were drawn correctly.

By dusk they were halfway to Jodhpur. They drummed onward above the darkening face of India until nine o'clock. Finally, arrived over the aerodrome in darkness, their eyes still burning from the earlier dazzling sun, they had descended, unusually grateful for respite. While the gyros whined down they had remained in their seats long enough to record the flight times and note in the logbook the few minor mechanical attentions the aircraft required. At last they had stretched their cramped legs and stepped down into the soft Indian night like men temporarily visiting from another world. After so long in the discipline of flight, they found it difficult to lose the beat of engines; and almost unbearably wearied, they became laconic and given to long silences.

On the fourth day they had risen once again with the last of the stars and they had flown on to Allahabad, which was the smallest and shortest aerodrome on the route, being barely nine hundred meters long. From there they held still easterly for Calcutta, and after refueling there they ascended once more to cross the Bay of Bengal. For four days eastbound they had been losing time by the sun and rarely managed more than five hours' sleep a night. Was that the true reason for what happened on that first flight with Malloy?

God damn it, van Grootes thought, here I am right back brooding on the same old thing. It should long ago have been forgiven and forgotten.

He rolled over, sat up with a grunt, and put his bare feet on the cool varnished floor. *There,* that was more pleasant. Perhaps he should call for an iced drink? No, a cigarette was more appropriate, since one did not receive cold drinks in hell. And now that it was being revisited the only escape was to pass on through. He saw that his hand was trembling slightly as he lit a match.

As a mark of respect for Malloy he had allowed him to occupy the left seat all the way from Amsterdam. At Calcutta he had decided his generosity had gone far enough. Returned to his proper place of command, he had sought the cool air at eleven thousand feet over the Bay of Bengal. Content at last to be physically as well as officially charged with the affairs of his aircraft, he had sat in pleasant silence as the evening closed in quickly. It loomed out of the east like a great silken curtain. The air was smooth and the sonorous beating of the engines so lulled him he had several times caught himself slipping into that state of suspended life which so often accompanies high and easy flight. He had often wondered if regular exposure to this phenomenon might permanently affect a man's personality when he returned to earth. It was as if all unhappiness and responsibility had been quietly jettisoned into the depths below. Occasionally it had seemed to him that time itself held still and he had experienced a haunting sense of eternity, of never having done anything else or having been any other place except in that exalted situation.

As they approached the Burmese coast they encountered the usual parade of cumulus build-ups. Gigantic foaming bastions of vapor rose as high as ten thousand meters. During the last of the twilight, when all color had left the sky, he had successfully managed to circumvent the highest and most formidable towers. Soon full night obscured everything outside the cockpit windows and it was no longer possible to judge the formations and weakest crevasses where an aircraft might slip through. With the sport of selecting his way denied, he had surrendered the mechanics of flying to the automatic pilot.

For a time then his duties were simple. He had only to hold fair and true on the correct compass course for Rangoon. That direct aim in degrees had been confirmed by Hofstra, who had held his key down and sought bearings from Rangoon itself.

Night approaches to the Burmese coast were almost always the same. Inevitably the aircraft would plow into a cumulus hidden in the gloom. After the initial jolts there would come the hammering of rain against the windshield followed by a miniature waterfall of chill water dribbling down from the drain trough behind the windshield. Usually his invasion of this upper wilderness was illuminated by prolonged flashes of sheet lightning, a forbidding spectacle unless a man had been there many times.

He had started descending some thirty minutes out of Rangoon. The change in the sound of the slipstream had roused Malloy from his dozing. He said in apology for his indolence, "I should really be ashamed to collect my pay for the last hour."

"KLM does not expect us to be supermen, just indefatigable. You will receive your reward in Java, at Bandung. There in a cool valley you will bathe and rest for seven days. You will smell the bougainvillaea about you, and a houseboy will care for you like a baby. You will sign a chit for everything, and if you want a beautiful girl the supply is inexhaustible. You will think—you will be *sure*—you have died and gone to heaven."

They had laughed together then and were two friends descending through the night. They remained on solid instruments down to five hundred meters, but he had not been in the least concerned since Hofstra had received the current weather at Rangoon. It was holding reasonably good—one-thousand-foot ceiling and four miles.

He had been pleasantly surprised when they had broken out exactly as predicted. He had descended according to the QDM bearings Hofstra received from the ground. Once in the clear, he had turned the cockpit lights far down and was able to recognize the vague outlines of a riverbank. All was as it should have been. He had banked for the airport as he had done so many times before and asked Malloy to switch on the main tanks and put the mixtures at full rich. Malloy had acknowledged the orders and about a minute later had moved the lever by his side when he was told to lower the landing gear.

Suddenly there were doubts and from that moment every detail was still sharply etched.

He leaned forward until his nose was nearly against the windshield and shielded his eyes against the subdued light in the cockpit. Ahead, where it should be, he could not see the aerodrome.

He heard Malloy call out, "Three green lights . . . pressure!" Confirmation. The landing gear was down and locked in position.

He had asked for fifteen degrees of flaps. And while he tried to find something recognizable in the blackness outside he had heard the second confirmation. "Fifteen degrees on your flaps."

He felt the extra solidity the flaps gave the aircraft. Concerned with not missing anything familiar outside, he had asked Malloy to advance the propellers to 2400 revolutions. He heard the engines snarl and then synchronize.

He glanced at the magnetic compass on the off chance he might have set the gyro wrong. It matched exactly. He was holding proper course. Still there was nothing to relieve the blackness ahead.

Suddenly the aircraft slammed into a wall of rain and he was glad he had not descended farther. Of course, here was the explanation for the void ahead. The aerodrome was hidden behind the squall.

He had slowed the DC-3 to 110 miles and asked Malloy to call out his speed and altitude. He heard him intone regularly, "One thousand . . . one ten . . . nine fifty . . . one fifteen . . . nine eighty . . . one oh five . . ."

He was about to ask Hofstra to request a final QDM when they broke out of the squall and he saw the flare pots of the aerodrome directly ahead. It was still raining lightly, but they were in a good position to land straight in—if a trifle high. He immediately called for full flaps.

Malloy complied instantly by moving the flap lever down. "Full flaps."

Almost at once it became apparent that his approach was higher than had first appeared. He pulled all power off both engines and pushed the nose of the DC-3 down at a steep angle. He was prepared to accept some increase in final approach airspeed, but he saw at once that the additional twenty miles was too much.

Rangoon aerodrome was laid out for the old three-engined Fokkers and the British biplanes, which floated down at very slow speeds. Now there was no question that his approach was too high and fast. Yet he had one trick left in his bag. Hoping the maneuver would not make Malloy uneasy, he pulled the DC-3's nose up until the airspeed read only eighty-five. If it was necessary to lose excess altitude quickly without gaining too much forward distance it was a perfectly safe procedure in the wonderful DC-3.

He switched on the landing lights and heard the engines backfiring as they swooped down for the border lights. The rate of descent was now too fast. He eased on a shade of power to smooth the touchdown and, as if his alter ego had spoken, he heard Malloy very distinctly: "I don't know this field, but it sure looks like a tight squeeze to me."

Why hadn't he packed up and departed immediately? He had only to shove the throttles full forward, call for the gear to be raised, ask Malloy to bleed the flaps up slowly, and climb back up to eight or nine hundred feet. There was plenty of room beneath the ceiling, and the visibility was only slightly reduced by the rain.

How many times had he reviewed that night? And cursed his aerial pride, knowing at last how extremely dangerous pride can be when nursed in the arms of a pilot. The prime element in all aeronautical events is man, and his pettiness frequently kills him.

As the flare pots marking the edge of the field vanished beneath the DC-3's nose and the loom of the landing lights began racing along the ground, it seemed he could touch down with room to spare. So? Desire and pride are the most dangerous combination of all.

All the way from Amsterdam he had been the mentor. The common business of flight had been Malloy's. The time had come to demonstrate superiority, the place well chosen for its familiar aspects. It was inconceivable that like some apprentice co-pilot he might overshoot.

Half of the aerodrome was behind the DC-3 before he had finally felt the wheels touch earth. He could still have gone around, yet in spite of a very distinct feeling that trouble was at hand he had refused.

He had jumped on the brakes and hauled back on the control yokes trying to gather all the drag available.

The brakes appeared to have no effect whatever. Water from the puddles splashed the slippery red mud of Rangoon against the landing lights and the far line of flare pots raced toward the windshield. And suddenly it was too late.

As the flare pots skidded out of sight behind the wings the landing lights picked up an embankment in the distance. And nearer there was a black ditch. Still standing on the brakes he had slammed on full left rudder and full throttle to the right engine. The tail swung wildly around in response and the DC-3 slid sideways into the ditch. There was a sickening crumping noise as the right gear and then the wing gave way.

There is an instant in calamity when every sense is stunned and recognition more slowly becomes pure awe. He had sat unbelieving of the messages relayed by his eyes and ears. In contrast Malloy had kept his wits and in a series of sure gestures cut the right throttle, both mixtures, and had turned off the fuel tanks. He cut the ignition switches and the master switch. The interior of the DC-3 went black. For several seconds it had seemed impossible to do anything except sit stupidly, listening to the light rain peckling on the roof of the cockpit.

"Let's get the hell out of here."

Malloy was thinking of fire. It could come in seconds.

From the blackness of the cubicle Hofstra pleaded in Dutch, "My glasses. I can't find my glasses?"

Malloy was already in the narrow passageway which led to the cabin. He had taken a flashlight from his flight kit. The beam swept past the stacked cargo in the bin beside him then fell upon Hofstra who was still strapped in his seat. He appeared to be paralyzed in position, his face white with fear. "I was cleaning my glasses," he whimpered in English, "and I dropped them."

As if he were going about a routine duty Alex swept the metal floor with the beam of his light. He stooped and picked up a pair of glasses.

"These *have* to be yours."

He slipped the glasses on Hofstra's nose and in almost

the same motion unfastened his seat belt. Then he hoisted him to his feet, and propelled him toward the cabin door.

The passengers blocked the cabin aisle although Malloy's flashlight revealed several still in their seats. Like Hofstra they seemed incapable of moving.

At the extreme rear end of the cabin someone was cursing in Dutch. A circle of light wiggled across the ceiling. It sprouted from Weber, the steward.

"Have you got the door open?"

"No, Commandant! It is jammed!"

The passengers had not panicked, but the rising sound of their protests and queries promised terror would soon take charge. Many of the passengers spoke only Polish or Yiddish. A few understood German.

"Please calm yourselves! We'll have you outside in a few minutes!"

The smell of fuel was becoming more apparent. If some fool lit a cigarette? Still, a shouted warning might confirm the hidden danger of ruptured fuel lines. Immediately the chance of panic was more certain than fire.

At the most two minutes had passed since the DC-3 had come to a halt. If we were going to flame, it should have happened by now, he thought.

"Come on, Van, let's kick those exit windows!" In this world there are men who are born for emergencies.

The exit windows were in the middle of the aircraft. Break the plastic, turn the red handles, and shove out. The windows fell away and at once the strong odor of fuel pervaded the cabin.

Strangely the passengers ignored all urgings and moved like invalids. Even the men seemed hopelessly dazed and required help through the openings where the windows had been. Yet when they were all out and counted, the evacuation could not have taken more than a few minutes.

The rain suddenly became heavier. Some of the passengers complained their clothes were getting wet. One man wanted to go back inside the cabin for his hat. It was crazy. A woman wept hopelessly because her new shoes were smeared with mud. They were escaped inmates from an insane asylum who obviously had no conception how terrible things might have been.

Van Grootes sighed heavily and pushed himself to his

feet. How many more years was he going to brood about that night? How many more years of life did a man have?

Moving like a great bear, he padded to the bathroom. He opened his battered leather toilet kit, extracted a vial of brown pills, opened his mouth wide, and tossed two pills inside. He washed them down with a glass of water and silently cursed the constipation which seized him after every time change. Curious that he should now remember he had been suffering the same disability when they had returned to the Rangoon aerodrome the next morning. Examining the wreckage of the DC-3 had been a dreadful experience. It had looked like a huge game bird, shot down and wounded. It was the first time he had ever put a scratch on an aircraft and only Malloy's quick action had saved it from total loss.

He looked up and caught his image in the mirror above the washbowl. For weeks after the accident he had avoided all mirrors and even when shaving or combing his hair he had contrived not to meet his own eyes.

It was more difficult to avoid the passengers, who were obliged to wait in the Minto Mansions Hotel until KLM sent another aircraft out from Java. And Hofstra was there, and Weber, and of course Alex Malloy. No one mentioned the accident either directly or by inference. There seemed to be a conspiracy to isolate Commandant van Grootes from all who were aboard that aircraft.

"Look here, I know I faulted and I am most grateful for your quick thinking after we stopped . . . Look here, I'm terribly sorry . . ."

Words that were never spoken. What could be said to people who had trusted a man with their lives and very nearly lost them?

There had to be an investigation, with the outcome largely dependent on what Malloy might say. He was the only spectator with a front row seat.

Yet Malloy had remained particularly aloof until the last night, when he suggested drinking a beer together on the porch of the hotel. There was a moon and just enough breeze to rustle the fronds of the hotel's potted palms. At last life seemed returning to normal. Was it because Malloy was being his most genial and it was like a soothing balm to discover a new friend?

"Alex?" It had been easier to look at the moon rather than risk embarrassing a new friend by questioning his eyes. "Our people in Amsterdam will expect you to write a report . . . your opinion."

"Yes, I know. I wrote it the next morning. Maybe you should read it?"

The man who had been a constant companion for better than a week, the man who had already become a valuable friend, rose and stretched and yawned at the moon.

"It won't take you long, because it's very short. I couldn't think of much else to say."

Van Grootes carefully combed his heavy gray hair, then returned to the bed. He sat down and pulled on his socks. To this day he could quote Alex Malloy's report verbatim:

I was serving as first officer to Commandant van Grootes on the night of March 5, 1938. The weather was overcast with rain and a standard night QDM approach was made to Rangoon aerodrome. On breaking out of a squall, the airport lights were observed ahead. Prelanding check was properly carried out and a final approach begun. It appeared to me we were high, but being unfamiliar with the airport I assumed there were obstructions along the perimeter which I could not see or were not lighted. Commandant van Grootes continued the approach and landed the aircraft. There was not enough distance remaining to stop the aircraft and considerable damage resulted.

In my opinion the proper procedure would have been to execute a missed approach. All mechanical systems in the aircraft were functioning normally and there was no reason to prevent the initiation of a new approach.

Succinct. The facts and a qualified opinion. What more could a man expect? Yet a fellow Dutchman might have reported differently. The Pilots' Social Association was strongly pro KLM until it appeared there might be some disciplinary action taken against one of their own. There were only thirty or forty pilots then, including two Germans, a Swedish count, one Australian, and two Englishmen. Until Alex and the other Americans arrived, the balance were all native Dutchmen. Certain things happen on every airline, and if no one was hurt the pilots' group believed some of the minor incidents were best left unresolved.

Of the Rangoon incident, one of the Dutch first officers might have reported, "I believe our difficulty was caused by overriding air in the immediate vicinity of the aerodrome." Or, "Braking action was poor to nil due to heavy rain. Commandant van Grootes should be commended for his quick action in making a deliberate ground loop before we slid into the embankment full on."

An even more imaginative first officer might have commented, "due to the rapidly approaching thunderstorm, which could have rendered the field unusuable beyond our fuel reserve, it was imperative that a landing be made immediately."

Van Grootes shook his head unhappily and reached for his shoes. He tried to dismiss the Rangoon affair from his thoughts. This long-nourished bitterness had to die someday. Or would it? Was this trip to Taipei more of a catharsis than a whole-hearted attempt to save a friend? Would Malloy have done the same thing if the roles were reversed?

Van Grootes finished lacing his shoes and stood up. He was ready now. The touch of malaria, which undoubtedly was not malaria at all, had miraculously disappeared. He knew this hour's retreat to privacy had been motivated solely by a long ago wounded pride. A man who had been absolutely right had simply told the truth and there had been nothing personal about it. In his eyes one lonely hard-headed Dutchman had bungled his responsibility as a pilot, and that was unforgivable.

Very well. Those who had been judged should be inclined to mercy.

5

Horn had hoped to call upon Sheldon Spencer during the afternoon. Perhaps, he thought, the man might become less negative if he understood we are not trying to make life difficult for him.

His telephone call to Far Eastern left Horn unsatisfied and vaguely suspicious.

"Mr. Spencer is in Tokyo. He will return the day after tomorrow . . . maybe. No, a definite appointment is not possible, because Mr. Spencer is very busy—always very busy. Call again, if you please. Your name again? Ah, yes. Captain Lew Horn. How do you spell it again?"

How do you spell Horn! Either Spencer's secretary was an idiot or he was deliberately hiding. Tomorrow Horn must discover why.

He glanced at his watch and found there was still enough of the afternoon to investigate one factor which had been troubling him.

As he crossed the lobby of the Grand Hotel the pace of his stride increased. Something must be done about the staff at the Taipei control tower. They would have been the last to communicate with Alex during his normal life.

Near the revolving door at the entrance he found Diderot sprawled in one of the overstuffed chairs. He halted although he would have preferred to keep going. There was something about Diderot which annoyed him. The man had seemed indifferent since his arrival in Taipei; his manner suggested he considered the battle lost before it had begun.

"Taking a quick nap?" Horn tried to keep the sarcasm from his voice. They were all weary, and he considered

Diderot arrogant when he flaunted his fatigue with a yawn.

"Without success. I looked for a long time at the fancy ceiling. What is it like to be a Chinese termite with all that carving for dinner?"

The man is too handsome, Horn thought, and the world has always been his to charm.

Diderot yawned again. "But the termites do not really keep me awake. I cannot stop thinking about Alex. I keep trying to put myself in his place and say to myself over and over again, Now what to do?" He shrugged his shoulders. "I am trying to imagine what it is like to have the responsibility—when it becomes more than just a word. That is what they do to us, you comprehend? They say the captain is responsible, yes? Well, we accept it. And we hear this word from the very first day we join the line. Whatever the line, it is all the same. For most of us it is only a word which brings extra privilege and pay. We think we know what it means, and how it must affect us if something happens."

He spread his hands upward as if he sought an answer from the ceiling. "But nothing happens. So we go on year after year holding our heads very high and being the big boss. *Alors*. What is it really like when people trust you with their lives and then lose them? What happens to the word 'responsibility' then, even if it is not your fault?"

He sat erect and searched Horn's eyes. "Do *you* know?"

Horn was suddenly uncomfortable. It seemed he could hear his own voice saying, No, I do not know, and yet he realized he had not even breathed a reply. For a moment he was greatly relieved to discover that he must certainly have been wrong about Diderot. It took wisdom and courage to question the cruel truth behind the avalanches of operational bulletins, most of which concluded with the phrase "Nothing in the foregoing alters the fact that the ultimate responsibility is that of the aircraft commander."

Diderot was saying, "I have been sitting here thinking how Alex must be one of the very few men in the history of flying who know what it is like. All the others, of course, died with their responsibility."

A silence came between them which Horn found increasingly disturbing. What would Brewster say if he posed the same question? Or any other line pilot? Would they also discover how casually they had treated the word? And be at a loss for a reply?

He asked Diderot if he carried a business card.

"Of course. Sabena keeps us well supplied. It is good advertising."

"Before we see Alex we should get rid of the obvious. One item is the remote possibility he misunderstood the altimeter setting given by the Taipei tower. I'd feel better if we had a talk with the controllers. I'd like to hear how they pronounce English numbers. I understand an impressive-looking business card can accomplish wonders out here. I thought we might take an hour or so and try to bluff our way into the tower."

Diderot was standing before he had finished. "It is better than my brooding."

In the taxi Diderot said he remembered his father telling him about two Air France crashes at Bahrain in the Persian Gulf.

"The first one went into the sea on final approach. As soon as the news reached Paris they sent out a special aircraft with an investigation team. On final approach to Bahrain it also went into the water and at almost the same place. In both aircraft the altimeters were set incorrectly."

"From the printed report on Alex it is impossible to know how the numbers transmitted by the controller might have sounded," said Horn.

"What was the altimeter setting?"

"Twenty-nine five five. Suppose Alex understood the controller to say two-nine-*nine*-five instead of two-nine-five-five. The difference would be about three hundred and forty feet. If Alex believed he was flying over three hundred feet higher than he actually was, then some of the things he did would make much more sense."

So little against so much, Horn thought. Altimeters were set according to the local air pressure. More than three hundred very important feet commanded by four-hundredths of an inch of mercury in a tube. And "five" in English if distorted by a microphone or careless pronunciation could sound like "nine" which was why it was standard radioese to pronounce that digit as "niner."

As they approached the control tower entrance a soldier who had been dozing on the concrete steps rose unhappily. He hefted his carbine as if to reassure himself, but he was a small and frail-looking young man and the gesture only seemed to mock the uniform, which was much too large for his frame.

The soldier examined their offered cards with dull eyes. Then he returned them and shook his head, once. The finality of the gesture was unmistakable. Diderot offered him a cigarette. The gift was not acknowledged in the soldier's eyes or in the slightest change of his attitude.

"We're not getting anywhere," Horn muttered.

Then a voice behind them asked, "Where would you like to go, gentlemen?"

They turned to see a small round man, bald of head and dignified. He dismounted from a bicycle, propped it against the wall, and removed a wicker basket.

"My refreshment from toil." His smile revealed impressive deposits of gold along his teeth, and his eyes sparkled with intelligence.

Horn at once presented his card and Diderot repeated the gesture.

"Ah! My pleasure. I am Wellington Kee, deputy chief controller."

There was handshaking and Horn, who was half again as tall as Kee, was careful to take his hand most gently, for he knew that the bone-cracking grip through which Caucasians so often proclaim their sincerity was as distasteful to Orientals as to Semites. He told Kee they had hoped to visit the tower and perhaps meet some of the controllers—exchange a few ideas about different procedures around the world.

Watching Kee's alert eyes, Horn sensed he had chosen his introduction well, for everywhere in the flying world there existed an unfortunate gap between pilots and controllers. Communication between the two groups was confined to routine radio exchanges. On both ends of the line the voices were impersonal and, if anything, stiff with politeness. A man who would never say, "Good day, sir," in ordinary conversation did so to his invisible partner. And controllers, suffering from some imagined difference in professional status, were almost pathetically pleased when line pilots troubled to visit their isolated posts.

"You have arrived at a fortunate time. My watch relieves the duty in five minutes. Welcome. I am extremely keen on learning from foreigners. We are so isolated on this island. My dream has always been to travel everywhere in the world." He laughed then repeated, "Everywhere."

As he escorted them into the control room Kee spoke sharply in English to the departing crew, castigating them for their inhospitality in drinking all the tea.

"Our Belgian and American guests come in friendship and what do they find? Dirty teacups!"

He turned to Horn and Diderot. "I apologize for my colleagues. If they do it again I will see they receive a free trip to the mainland."

Then Wellington Kee laughed uproariously and Horn knew he was showing off his English as well as establishing his "face." For an instant Sylvia's soft voice echoed in his thoughts, and he saw her eyes explaining. Then he dismissed the vision.

Horn looked to the west, where the plateau baked in the sun. He decided it would have been impossible for the duty controllers to see any fire on the night Alex had crashed. Only the prolonged lack of response from his flight would have confirmed their suspicion that something had gone very wrong.

Two of Kee's assistants sat at the console. Below them stretched the runway and taxi-ways and beyond, softened in a layer of blue smog, lay the city of Taipei. Horn turned to look behind him and saw the Keelung River flowing toward the red tiled roofs of the Grand Hotel.

Traffic was very light. A military DC-3 was taxiing to a parking area, a Pan American 707 waited for take-off clearance, and a Far Eastern 727 was on final approach. Horn watched the 727 enlarge from a speck over the plateau, saw it seem to hang in the air as it passed the region of the outer marker, and then observed it sliding down the invisible glide path to the runway. Even, he thought, as Alex should have done that night.

As he listened to the spasmodic talk of the controllers Horn became convinced they were displaying their best aerial manners. Considering the amount of traffic, the tower was certainly overstaffed and yet each man's zeal for the work seemed intense.

Although Horn listened carefully, the numbers "nine" or "five" were not pronounced. He was vaguely disappointed. Other numbers pronounced by the controllers were distinct, even though delivered with a slight Oriental lilt.

"You run a tight ship, Mr. Kee."

"Sometimes it is more like the Tower of Babel. You should be here when we have Japan Air Lines on approach, Cathay Pacific in the pattern, and Philippine Air about to take off. Thank God for English and its lack of gender."

Horn was about to tell Wellington Kee the real purpose of their visit, then changed his mind. Sylvia again. She had said something about all departments of the government being interlinked and every employee on guard for his own rice bowl. Yet how could he persaude Kee or any of the others to repeat "two nine five five" without arousing suspicion?

Wellington Kee excused himself a moment then returned almost immediately bearing his wicker basket. He removed the spotless napkin and flourished it with the air of a maître d'.

"If you please. My wife would be honored if you would share what she has prepared."

Horn and Diderot declined. They had just finished lunch . . . Mr. Kee was too kind. As far as they knew, their lines were not contemplating a new route through Taiwan. Ah, yes . . . the photos of Wellington Kee's wife and children at the beach were charming. He was a lucky man.

As Wellington Kee displayed his personal treasures with the eagerness of a small boy, Horn marveled that such an ordinary man might have been even partly responsible for the deaths of so many. Although he was probably innocent in this case, the power of a petty error being magnified into a catastrophe was still within him.

Uncomfortably aware of the warmth in Kee's open smile, Horn could not bring himself to ask if he would pronounce "two nine five five." Instead he inquired how it was that Taipei tower transmitted the altimeter setting in inches of mercury rather than in millibars according to custom in most of the world.

"I do not know, Captain. I suppose it is the American influence. Like Coca-Cola."

Again Kee laughed, this time Horn thought, with a trace of forced heartiness.

"Do you ever have any confusion about it?"

"Nothing serious. All incoming pilots who are accustomed to millibars carry a conversion scale." He paused and looked up into their eyes. Then emboldened he said, "My brother has a car, a nice Buick. Tomorrow afternoon I am free. I show you Taipei if you like. There are many wonderful things to see. My wife would make a lunch for us . . ."

His statement remained unfinished as if he knew the invitation would be declined before it was uttered. As if, Horn thought, he knew at last these tall foreigners were not new friends and their visit could be potentially troublesome.

There was the rebuke of the betrayed in his eyes, Horn decided, and he wished he could wipe the impression away. For now he must ask him the prime question.

"Mr. Kee, do you know who had the duty on the night of Far Eastern's crash?"

The disappointment in his eyes became complete. Horn saw his move to the defensive although his new wariness seemed tinged with regret.

"Unfortunately."

There was no need for elaboration. The way Kee uttered the one word was enough. Somehow he must be persuaded to recite the vital numbers.

Horn took his sketch pad from his pocket. It was his camera, the lens through which he viewed the world.

"Mr. Kee, you have been so hospitable I think we should respond. Our cards give only our airline address. You should know how to find us at home if you arrive in the middle of the night."

There was a question in Diderot's eyes and then understanding as he accepted the offered pad. Horn remembered his address was a typical Flemish tongue twister—something or other Vooruitgangstraat.

"Help Mr. Kee pronounce it or he may have trouble when he travels to Brussels."

While Diderot complied Horn wrote a New York address on the pad. "You'll have no trouble with this one."

Kee accepted the paper, glanced at it and dropped his hand to his side. He seemed confused. In only a few moments he had seen the pleasure of a vicarious voyage denied, and now once again become available.

He raised his hand very slowly as if the writing might be frightened away if he failed to control his anticipation. His hand quivered as he said softly, "Two nine five five Riverside Drive, New York. And the telephone—three six one two nine five nine. I thank you."

Horn held his breath. It had been done. Kee's voice had sounded completely natural.

"Is that how you always say 'nine'?"

"Yes? Why please?"

"No reason really. I just assumed controllers would say 'niner.' "

"Ah, sometimes when we are working aircraft. But only sometimes."

Horn offered his hand and Kee's fingers touched him softly. "Be sure to come and see us. I will arrange for you to visit the control tower at Kennedy."

"And in Brussels I will do the same. Your wife will like our shops."

"I hope not too much."

The smile was renewed on Wellington Kee's face, yet Horn noticed it was not the same. He had suddenly become a man plodding through formalities. How many years had he taken it for granted that he would one day tour the world? Now the illusion had been torn from him and exposed as just another sterile dream by those who should have been more tender. He had been notified by both their voices and their eyes that they never expected to see him again.

He is a very brave man, Horn thought, for he still managed to say, "It was very good of you to come here. I am sorry I cannot show you more of Taipei."

They were silent nearly all the way back to the Grand Hotel. And Horn decided that Diderot must be far more sensitive than he had supposed. He obviously understood how they had destroyed another man's precious dream.

As their taxi labored up the hill to the hotel, Diderot said, "It *could* have happened, but . . . I doubt."

Horn was saddened. "After this is all over I am going to send Wellington Kee my correct address. I will tell him I moved and hope he will come."

6

MEMORANDUM from the Honorable R. D. Chew, Judge, Taipei District Court.

Re: Captain A. Malloy, employee Far Eastern Airways, vs. Republic of China—The People.

1. Having duly considered the evidence offered against Captain A. Malloy, a U.S. citizen, I find him guilty as charged. In all respects was the defendant guilty of negligence. Said neglect brought about the deaths of 14 persons and serious injuries to 46 additional persons. Therefore negligence must be considered criminal.

2. Pending further conferences with my colleagues and in the absence of additional information or evidence, I propose the following penalties should be invoked upon the prisoner:

Penal servitude, 5 years (less time in sanitarium)

Fines, $5000 Taiwan.

3. I will also recommend revocation of all licenses within the jurisdiction of the Chinese CAA.

• •

After his lunch Oliver Chatsworth went to his room with the firm intention of taking a nap.

"I'm aging," he mused. "And in precisely fifty-one days I shall be put out to pasture."

While he waited for sleep he considered the prospect of retirement. There was a wall in his cottage at Didcot, Berks, where his whole career was recorded. From floor to ceiling there were yellowing photographs of aircraft—every type from the beloved old Handley Page Hannibals to Viscounts, Ensigns, and Boeing 707s. Many of the aircraft served as backgrounds for a much younger Chatsworth, a jaunty figure in heavy leather flying coat, helmet, and goggles.

He smiled in his drowsiness as he recalled a long ago exchange with his wife. She had insisted he always assumed a special stance in the photographs—his "standing by an aircraft look." And he had replied that in his opinion he invariably looked like an Antarctic penguin in search of a fish.

Later in the chronological gallery it was obvious the young aviator had grown a mustache and goatee. Quite. When enclosed cockpits became the regular thing a chap would have looked a bit silly carrying one's helmet and goggles about. *Something* had to decorate the Chatsworth façade.

Yes, he thought, it will be a strange experience to keep one's foot on the hearthstone. William Oliver Chatsworth, husband of one, father of two, pilot of the line—ex. *Requiescat in pace*. Please send expressions of condolence to your favorite charity. And let us remember that the victim who squandered the best years of his life aloft had a jolly good time in the doing.

Now this wretched business with Alex. How astonishingly easy it is to loft one's mind from an air-conditioned room to a winter night when Alex was a passenger in an aircraft commanded by the very imposing Neville Keith-Harris. Indeed, *there* had been a chap who had simply rolled over and died one year after his retirement. Some said of a broken heart. Keith-Harris had learned to fly in the World War I RFC and afterward had been one of the original Instone Line pilots which subsequently became part of Imperial Airways. Which in turn eventually became BOAC.

War had come again, and in the autumn of 1941 Keith-Harris had been ticked off to fly BOAC's much maligned "return ferry service" across to Canada. The task was to deposit with care those ferry pilots who had flown the sorely needed Hudson bombers to the U.K. They were hurried back to Montreal so they could bring yet another bomber. Two unfortunate crashes after take-off from Prestwick had caused the surviving professional passengers to regard the service with the utmost suspicion. And Alex Malloy had been one of those pilot-passengers.

Chatsworth allowed his thoughts to drift through a winter's night sky over the North Atlantic. He envisioned an LB-30, a modified transport version of the American B-24 bomber, soaring beneath the frozen stars. Not a bad aircraft, considering it was designed for a different task, he reflected, but a poor ice carrier. To avoid ice many flights were conducted at eighteen or twenty thousand feet, hopefully above all cloud. The aircraft heaters were inadequate to the temperatures at the higher altitudes, and in winter the passengers suffered agonies from the cold. Even on the flight deck hands and feet were numb, but at least the working crew had oxygen masks. The passenger-pilots, huddled together like cattle bound for market, sometimes slipped away into temporary limbo from lack of oxygen. While they were welcome to enter the flight deck, borrow a mask and refresh themselves, few availed themselves of the privilege. They were too much of an independent go-to-hell lot and the recent crashes had created a hostile barrier between passengers and crews. Chatsworth, assigned to the new BOAC base at Montreal, had been obliged to share their misery.

Keith-Harris was in command, Alex Malloy was also one of the freezing passengers. Outside beneath the stars an invisible wind, common to the route and very powerful. The destination as usual, Dorval Airport.

The events were easy to recall, but the various personalities also had to be remembered. First Keith-Harris, a supremely haughty oak cast of a man, regarded by his crews as a reincarnation of Attila the Hun, Machiavelli, and Ivan the Terrible. Convinced that his considerable hours aloft entitled him to take an Olympic view of his fellow man, he was intolerant of the slightest frivolity, a God in the pantheon of such greats as O. P. Jones, Kelly Rogers, Wilcockson, Kingsford-Smith, and Alan Cobham.

For that flight he had drawn a rather scratch crew. A chap named Bottomley was first officer, somewhat a timid sort. The engineer and the wireless officer? Chatsworth didn't remember them. But the navigator was . . . Proper?

No, *Prosper*. A lad of nineteen making his first unsupervised crossing, a fact of which Keith-Harris, who demanded the best crewmen available, had not been advised.

"I trust you know your numbers, lad, because I am impatient with sloth. When I ask our position I want it immediately. And, mind you, precisely."

Prosper was trembling with assorted fears long before they entered the aircraft. In addition to the usual Icelandic low an ugly front bisected the course between the southern tip of Greenland and Ireland. Ice and moderate to severe turbulence were predicted in cloud with beam winds on the order of sixty knots through the frontal area.

Surveying the flight plan over his royal nose, Keith-Harris had worried his navigator. "I trust our touchdown at Dorval will not differ more than five minutes from your estimate. I like to keep things tidy, Mr. Prosper."

The flight was three hours out before the met forecast was resoundingly confirmed. Somewhere south of Iceland Prosper managed a three-star fix which placed the aircraft approximately on course, but fifteen minutes behind flight plan. They were picking up some ice, and the bloody racket it made spinning off the propellers and pounding against the fuselage unnerved him. The turbulence kept sending his carefully sharpened pencils, his dividers, and computer scurrying across his chart, and in spite of the chill on the flight deck he began perspiring mightily. He would scribble a number, then search minutes for his eraser. Once he stepped forward to check the magnetic heading on the compass, but the rubber tube of his oxygen mask brought him up sharply as a tethered hound.

Everything was going wrong. The forbidding bulk of Keith-Harris was directly forward of his navigation table. Bottomley, the first officer, must not have troubled to bathe in weeks. Prosper was certain he could detect the odor even through his oxygen mask. The wireless officer sitting opposite him just announced communications were impossible. Even the engineer irritated Prosper, bumping into him each time he passed back and forth between the fuel transfer pumps in the cabin and his flight deck duties.

When Keith-Harris commanded his navigator to extinguish the tiny light so he could judge the outside weather situation, Prosper's confusion was complete. How could anyone navigate under such conditions? To make things worse the pilots back in the cabin suddenly burst into song —Alex Malloy leading his comrades in a chorus of "Many Brave Hearts Are Asleep in the Deep." What else to pass the time when smoking was forbidden?

Odd thought Chatsworth, that not one of those LB-30s ever exploded. The smoking lamp was never lit, because the fuel transfer system had a nasty habit of inundating the cabin with petrol. Rather silly prohibition, since sparks from the wireless flickered merrily within inches of the transfer hoses. It must have been the superventilation, which also froze the passengers. There were drafts and counterdrafts and minor cyclones which somehow failed to alleviate the all-pervading stink of the single toilet situated behind a green curtain in the tail. A passenger could take his choice of sleeping in temperatures identical to those outside, or watching the red-hot glow of the superchargers beneath the engines. Vicarious heat was better than none.

Alex Malloy's serenade soon irritated his highness in command, who kept muttering that the bloody Yanks were a pack of savages. But even Alex's ample lungs required oxygen, and after a while he disentangled himself from the limp bundles of arms and legs belonging to his near neighbors and crawled forward to the flight deck. The engineer handed him a mask, and Alex inhaled gratefully.

Prosper's light was on a rheostat and he had dimmed it until it hardly provided any illumination at all. God almighty, symbolized in Keith-Harris's backside, might complain.

"Wireless" was fussing with his knobs and occasionally tapping his key, demanding and then beseeching response from the indifferent world below. His headphones were askew, high on the sides of his head, and chirping like a brace of indignant birds. Yet always he remained the eavesdropper; no signals were addressed to him.

Forward, beyond the looming figures of Keith-Harris and his first officer, the crammed instrument panel was illuminated by small flourescent spotlights. Each man, his natural features distorted by an oxygen mask, appeared as some less than mortal creature risen from the depths and commanded to preside over the little territory about him.

The accumulated ice rendered the windshields an

opaque marble. No one on the flight deck spoke. Was it the lack of communication that first caused Alex to suspect all was not as it should be, since most crews find reason to lift their masks long enough for at least a brief exchange?

The overburdened aircraft eventually passed out of the ice and once more the only sound was the rhythmic beat of those ever so sweet Pratt and Whitney engines punctuated by the erratic peepings in Wireless's headphones.

The oxygen had cleared Alex's wits. He noted the altitude holding at 18,000, the airspeed indicating 140, and was troubled at the amount of power being used for such low speed. Accumulated ice still weighed heavily on the aircraft. Certainly the English crew had the foresight to take on extra fuel for just such a handicap. Or would they? All of the windows and the astrodome above Alex were opaque with ice, and he wondered how long it had been since this child navigator had taken a star sight?

There were certain other signs which to Alex's experienced eyes were unsatisfying. First Officer Bottomley was doing the actual flying, not an unusual procedure, but the commander seemed strangely ill at ease. Anxiously preoccupied with tuning and then retuning the automatic direction finder, he would frown as he watched the needle swing and shake his head unhappily.

Prosper and his chart table were directly beside Alex's leg. He looked down upon the laboring youth and noted that his fingernails were dirty and beads of perspiration glistened on his forehead. Writing down numbers, changing them, twisting his computer, he appeared obviously bewildered doing the same things over again and over again, pausing only to lift his mask for a moment to blow on his white fingers.

Leaning as far forward as his mask would permit, Alex checked the magnetic compass course. Two hundred and thirty-five degrees? It seemed a good bit south of west for this zone. A temporary detour to avoid more bad weather ahead? An adjustment for a return to the proper course line?

After a few minutes Prosper wrote a number on a slip of paper and went forward to clip the paper beside the compass. New course. Two hundred and thirty degrees. Keith-Harris did not look up from the direction finder.

"You must have some blast of wind from the south," Alex finally said to Prosper.

Prosper, who had been increasingly aware of the intruder looking over his shoulder, now decided he must appear the veteran of many crossings. He took up his dividers and using the points pretended to be solely concerned with scratching at the dirt beneath his fingernails.

"It's a bit brisk tonight."

"How long have we been on this course?"

It is not the affair of passengers to question such matters, but Prosper hoped that if he obliged, the American would go back where he belonged.

"An hour and ten minutes. Now if you don't mind just slipping back—"

"We're bound for Montreal and you're steering two hundred and thirty degrees? That makes for a hurricane," said Alex incredulously.

"Yours not to fret, sir. Just pop on back to the cabin and have yourself a nap. The captain objects to visitors who overstay—"

"I'll be damned if I'll go back until your high-falutin' captain explains how we can make Montreal on a course of two hundred and thirty degrees!"

Keith-Harris suddenly became aware of the discord behind him. Turning in his grand manner, he stared at the stranger. "May I inquire just what you're doing here? If you are seriously in need of oxygen, inhale a pound or so and be off."

"Someone is crazy up here. The course you are flying will take us to Bermuda, if we don't run out of fuel before we get there."

In all of his flying experience Keith-Harris had never been challenged. "Have you been drinking?"

"No. But I'm a damned poor swimmer and you had better get yourself oriented right now or—"

"Or *what,* sir? BOAC has not informed me that you are in command of this aircraft."

"Or I'll *take* command. This kid you've got working the numbers is confused. He subtracted the variation instead of adding. I've watched you try to take a bearing that would make sense and you haven't been able to do it."

Turning uncomfortably on his bed, Chatsworth found

himself wide awake. Why do I keep remembering? he wondered.

He sat up in the bed and toyed with his goatee as he sought anxiously for additional details. Adjustment of a flying course for magnetic variation is easy and elemental, yet so many navigators have done it incorrectly that there are several jingles to assist the uncertain. The harassed Prosper had even forgotten the jingles.

Once his attention was called to it, Keith-Harris undoubtedly realized they had been flying a wrong course. His concentration on the direction finder and his marked disapproval of the bearings he obtained would indicate he was about to order a change of course when Alex interfered. He would certainly have done so once he had examined Prosper's grubby calculations. The impasse which ensued was due exclusively to the inherent nature of Keith-Harris himself. The man was born pig-headed. Possibly he had mistaken Alex for a Canadian and classed him as a bloody colonial or, worse, knew him even then as an American, which would definitely classify him a bloody rebel. Even more significant, he probably realized Alex was right.

Those personal factors boiling within Keith-Harris caused him to announce in a tone no one could possibly misunderstand, "You will return to the cabin immediately or I will climb to twenty thousand. Since your companions are without oxygen, I should think you will become extremely unpopular."

But Alex stood his ground. "I'll give you ten minutes to take up a reasonable heading. Otherwise all eighteen of us are going to come up here and take over."

Alex tossed his mask contemptuously on Prosper's chart table and lowered himself into the black depths of the cabin. Had Keith-Harris persisted there would have been the first case of aerial piracy.

On schedule, exactly ten minutes after his ultimatum, Alex returned to the flight deck. Keith-Harris had changed course—277 degrees for Montreal. Without a word to Keith-Harris or his crew, Alex once more vanished into the freezing darkness, where he remained in silence until they landed safely at Dorval.

Then he proceeded at once to the BOAC office, where

he filed a formal complaint against Prosper as being incompetent and recommended that Keith-Harris be given a reprimand for "careless indifference to the course being flown."

God, momentarily descended from upon high, discovered a droplet of mercy within himself. "Look here," Keith-Harris had said, "I do admit I was tardy in correcting. I'll survive, but Prosper needs a break. Would you withdraw your protest? After all, these things do happen in the best of families."

"I am not in your family."

"Prosper may very well be given the sack."

"He should be."

"He'll never make the same mistake again."

"He'll make others."

"But damn it, man. You've got to consider his wife and children."

"I am."

And that was the end of it. Or was it? Alex's protest had included a detailed outline of the consequences if the wrong heading had been held for another hour. Disaster was obvious. So Prosper was switched to a ground job—provisioning, was it not?

Keith-Harris had the option of making his next trip as first officer to someone much his junior or spending two months on the ground repenting his sins. His choice was automatic and surprised no one who had ever known him.

Alex? He refused to express the slightest sympathy for either man. And where now was the accuser?

He reached across the bed for the ringing telephone. "Chatsworth here."

The voice of Lew Horn reminded him he was expected in the lobby. Sylvia had said they must be punctual.

"Yes, of course. It's later than I thought. I'll be right down."

"Were you sleeping?"

"No . . . thinking. Not too successfully I fear."

He replaced the telephone. That touchy incident on the flight deck might serve as a perfect example of why it was necessary to know the fundamental nature of a man involved in any flying accident. There was a need to know many other things besides his name and his professional qualifications.

No, the afternoon had not been wasted. Technicalities be damned. There, over the North Atlantic on a winter's night, reviewing a calamity that did not quite happen, Chatsworth decided he might well have discovered a priceless token.

• •

Horn, who supposed he was the most shocked of all, could not at first find voice to greet the stranger who cowered in the wheelchair. Always he had thought of Alex Malloy as a man tall as himself, lusty, and powerful of speech and manner. He had been a duly honored noble among his comrades. Who was this shell of a creature with his sunken cheeks and pleading eyes buried in the sockets of a death mask? His hands were heavily bandaged, but he hugged the chair with his forearms as if it were the last of life itself. When he tried to smile at his visitors, the movement of his mouth was tentative and experimental.

"Hello," he murmured softly and then seconds later added, "friends."

Horn glanced at Sylvia, angered that she had not warned him of this moment. Then at once he was grateful, because with foreknowledge the actual confirmation might have been unendurable.

"It's good to see you, Alex," Chatsworth said finally.

Horn admired his ability to sound as if he meant the greeting. It could never be good to see a long admired idol struck down.

It's been a long time," van Grootes rumbled. The embarrassment in his voice was unmistakable.

Horn found a vacancy in the corner opposite the narrow bed. With his back to the wall he slowly lowered himself to the floor.

"Sit on the bed some of you," Alex was saying. "I never knew I had so many friends. I must owe all of you money."

No one laughed. The bed screeched obscenely when Diderot and Chatsworth put their weight on it. Moller held the single chair for Sylvia, and van Grootes leaned against the door.

"Sylvia told me why you have come."

For a moment Horn was certain the thin voice was going

to break, but at the last moment Alex seemed to reach deep within himself and give it strength.

"She brings me a few letters every time she comes . . . from all over the world. Had one from Bud Rude in Alaska the other day. Used to fly together on Trans-Ocean during the Korean business. . . ."

His words drifted away as if he knew his audience was lost. He held up his bandaged hands. "If you're wondering about these, well, they will be all right in time."

We are witnessing a man living in his own hell, Horn thought.

"You look like you were run over by a tank," Moller said.

Grand prize, Horn thought, for tact. At least he had broken the terrible silence.

Chatsworth moved into the breach. "Met a chap in London, Alex. Said you owed him a gallon of whiskey because of a wager you lost concerning the altitude of the highest peak in Western Samoa. Name was Walts, Watts . . . something of the sort."

Horn could not detect any reaction in Alex's eyes. They had gone dead again. He did not seem even to be listening when van Grootes spoke. "Some of your old friends at KLM send you their regards—Elleman, Koppen, Duimelaar, Bruynestein, Hondong."

Still no acknowledgment in those eyes.

Finally Diderot managed to catch Alex's attention. "Before I left I had trouble with my father. He wanted to call the Generalissimo and tell him he must be senile to allow such things in Taiwan. And since Madame's French is supposed to be so good he wanted to tell her—"

"How is your pop?"

"Splendid. He still flies on good days."

Then seeing the incomprehension in Alex's expression, he added, "Only for the sportive you understand?"

"Ah."

Another silence. Alex rolled his wheelchair forward until he was within reach of Sylvia. She touched his bandaged hand.

Moller said that he brought hearty greetings from Rudy Mayr, who was now flying 707s from Frankfurt to New York. He had learned of Alex's troubles and wished to say that he would be available if he could help. Alex seemed not to hear him.

Then Horn explained that before he had left Paris he had telephoned headquarters of the International Airline Pilots Association. They were very unhappy about the situation and were considering what might be done to effect a change.

Alex only blinked his eyes. "How is your wife?"

"Fine." There was no reason to complicate the tension in the room.

The conversation limped along. In the hall beyond the door someone dropped a tray and Horn thought it sounded like an explosion. He found it almost impossible to resist looking out the window. Dusk had fallen and a thin wash of color lingered in the sky. How often, he speculated, had Alex sat staring at the same sky through this same window. Alone with the ghosts of his passengers.

With a strange apology in his voice Alex explained how Far Eastern Airways had supplied him a defense lawyer who had done his best. But the company needed all the government friends it could find just now and it was difficult to back him against the official authorities. The company did not wish to be accused of arbitrarily defending a pilot who according to the Chinese Civil Aeronautics Administration had gone out of his way to kill people.

At least, Horn thought, there was now no need to pussyfoot around any longer.

"Why is your co-pilot Leonard Wu so uncooperative? As I interpret his testimony, it does not directly damage you, but it certainly does not help."

"I don't know. It was the first time he had flown with me. He's new with the line, so he's on probation. I believe he is convinced that whatever he says, it might be the wrong thing and he might break his own rice bowl . . . just when he had it full."

Horn thought he heard a hint of the old Alex in the beginning of his reply but toward the end his spirit vanished again.

During the ensuing silence van Grootes drummed his huge fingers on the linoleum floor beside him.

"We heard the words on the flight recorder. Was it Leonard Wu who said he had an MDA light?"

"Yes. I had one too, but I didn't say anything aloud, so my reaction was not recorded. As soon as I saw the light I thought, Alex you'd better get the hell out of here. I was actually reaching for the throttles when we hit. I am sure my reaction was slow, because at that moment in the approach an MDA light just didn't make any sense. It was too soon and my pressure altimeter still said we had a thousand feet."

"You had received an outer marker light?" Horn asked.

"As bright as the sun in the sky."

"And your direction finder needles swung around?"

"Number one needle was on the outer marker and swung in the normal fashion. Number two was still on Hsinchu, and Leonard Wu was actually changing frequencies when we hit."

"Why would Wu deny seeing the outer marker light?"

"He doesn't. He refuses to commit himself one way or the other."

"How about the audible signal. Wouldn't he have heard that?"

"In the wreckage they found his audible signal switches in the off position. He was working traffic control and would not necessarily be monitoring everything."

"Did *you* hear an audible signal?" Moller asked.

Alex brought up his bandaged hands to rub at his eyes. No sound came from him, yet it seemed to Horn that he could hear an inward groaning.

"I can't remember. And I have worried about it endlessly. I have relived hundreds of other approaches and realized I have never paid much attention to the audible signals. I have always kept the audible control on very low volume, since I am convinced it is the sort of thing you miss only when it fails to sound off. Because I continued with the approach, I can only assume that I actually heard the proper signal."

"Was the audible switch on your side in the on position?" Horn asked.

The answer was uttered as if each word seared his tongue. "Everything on the left side forward of that airplane except the captain . . . was destroyed."

And one soul more than was officially listed, Horn thought.

He watched Alex rub at his eyes and wondered how much longer he could endure such torture. Yet there were other questions that had to be answered before they could hope to rescue him. Why had Alex committed himself to a final let-down without using the glide slope, at least as a countercheck on his situation? In court he had testified that the system was unreliable. According to his testimony the two pinlike bars which were supposed to translate the most delicate electronic whispers sent from the ground often behaved so eccentrically at Taipei that few pilots had any trust in their indications.

For a moment Alex's eyes came alive and he raised his head like a wounded lion with yet a great deal of fight left in him.

"During the last two years there have been twenty-three erratic behavior reports on the Taipei localizer. In every case the Chinese stated their monitoring system indicated normal operation. What the hell can a man do? We had to learn how to get along without it. The best way if the weather permits is to request an ADF approach. Is? . . . Was? I suppose I'm in no position to say which is the best way . . . to do anything."

Horn wondered if Tseu the flight engineer had seen the outer marker light. He was about to ask, then changed his mind. Tseu would not have had a chance to confirm or deny before he died. Just now a mention of his name might be more than Alex could tolerate.

"I know you've all come a long way to help me, and I cannot express . . . thank you. I have relived those last minutes over and over. So many times I have divided the events into microseconds. I still believe I was justified in starting a descent, but obviously—"

Horn quickly changed the mood. It was better to stay with technicalities. "Has the outer marker system at Taipei ever been reported as unreliable?"

"Once. A charter outfit reported receiving normal indications when they were actually four miles from the marker. According to the Chinese CAA, an investigation was made and the equipment found to be operating normally. They stated the charter captain was a stranger to the area and was mistaken in his position."

"These are the perfect people, then. Nothing ever goes wrong with their equipment?"

"It's very difficult to challenge them when two other aircraft make normal approaches and landings just before and just after your own failure."

"Did they report anything out of the ordinary?"

"No."

Thirty minutes, their allotted time, had passed and no one had mentioned Tseu, or Alex's hands, or what it might have been like after the impact. Horn was pleased with the unity of his delegation. Here were men of five nations who seemed to understand there were certain things better left unsaid.

Chatsworth had been studying the linoleum floor as if it might hold the answer to his question. "Can you give us any clue, no matter how absurd, as to why you think the light and audible signal came on when you were almost seven miles from the outer marker?"

Alex bent his head. He closed his eyes and brought his hands to his forehead. "I only wish to God I could."

By unspoken consent they gathered in Horn's room. There was heat in their arguing, but no malice. Horn saw the verbal explosion which followed their parting from Sylvia as a natural development. There had to be some relief from shock, some bolstering of egos after viewing the ruins of a man who might have been any one of them. How much easier it would have been to stomach if Alex had always been a weakling.

"I have rarely in my life been so depressed," Chatsworth lamented.

"I could hardly look at him," added Willie Moller.

"His eyes! Was there some brain damage?" Diderot asked.

"Nothing in the report."

"There was nothing about his hands either."

Horn said, "Let's remember he undoubtedly looked much more himself before he crashed."

Van Grootes told them how he had managed a few moments alone with the nurse in the corridor. She had been on duty the night Alex had been brought to the sanitarium along with several of the ambulatory passengers. One man had told her how the rice paddy became a sea of fire except for a small area. The man had recognized the captain in that area with other survivors and he appeared not to have been injured. Then he observed the captain go back into the flaming wreckage and return moments later dragging a smoking body. It was Flight Engineer Tseu.

"Why didn't Sylvia tell us about his hands?" asked Chatsworth.

"My guess," said Horn, "is Alex insisted she *not* mention his hands and certainly not how they were burned. He has always sneered at heroics."

"That may be," Moller brooded. "We have all admired him or we wouldn't be here. But I now believe we should mind our own business."

"What do you mean by that?"

Horn was angry with Moller, more angry, he suddenly realized, than he had any right to be. Moller was entitled to his opinions. And he was an intelligent man.

"Because I think Alex is lying. I don't think he ever saw an outer marker light, or heard the signal, or saw his needle swing."

"Alex was never a liar. He always—"

"A man can change," Diderot interrupted. "Sometimes a man will do strange things to—how do you say?—save his own skin."

Chatsworth kept his voice deliberate. "From the moment he hit the ground Alex must have yearned to justify his actions. I daresay that under the circumstances it might not be too difficult to persuade himself he actually *had* seen a light and heard a signal."

Van Grootes said, "So far as we know, Alex was the only person in that cockpit who saw the outer marker light. His co-pilot will not confirm or deny it. There is something fishy here. Too many things do not add up. If this accident were presented to me cold and I were to judge from what I have so far observed, I would certainly judge it pilot error. Analysis? The pilot simply abandoned his instrument approach because he thought the weather was reasonably good below the overcast and he expected no difficulty in seeing the aerodrome once in the clear. We all know how many times it has happened."

Chatsworth challenged him at once. What was the co-pilot doing all this time? Sleeping?

Moller said that a lie told enough times became fact, as witness the deceptions of Hitler. In his first desperation Malloy may have questioned his decision. But soon he would think of positive reasons for letting down, and if he chewed on those reasons long enough they would become actual events. "Now he may *think* he is telling the truth, but you damn well bet it's a lie!"

Horn had heard enough. He strode across the room to the door. "Until now I've been under the impression you were a very special group. Apparently I made a mistake. You sound like a covey of bureaucrats. Blame the pilot. Enter that in the report and go home to forget about it. The pilot can't sing out from his grave and say now wait just a god damned minute, there was something you never bothered to check!"

Horn swung the door open. "You all came a long way to be here. Now here's the exit. If you're already convinced Alex is lying, you might as well leave. And by God I hope you don't spend too many nights wondering if you gave him a fair chance!"

He waited. There was no movement until Moller pushed himself slowly to his feet. "I'm sorry. I guess I will go home."

He looked at the others as if hoping for company, but their faces were nearly expressionless. Then he bent his head slightly and, avoiding Horn's eyes, moved deliberately past him.

After he had gone Horn searched the faces of the others and found little encouragement. "If no one else wants to leave, I'll close the door."

There was no response. They sat looking at the floor. Horn gently closed the door as van Grootes broke the stillness.

"I will not give up yet, but I would be the liar if I did not admit my distress. My impression is that Alex has aged terribly since I last saw him. There is such a thing as not having enough flight time and also . . . having too much. Alex is an old man now, at least by our standards. All of his faculties are slowed down and there is a point where experience fails to compensate . . ."

His voice fell away and Horn knew he was thinking of his own aging.

Chatsworth said, "This afternoon in Alex's room I wondered if he was not trying to tell us that he knew he was guilty, but could not quite bring himself to admit it. I can only suggest we carry on until we're satisfied nothing is left undone. I shouldn't think we'd need more than another few days."

Horn quickly seized upon the Englishman's firmness. "Let's think of the man," he insisted. "They examine our eyes and find them twenty-twenty or better and our ears to make sure we don't lose more than thirty decibels at four thousand vibrations per second. They look at our gizzards and our spleen and confirm everything is fine. They make sure our EKG stays on the tape and they pass us for flight for another six months. But when do they ever examine the mind? It's not our eyes or ears or hands at fault. If it was pilot error, then I think we should find out what made Alex's thinking go wrong."

Quietly then they began to divide the possibilities still to be explored. They did not mention their company was now one less.

7

Medication, Treatment and Progress Record. Continuation Sheet.

FLOOR: First. West wing.

DUTY DR.: G. N. Low

REMARKS: (Note progress of case, complications, consultations, change in diagnosis, condition on discharge, instructions to patient or other persons.)

At approximately 18:30 hours Nurse Tshen informed me patient in Room 12 became hysterical. (A. Malloy. Male. Caucasian.)

Fearing he might attempt to take his own life, Nurse Tshen requested assistance. I diagnosed the case as acute depression aggravated by present mental and physical difficulties. Therefore I administered 50 mgs. Demerol. Patient remained quiet through the end of my duty period.

SIGNATURE: G. N. Low

• •

While he was waiting for Sylvia, Horn telephoned the American Embassy. Since it was long past office hours, he placed the call more to distract his mind from the image of Alex rather than in the hope of receiving an answer. To his surprise a man's voice answered and identified himself as Fry, the vice-consul. He sounded young and weary as he conceded that he was well acquainted with the case of Captain Malloy.

"Have you people done anything to help him?"

"Not directly."

"But he is an American citizen. How can they hold him

prisoner without some official reaction from his own embassy?"

"Captain, I assure you we are very interested in the Malloy case. But this is the Republic of China and the Chinese are making the rules. Too many Americans ignore the fact that if they break a law in any foreign land they are subject to prosecution by the local authorities. There is very little we can do—"

"You are equivocating."

Horn knew he was tiring and yet he had a demanding night before him. He must remain alert for any clue Leonard Wu might offer. And as always his impatience with bureaucrats tried his self-control.

The vice-consul sounded almost wistful. "I wish I could be a little more equivocal when some of our tourists come in here with minor problems like traffic violations. The Chinese, along with every other neighbor we have on this earth, have some difficulty understanding why Americans away from home seem to think they can do as they damn please. Are you still listening, Captain?"

"Yes. It's refreshing. You don't sound like the usual government employee. What was your name again?"

"Sam."

"Uncle Sam?"

"If you must be funny, that's your privilege. Fry is the last name. Spelled F-R-Y."

"Then there is nothing more that can be done through your office?"

"At the moment we believe a hands-off policy is best for Malloy. When the verdict is handed down, then we will try to file an appeal."

"Do you think it would help if I talked to the ambassador?"

"Negative. The Chinese would certainly resent any official interference and it would do your friend more harm than good."

"I suppose you know what you're talking about."

"Comments like that are what I deserve for working so late. Captain, I assume you know what you're talking about, so let's switch positions, and I expect you to be as honest with me. I fly the airlines a great deal and happen to be a charter member of the sweaty palms club. Now remember, you're not talking to a captive audience on the airplane's public address system."

"Go ahead."

There was something about the sincerity in the vice-consul's voice Horn was beginning to like. The man had not once demurred.

"With all the safety features you people are always telling us about, why does a thing like this happen?"

"One of the reasons I am here is to try to make sure it will never happen again."

"Now *you're* equivocating."

"Touché," Horn said slowly. He added a thanks for Fry's time and hung up. Ruefully he thought that he should have known better than to cross words with a professional. Frustrated, he began his habitual pacing. It was still half an hour before Sylvia would arrive. He knew without question that he would be waiting for her at the hotel entrance at least ten minutes before the appointed hour of nine.

He paced in silence, wall to wall like a prisoner long confined. To divert his thoughts from Sylvia he tried to concentrate on his painting, those exciting little oils which were never realized except in his imagination. Yet now each painting was stillborn. There were too many distractions, and even pacing failed to quiet his racing thoughts.

He halted momentarily in the middle of the room. What was this obsession with flight? Why, except for the bonds of friendship, was it so important that Alex Malloy be vindicated? And when, now that the possibility of mental deterioration had been raised, had he last seen Alex unquestionably the complete man to be admired?

It would have been at Lorenzo's funeral, three years ago . . . four? At the time Malloy was employed by the Boeing Company as a test pilot and in that capacity checked out many foreign pilots, among them, Étienne Diderot of Sabena. When notified of Lorenzo's death he had come at once to Long Island, where the final ceremonies were to be held. They were two of a kind—pioneers, fierce in their way and often irascible.

"I loved the man," Alex had declared. "He was a thief, a lush, and a born swindler. He was an ignorant oral copulator and without question the meanest son of a bitch who ever left the ground. But the sky will never be the same without him."

Lorenzo had flown Pilgrims, Curtiss Condors, Vultees, Fokkers, Fords, and Stinson A's, all during his service with American Airways. It was a time of confusion and constant jockeying for position among the airlines, and often enough the actual flying under comparatively primitive standards was no more devious than the desperate maneuvers behind office doors.

"Why does a thing like this happen?" the vice-consul had asked.

Sir, in your innocent way you posed a most embarrassing riddle. As yet an unequivocal answer is pending. For this disaster there were innumerable possibilities. It just could be because Alex *had* flown through that experimental era with men like Lorenzo. He just might have reverted to the old style techniques at just the wrong time?

Pacing still, Horn remembered when he had been a copilot, very low on the totem, a time when "peeking" was still accepted procedure. Each airline published *limits* to which a pilot was authorized to descend. At Buffalo it was four hundred feet, at Newark and Cleveland three hundred feet, and at Burbank six hundred feet. Yet very few pilots found *any* of the restrictions to their liking, and since the airlines were interested in completing schedules the practice of "have a look-see" was condoned. How much below the authorized height a pilot might venture depended upon the individual. Some were known for their temerity and a much smaller number for their timidity.

The stool pigeon in the tail of modern aircraft had put an end to all that. And the in-flight recorder had told most eloquently of Alex's premature descent. Was he just having a look-see?

Lorenzo might have tried the same thing. The fact that he died with his boots off was no indication of his fundamental character. In a way his funeral had represented the departure of a special breed, the beginning of the end of a kingdom ruled more or less benignly by those stalwarts who had started flying in leather jackets, helmets, and goggles.

Sixteen of Lorenzo's contemporaries assembled to do him final honors. Some were certainly scalawags and others as surely heroes, but there was an air about them, an almost visible independence common to them all. A few still adorned their upper lips with the thin pencil-line mustache of the pioneer airman. And, Horn remembered, they behaved like the surviving members of a once proud family. In America they were the Benny Howards, the Roscoe Turners, Dick Merrills, Alex Malloys, Bernt Balchens, Doolittles, and Billy Parkers. In Germany there was Udet and Rudy Mayr, and in France Mermoz, Nungesser, and Detroyat. They were men of the world—all of a kind.

It had been Lorenzo's wish that his ashes be scattered to the four winds. Possibly, Horn thought, he had chosen such final rites simply because it was illegal.

They had gathered in a circle about Horn's little biplane, screening the ceremony from unsympathetic eyes. They watched as he held out the tin can girded with a pink label identifying its contents as the "Remains of A. S. Lorenzo." The words were encircled by an olive branch design, and now Horn remembered what whoever had done the typing had keyed over the R in "Remains." The callousness displeased him. Lorenzo the man deserved a better farewell.

They had all recognized that the windswept cockpit of Horn's aerobatic craft would make disposal of the ashes difficult. So with the air of conspirators they had opened the can and transferred what had once been A. S. Lorenzo into a brown paper sack.

"If you are careful not to punch too big a hole it is bound to be very beautiful," Alex said solemnly.

Horn had taken off and climbed seaward into a dazzling sun. Five miles off the Long Island shore he had throttled back and turned exactly west.

He trimmed the little craft carefully, then took the bag from his lap and held it out to the slipstream. He twisted the corner of the bag until there was a small hole and opened his fingers. A thin sand-colored line streamed straight back like a miniature contrail and Horn was pleased. Alex had been right. In the sunlight it was somehow very beautiful.

Then suddenly the contrail had ceased and he knew that Lorenzo was gone.

A eulogy for Lorenzo would have been difficult to compose. No monuments would ever be erected to commemorate his achievements. He had simply learned to fly an airplane in his youth and continued flying for the rest of his years. He had been no Balbo, or Nobile, or Levchenko, Hughes, Crosson, Byrd, Hawks, or Post. Neither his name nor photograph had ever graced the scrapbooks of young Lew Horn, because he had never won any air races or trophies, flown to unexplored regions of the earth, or tested exotic aircraft. He had been an ordinary airman flying his craft through all kinds of weather without accident or even notable incident. Higher pay, if routine labor was involved, would never have lured him away from flying.

When Horn had finally released the paper bag he did think of a eulogy and, embarrassed at his sentimentality, found himself murmuring against the roar of the engine, "But he did know why the birds sing."

Then in keeping with his mood he had tightened his shoulder harness and rendered the sort of salute he considered appropriate. All the way back to the coastline he had executed his best barrel rolls, Cuban eights, hammerheads, and sixteen-point rolls. And Lorenzo's mourners had approved.

At the wake that night Alex had led them in song, and Horn had marveled at the *esprit* which so obviously bound them together.

Where then was that instinct now? Perhaps this disaster would have been much easier to accept if Alex had been killed. He would then have been part of just another ugly statistic.

Pacing as if a clear solution depended upon his continued movement, he thought it would have made little difference if Alex had been a salesman, engineer, clerk, or merchant. Something wholly unforeseen had struck him down with the force of a thunderbolt. His most grievous wounds were not physical but spiritual, and his soul cried out for a miracle. He was no longer desperate. Even desperation requires a spark of hope.

Leonard Wu's flat was all of one room, large and sparsely furnished with several rattan chairs and a few dark mahogany tables. Several glossy photos of Chinese cinema stars adorned the walls.

Horn was surprised at Wu's physique. He was very tall for a Chinese and his shoulders and muscled forearms were those of a gymnast. His tee shirt and tennis shoes seemed a natural part of him.

Wu led them through a pair of double doors to a small open court and asked them to be seated. He spoke to Sylvia in Chinese for a moment and then apologized. "In difficult situations it is easy to be rude without intending to be."

His manner of speech reminded Horn strongly of a purring cat. And his movements were strangely feline.

"My hospitality is as limited as my manners. I am a bachelor and take poor care of things. I have not anything to offer you to drink."

Horn made a negative gesture. For the moment he was certain that the less he said the better. Since their arrival he had been watching Sylvia. Her quiet dignity lends a sense of majesty, he thought. Little wonder Wu treated her with marked deference.

Wu was saying, "We should never underestimate the power of Chinese women. Our ancient emperors ignored them and found themselves the ruled rather than the rulers. Sometimes I think nothing has changed."

Horn saw him glance at Sylvia. A thin smile crossed his lips, then he stared up at the black sky.

"Sylvia has informed me why you are here. I do not know what I can tell you that is not in the official report."

Horn hesitated. He had expected banalities for the first few minutes and at best vague hostility if Wu actually had anything to hide. Yet Wu appeared totally at ease.

He began quietly, almost as if he were indifferent to what Wu might answer. "There are certain questions which seem to us inadequately covered in the report. For example, why were you making what appears to have been a routine ADF approach when the glide slope was available?"

"Captain Malloy was making the approach. It was his decision."

"But you were assisting him?"

"Any decisions were made by the captain."

So? The pattern was set hard as concrete and Wu's apparent openness was an illusion. Strange how the strongest of men were willing to shift the blame when directly confronted. Or was his physical appearance only the result of a weakling striving to attain strength through consistent exercise. There were such men, Horn reminded himself.

Yet he must be careful now. He must remember how Sylvia had arranged the interview. It was a matter of face and he must be cautious lest he violate the rules.

"I am sure a man of your standing and experience must be unhappy about the charges against Alex. Those of us who fly for other lines think it is a disgrace. Have you considered that if Alex is convicted, some of the international publicity might rub off on you? It might be something you would have to live with for a long time."

Wu's eyes remained indifferent. "I have said everything there is to say."

"We studied the questions presented to you at the official hearing and it struck us that your presence in the cockpit was considered unimportant. The questions asked you by the Chinese CAA were elementary and, if I may say so, meaningless to the final result."

Wu failed to respond. He was staring at the sky again as if merely waiting for time to pass. Obviously he knew how simple the questions had been. Did the flight depart on schedule from Manila? Yes. Is your airman's certificate and medical current? Yes. Totally unrevealing.

"Was there some reason why you have never been called into civil court to either confirm or deny Alex's testimony?"

"Captain Malloy was in command of the aircraft from the time of our departure at Manila until our arrival here."

"You mean disaster here."

Horn was angry at himself for descending to sarcasm. I have no right, he thought. I was not there during those terrible moments and this man was.

"If you wish to put it that way."

"Are you suggesting you had nothing to do with the flight? Do first officers on Far Eastern just sit and look out the window? As a matter of fact, did you look out the window?"

"When?" Wu was becoming sullen.

Horn sensed he must keep pounding at him or he might

slip away entirely. And according to Alex, he thought, my lack of mercy should be the seal of our profession.

"It might help if we knew you were looking out the window, say a few seconds before you hit."

"No."

"Why not? What were you doing?"

"I was busy on the radio, working Approach Control, and later the tower."

"What else were you doing from the time you started descent?"

"I did not start the descent. Captain Malloy did."

Horn warned himself to be overpatient. He had used the English word "you" in the plural sense and Wu interpreted it as singular. Or was he deliberately searching for escape time?

"Were you looking out the window during any part of the descent?"

"No. I was busy tuning radios, checking my approach plate, watching the power—"

"Wasn't Engineer Tseu handling the power?"

"Yes, but I kept an eye on it too."

"Then wouldn't it seem to any knowledgeable person that you were very much involved with the flight of that aircraft until the moment it hit the ground?"

Horn threw the question away as if he were uninterested in a response. I must try, he thought, to make him want to convince me he was not just along for the ride.

"Captain Malloy was flying the aircraft. I was very surprised when we hit."

"Why were you surprised? Wasn't it your voice on the tape saying, 'I have an MDA light'?"

"I was also surprised to see that light."

"Why?" Horn leaned forward in his chair pleading. "Why, Mr. Wu? Please tell me why?"

At once he saw that he had gone too far. Wu drew back and looked at Sylvia accusingly. "You asked me to talk with your American friend. I did not expect this sort of conversation."

"Captain Horn means you no harm. He is only trying to help Alex."

Wu replied in Chinese and the purring quality left his voice. For what seemed to Horn like a very long time the exchange continued between them. At last she seemed to have soothed him.

"Mr. Wu has been explaining to me that he is on only temporary leave from the Nationalist Air Force. His present civilian status could be terminated at any time if the authorities are displeased with him. That would be very bad for his airline career."

Wu said, "Mr. Spencer told me I cannot go back to work until the verdict on Captain Malloy is announced."

"Why not? What difference would it make?"

"Mr. Spencer says it would be inappropriate."

And, Horn thought, whatever Mr. Spencer says is obviously holy law in Taiwan.

Feeling his way, he asked, "Does Mr. Spencer think Alex is going to be found guilty?"

"I cannot speak for him."

Nor will you for yourself, Horn thought as his hopes faded. Wu had no intention of committing himself to anything. There was one possibility—remote, a gamble, but now there was little to lose.

He glanced at Sylvia. She would keep her serenity. He stood up and advanced on Wu. There was no mistaking his determination.

"Now you listen to me very carefully. The flying business is a small world and we know you lied about your flight hours when you applied for your job. We also know you had great difficulty getting through the Boeing school in Seattle. A written report to your Mr. Spencer may not get you fired tomorrow, but you can be sure such information attested by five international captains will go in your fitness file and keep you from promotion for the next ten years. You might even find yourself back in the Air Force. Do I make myself clear?"

Standing over him, Horn waited for the silence to end. Wu appeared stunned. Then the gamble had been won. Every pilot since the Wright brothers exaggerated his flight time, and Wu was obviously no different than any others. And the majority of pilots, foreign or otherwise, passing through Boeing's tough schooling had difficulty at one time or another. The rest was guesswork. He had no idea if a negative view of Wu expressed by five foreign experts would have the slightest effect on his career.

Finally Wu broke the silence. "I have nothing against Captain Malloy. He is a nice man. I have told you all I can."

No progress, thought Horn. He must gamble once more, a final attempt to unlock the brain of First Officer Wu.

"All you can? Then someone has told you to keep quiet. Or was it an order?"

No reply. Wu was retreating again into the shell of his fears. It must be all or nothing, Horn decided.

"Why have you holed up here ever since the crash? Why have you refused to discuss that night with anyone unless they were officials of the CAA? You haven't said anything except that you happened to be riding in an aircraft that suddenly flew into the ground, all to your complete surprise. *Why?*"

Wu worked his lips but no sound came from them. His rattan chair squeaked as he shifted position. "I was advised to avoid discussion of the subject because a number of lawsuits are pending. Also our newspapers are very inaccurate with such matters, and what I said if quoted wrong might be damaging to Captain Malloy."

Logic for the first time, Horn decided. Could he have been wrong about Wu or was he simply skipping out of range? There was after all nothing to prevent him from insisting they leave. Or was the man just not very bright?

"You can help us very much if you will. And I promise we will be completely discreet. Were you on solid instruments at the time of the crash?"

Wu hesitated and then nodded affirmatively. Horn wanted to cheer, for he had confirmed what Alex Malloy had said.

"Is that why you didn't bother to look outside? Because you would not have been able to see anything if you did?"

"I did not think about it. As I told you, I was busy working traffic control and the tower—"

"With your eyes closed? What *were* you looking at?"

Horn paused. He wondered if he dared keep pressing, for now Wu's forehead glistened with perspiration. Yet if he relented, the logical progression he needed might be lost. He plunged ahead.

"The instrument panel on your side is exactly like the captain's. Right in front of your nose then there were two radio direction finder needles. Before you hit did you at any time see those needles turn and reverse their bearings, indicating you had just passed the outer marker?"

Here was the crux of the whole interview. It was Wu's voice on the tape which had said they were passing the outer marker.

"Yes," Wu sighed.

"Did you seen an indicator light for the outer marker? It would be the same on your side as the captain's."

"I do not recall."

"You don't recall?" Horn snapped his fingers angrily. He was disappointed. Alex had insisted he had seen a light.

"Perhaps I could have missed it. About then I had my head down switching frequencies."

"A function you claim you were engaged in when you hit the ground. Did you see the outer marker light at any time?"

"No."

"Did you hear the audible signal?"

"I was not listening because I was busy repeating our clearance and listening for the weather."

The man is purring again, Horn thought. He seemed sure enough of himself to be telling the truth. He had even become slightly patronizing. Patience.

Horn returned to his chair and his tone became conciliatory. "I understand how difficult it must be to remember exact details, but would you give me an opinion? Just before you struck the ground was it your firm impression that you had actually passed the outer marker?"

The question was such an obvious trap Horn had little hope he would offer a believable reply. If he believed they had *not* passed the outer marker, then he was guilty of failing to call Alex's attention to the dangers of a premature descent. He would certainly become an accessory to the alleged crime.

Horn waited through a long silence. He tried not to show his excitement when Wu finally admitted it was his impression they had passed the marker.

"Is that why you were so surprised when you suddenly saw an MDA light and realized you were too low?"

"Yes." Wu's voice was almost inaudible.

"Why didn't you say that in your testimony?"

"I was not asked."

"Well you should have volunteered."

Horn made no attempt to conceal his disgust. He beckoned to Sylvia, who spoke briefly to Wu in Chinese and then followed him to the door.

Wu did not rise. When they left he remained staring at his tennis shoes. Horn wondered if his attitude of dejection was genuine or simply an act to be rid of them.

"He is a stupid man," Sylvia whispered. "He cares only for his face."

Later, on the way back to the hotel, she briefly touched his hand. "You're so quiet. Are you afraid of my driving?"

"No."

He had been barely aware of the traffic except for the occasional bursts of light which splashed across her face. He was grateful for the lights.

"Then why do you keep watching me? I think you are afraid to look ahead."

"Yes. You are driving too fast . . . for me."

"I am only going thirty."

"Still too fast. I wouldn't mind if this journey took several years."

Was she still smiling? Now, watching her profile, it was hard to be sure. A car approached from the opposite direction, and her eyes were better revealed. He thought he saw disappointment.

"Yes. Many years."

"You're a wonderful person. I think your wife is very lucky."

He resisted an urge to tell her about Barbara. The doors to lost kingdoms should be permanently sealed. And yet how could he tell her without offense that at this moment he was magically content, more at peace with himself and the world than he had been for a very long time.

She broke his reverie. "After watching you with Leonard Wu, I am sure I can now tell you something I was afraid might discourage you. Far Eastern Airways' contracts with the government have been so tight it has been difficult to start any competition. Unfortunately there is only one Chinese on the board of directors and all the executives are Occidentals. All of the flight captains are Occidentals. This has been very bad for local 'face,' and about a year ago a group of prominent Chinese formed a new company, Formosa Air. They have just been issued a temporary permit and have ordered two Boeings. They will take their pilots from the Air Force. Very good for 'face.' "

"You're still driving too fast." He was reluctant to abandon his most pleasant thoughts. "I was hoping you were lost."

"Alex's accident provided a golden opportunity to discredit the safety record of Far Eastern. Hauling Alex into public criminal court and proving him incompetent or negligent, with all the newspapers daily informed, is very deliberate."

"But the judges? Are they involved with the new line?"

"No. But this is China."

"That's the second time I've been told that today. Very firmly."

"For more than two thousand years Chinese justice has been tempered by need or convenience. The judges have gone through the motions of a trial. Once they officially announce their verdict they would lose great face for themselves and the government if they changed."

"Then you believe they will find him guilty?"

"I don't know. For what good it does, I pray. And since I have come to know you even a little, I have hope. There are only a few days left."

She reached out in the darkness and once more touched his hand. "You must hurry."

Diderot was lonely. He had explored the vast and complicated environs of the Grand Hotel in a futile effort to find someone to match his restless energy. Van Grootes and Chatsworth, pleading near exhaustion, had gone to bed. He considered calling Moller's room, intending to argue against his withdrawal from the delegation, then changed his mind. Let the *boche* sleep. He might be of better mind in the morning.

Diderot ordered an Amer Picon in the lower bar and spent some minutes flirting with a young American woman who affected Chinese dress. The promising liaison was terminated when three Japanese businessmen entered the bar and joined her. They were drunk and noisy, and their laughter made Diderot all the more lonely.

He left his Picon unfinished and climbed the stairs to the lobby. For a while he watched the colorful dispersal of a formal diplomatic party and was pleased to hear frequent phrases in his native tongue. The curse of all Frenchmen, he thought, is that like so many of our wines we do not travel well. We are belligerent provincials. If something is not French it cannot be very good, and if it is French then there must be something wrong with it. We seem to agree on only one thing—Jeanne d'Arc was probably a virgin.

When the diplomatic cars with their bright little flags had swallowed the last red sash and sequined gown, Diderot turned away from the hotel portico and started for his room. He was delighted to find a letter had been slipped under his door. Recognizing the unmistakable flourish of his father's handscript, he tore open the envelope immediately.

My Dear Étienne:

I tried to telephone you in Brussels, but you had already left. There was something I wished to tell you regarding our friend Alex. It might have some value and possibly help.

After my nap today I went to the Club Vieilles Tiges, where as usual I found old comrades. It was a relief to abandon our usual lies about long ago exploits and discuss your own present mission. A great deal of senile nonsense was exchanged, but some of it made sense. Bearing in mind that we could not appreciate the real situation out there, you may wish to consider this.

Could it be possible that Alex was the victim of an idée fixe? Only a few years ago there was a series of accidents because of erroneous navigation. The pilots were taking bearings on the wrong direction finder station while they had absolutely convinced themselves they were listening to the correct one. My friend Marcel Teran (Air France) met his end that way. Thought he was depending on bearings from Seville when he was actually receiving a station in the Azores.

My old friend Dabry was here today. Remember he once introduced you to Didier Daurat, who originally managed Air Bleu and also arranged for you to shake the hand of Mermoz himself? You were only ten or so. Never mind, my mind wanders.

Dabry told me of a flight when he was approaching Iceland and receiving quite logical and steady bearings from Keflavik. But finally he became suspicious and after investigation found his direction finders were reacting to signals from Dakar. He admitted he had surrendered to an idée fixe.

Could the same condition have influenced Alex? Could he have been too relaxed—that flight from Manila too much his habitude?

Did I ever tell you what happened to me when I was based in Algiers? It was just before Aeropostale in Africa and Latécoere was trying to establish a line from Toulouse all the way to Argentina. A man eater that enterprise proved to be, with more than a hundred pilots and mechanics killed before the job was done. Great names involved—many of my old comrades. Besides Mermoz there was Guillaumet, Reine, Saint Ex (I always thought him a better poet than pilot), Delaunay—I wander again. These names can't mean much to you.

I was still in the Army, then a rated flying sergeant. You were with your mother in Toulouse. We thought it healthier for you. There was some sort of infantile disease running through Algeria then . . . can't remember.

We were flying Potez 25s with Lorraine-Dietrich engines—water-cooled. My escadrille was stuck with the job of flying the southbound mails, across the Sahara and terminating in Nigeria or Senegal. We were a cocky lot (damn fools really), and it didn't particularly concern us that the Moorish tribesmen thought us worth a heavy ransom if we went down in the desert. In Mauritania they were really tough. I recall Reine and Serre were prisoners for about four months (I knew them only casually), both Mermoz and Delaunay had troubles, and Erable and Pintado were killed. A man named Gourp, whom I remember very well, was wounded, lashed to a camel, and rescued too late. He died in Casablanca. And the Moors had a nasty habit of cutting the balls off Frenchmen. Given the choice then, I would rather have lost my head—now I'm not so sure which is more important.

I wander, son. Forgive me. All this is not my point at all.

We always flew two Potezes in case one of us went

down. The distance was three thousand kilometers and the flight took us four days. The first night we rested at a place called El Golea in the desert and then at dawn the next morning we started for a place called Bidon 5. And that was just what it was, nothing more than five cans sitting out in the middle of the desert. Finding the place was difficult. (Bidon 5 is still there I understand. Still one of the most isolated places in the world.) Of course we had no radio aids and there were few landmarks in the desert. We relied on our compass and a line of tin fuel cans an expeditionary party had painted white and set down every five kilometers.

Patience, son. I am getting to my point. It bears directly upon your present mission.

Following the cans to Bidon 5 was easy in clear weather, but when a "haboob" hit the Sahara, the sand and dust obscured everything and was lifted much higher than we could fly. Even higher than you can today in jets, I think.

One afternoon my friend Lucien Hamot and I were about one hour out of Bidon 5 when we ran into a haboob and serious trouble. We lacked fuel to turn back and had no idea what the wind was doing to us. We signaled each other with our hands and separated for fear of colliding in the murk. That was the last I saw of Hamot for some time.

About twenty minutes passed and I had not seen a single can below. I was grinding dust with my teeth and even having trouble breathing. What to do now? What was the wind doing? None of us knew much about instrument flying then, so I kept losing altitude trying to look for a can and get back on course. I calculated enough time had passed for me to have missed two cans on the line, maybe more.

I was becoming more and more unhappy when I saw something dark looming ahead and realized it was a rock cliff. I hauled back and climbed immediately, which is one reason you still have a living father. Then, of course, I was committed to the higher altitude.

I lost all contact with the desert floor and concentrated on compass, ball and needle, trying to stay right side up. I crossed myself several times and wished I had become an apothecary like your grandfather wanted me to be.

I calculated my remaining fuel and started to sweat. I know now I was ripe for an idée fixe.

Do you remember when I began teaching you to fly? Fly it or it will fly you? Think ahead of your craft, and the faster it is the farther ahead you must think. And I told you that no matter what is said to the contrary, any aircraft can kill you—like a woman they respond to affection and respect, but they can bite hard if you hold them even momentarily in contempt.

And the rule of doubt? If you doubt your position *admit* you are lost. The worst thing you can do is start turning left and right, just hoping.

The wise airman holds fast to his initial course which he calculated in the sweet time of reason before the flight. Had I followed the rule that afternoon over the Sahara I would not have had such a narrow escape. I started thinking about what the wind must be doing to me and turned away from my original course. After all, Bidon 5 could not be more than another ten or fifteen minutes' flying time ahead.

When my chronometer told me there could not possibly be more than three or four minutes to go, an extraordinary thing happened. I broke out of the dust storm into dazzling sunlight. Visibility was excellent, and there on the horizon was the familiar pattern of Bidon 5. I cheered. God was in his heaven and I could taste the glass of Armagnac the mechanics would have waiting for me. I looked around the sky for Hamot, but there was no sign of him so I assumed he had already landed. "Where have you been?" I knew he would ask. "Exploring Africa?"

I loosened my helmet strap and even pushed up my goggles. Life was returned and remained very good for several minutes. Then I became suspicious.

I had started a long descent to increase my speed, but Bidon 5 did not come any closer. Finally I realized that the shimmering image of five white cans in a familiar pattern was still on the horizon. It was a mirage and I was truly lost.

Emptiness everywhere. I leaned the engine mixture and flew slowly in gentle circles to conserve fuel. I had now no assurance that Bidon 5 was ahead or behind me in the dust, or to east or west.

Suddenly something passed between me and the sun.

A dark shadow flashed across the cockpit. I thought, Surely a buzzard has spied his next meal.

I looked up and saw Hamot in his Potez. He slid down to my wingtip, patted his helmet, and signaled for me to follow him.

In less than ten minutes we both landed at Bidon 5. I had three liters fuel remaining—enough for as many minutes.

Thanks to Hamot, who was not possessed of an idée fixe, I was able to swallow a glass of Armagnac and borrow more years of precious life.

It need not have been so because I had pursued my idea beyond the limits of return. I had nursed the thought that my destination should appear at a fixed time and when it failed to appear I became desperate. My eyes "saw" Bidon 5 because it was *due* to appear and desire ruled my brain.

Think about this.

Affectionately,
Papa

Diderot smiled and carefully reinserted the pages in the envelope. Yes, he would think about Bidon 5 and in the morning he would show the letter to Horn, whose French was remarkably fluent if hopelessly stilted. Yes, it was a possibility. Alex could have expected the correct signal from the outer marker at approximately the time he claims to have received it. But the possibility should not be suggested to Horn before he had a chance to read the letter. Else he might acquire an idée fixe.

Thinking of his father, Diderot walked slowly to the window. The need for sleep had come strongly upon him and yet, inexplicably, he was reluctant to surrender his awareness. His thoughts were a shambles of conflicting impressions. Was this impromptu delegation of Horn's actually a waste of effort as Moller had declared it was? Horn was an American, typical of a nation of idealists who had historically charged into battle without careful weighing of the consequences. They were little boys most of them. Was Horn's drive to vindicate another American who appeared to be anything but innocent simply another example of American naïveté? If so, there were more important things to do.

On the other hand it was ridiculous to suppose that a man of Alex's experience imagined the signals and was thus betrayed into making an immediate descent. Could he have heard *something* almost identical to what he expected? And quite satisfied, have then acted on his idée fixe?

Diderot wished that his father could meet Lew Horn. In a way he was like that fabulous Argentinian Vicente Almendoz de Almonacid, who had spent an eventing at the Diderot home one night long ago and left an unforgettable impression: the first man to fly the Andes at night, Légion d'honneur, Croix de Guerre with innumerable palms, a man capable of such devotion to a cause he had challenged an Argentine official to a duel when he refused permission for French planes to fly the mails.

Horn was of the same rare breed, he thought. But joining their company did not always make good sense.

At last resigned to sleep, he reached to pull the curtain across the window. Half done, he hesitated, for in the driveway beneath his window he watched a pantomime which interested him greatly. The angle was such that he could see a car halted beneath the hotel portico. He recognized it as Sylvia Malloy's.

Horn was standing beside the car, his tall frame bent down so that his face would be nearly level with that of the occupant. He was talking with great animation and after a moment Diderot saw a feminine hand reach for Horn's. He held the hand for some time, much longer, Diderot mused, than would have been normal for a simple farewell.

Finally he saw Horn straighten up. Almost immediately the car started from the portico and passed beneath his window.

Horn stood watching its departure, then he raised his fingers to his lips and gestured a kiss toward it. Slowly then, head bent as if in deep thought, he turned to mount the entrance steps.

Diderot closed the curtains. Papa, he thought, was it not you who once told me that to fall in love with the wife of another man was civilized, but to fall in love with the wife of a friend was anarchy?

8

The sunlight roused Horn from the deepest sleep he had known since his stay in Paris. For a moment he lay confused. The architectural confines of the room could have been any one of the innumerable hotel rooms about the world to which his flying life had committed him. Then as the details of the great fan above the bed became more significant he remembered where he was. He glanced at his watch and immediately rolled out of the bed. It was seven thirty and he had overslept.

Forty-five minutes later Horn entered the offices of Far Eastern Airways on Chungshan Road. He was irritated with himself. It had been his intention to be waiting for Sheldon Spencer when he arrived and thus thwart any attempt to avoid an interview. Now, standing before the young Chinese clerk on the third floor of the building, he was obliged to become a supplicant rather than a challenger.

It was easier than he had expected. The clerk appeared impressed with his airline business card and disappeared into an adjoining office. He returned after a few minutes and ushered Horn through a door labeled "Flight Operations."

A man sat behind the desk reading the *China Post*. After a moment he lowered the paper and studied Horn with obvious distaste. "Good morning. What can I do for you?"

"I've come to see you about Alex Malloy."

"I know. News travels fast in Taipei. I knew about your arrival an hour after you reached the Grand Hotel. I am mystified at what you think you are going to accomplish."

"Mr. Spencer—"

Horn thought he should probably have addressed the man as "Major." There was a group photograph of several American Air Force officers on the wall. They were posed before a jet fighter of the Korean War vintage. Spencer was in the center looking very forthright. A pair of major's leaves adorned his flight jacket. Now the face behind the desk was less fleshy, but the brush of black hair appeared unchanged and the eyes even colder.

Horn glanced at the empty chair against the wall. What a heartwarming reception! Possibly his host issued an invitation to be seated only after receiving a request through channels.

Spencer carefully laid the paper on the desk and made a church roof with his fingers. Horn saw the flash of a large military ring.

"I was hoping—"

"I suggest you and your friends go back where you came from as soon as possible. You might do Alex more harm than good."

"How could that be?" And how, Horn wondered, was he so suddenly finding himself on the defensive? "How can Alex be any worse off than he is?"

"Easy. If the Chinese think a group of Caucasians are trying to tell them what to do they might throw the book at him. Left alone, my guess is they'll be lenient."

"Your guess?"

"The Chinese are a practical people. They are not out for vengeance, and for them there is no real percentage in persecuting Alex."

Horn sat down in the chair without an invitation. He wiped his brow. There was no air conditioning in the office and the raucous street noises floated through the open windows on updrafts of hot moist air. There were shouts of peddlers, varieties of clickings and horns, the blatting of motorbikes, and farting of diesel truck exhausts. Dominating all the sounds was the whine of a bamboo flute.

"Alex," Spencer was saying very carefully, "is an old-timer, and like so many others he has old habits that are hard to break. I assure you I have spent many long hours going over the facts of that night. Since this company is operating under the tolerance of the Chinese government it was my duty to make Alex look as good as possible."

"We have read the report—thoroughly. It is our impression that Alex was telling the truth."

How easily have I discarded Willie Moller's opinion, Horn thought. In combat a defector becomes the enemy.

"Alex is still with his hallucinations. He is not the first man to see something that was not there on a rainy night or mistake a grouping of lights for something he wanted to see. The setup was perfect for the type accident that has happened many times."

"What about the glide slope?"

The answer, Horn hoped, would be a test of Spencer's frankness.

"Alex never had any intention of using the glide slope. He hit the ground almost two miles before he could possibly have received an on-course indication."

"It is my understanding that because of an unreliable record it is common custom to ignore the Taipei glide slope."

Spencer's voice took on a note of haughtiness. "This airline does not operate on common custom. There is nothing in our manual which permits any Far Eastern pilot to ignore approach aids."

"Even if the indications are obviously unflyable?"

"The glide slope was operating normally on the night in question." Spencer pulled a manila folder from beneath the newspaper. "The system reports are all in here."

He gently caressed the manila folder as if within were hidden invaluable secrets. "I saw Alex two hours after the crash. He was in no shape to recall anything clearly. You must realize that Alex, First Officer Wu, and Engineer Tseu were separated from the main part of the wreckage when the whole front end broke away. Only a totally irrational man would have gone back inside that fire just to pull out what was left of Tseu."

The street noises reached a sudden crescendo and then subsided again. Horn admitted to himself that so far all the points had been made by the cold man behind the desk. There were holes in his logic, but the weight of evidence was difficult to deny. He forced himself to match Spencer's arrogant calm as he explained Chatsworth's service with BOAC, van Grootes's with KLM, and Diderot's with Sabena. Once again, he though, I have managed to deny the existence of Moller.

"We are all recently qualified on 727s and DC-8s. We had in mind chartering one of your airplanes and with you aboard, of course, carefully repeating Alex's flight from the time he was cleared to descend for approach . . ."

Spencer was holding up his hand, a trace of a smile on his lips. He reached into a drawer and brought out a second folder. He patted it gently as if like the other it also contained jewels of great price.

"If you had been here a few days after the crash I would have arranged for you to ride along while I did just that. I even chose a Chinese first officer with approximately the same level of experience as Leonard Wu. The flight was scheduled at exactly the same hour. By chance there was a similar overcast and I requested special clearance to divert from normal procedure so the possible point of impact would be the same. I duplicated Alex's gross weight by carrying fuel instead of passengers. There were only two differences in our flights. One, it was not raining, so I had better visibility. And two, I deliberately set my altimeter to read five hundred feet low." Spencer scratched his chin with his military ring. "I am sure you will understand that I did not intend to duplicate Alex's flight quite to the point of finality."

For the first time since his departure from Paris Horn sensed a weakening in his resolve. They were too late. All that could be done had been done. And there was such an over-whelming accumulation of evidence that a master had erred. Now even Spencer sounded convincing as he held out the second folder.

"You are welcome to read this. Frankly, I was quite surprised at the results. When we broke out of the overcast and started descent I experienced a very marked series of visual hallucinations. Even though I am very familiar with this area, I mistook the lights of Keelung for the lights of western Taipei, and I was certain we were much higher over the dark sectors where Alex actually hit. I would have been unable to state my exact position when my MDA light finally snapped me to attention."

Something came to Horn, words that Sylvia had said: "I

hope you understand that if your findings confirm his guilt you will kill your friend."

And for an instant in his thoughts he saw Alex Malloy's anguished eyes. It was enough to restore his determination. He stood up. "No doubt you did a thorough job, but to satisfy ourselves we need an airplane. We are willing to pay the going rate for it and accept any convenient block of time—midnight to three in the morning if nothing else is available."

"We simply cannot spare anything at this season of the year."

"Or any other season?"

"Take that chip off your shoulder, Captain. Because of the accident we're short one aircraft. The others are operating around the clock when we're not doing maintenance. Compared to yours this is a little airline. Our resources are not so extensive."

Horn leaned across the desk. He kept his voice even. "What the hell is the matter with you? You know what we are trying to do. He's your own man. He needs your help. If you won't lend us an airplane we'll have to find one on our own."

"I would not advise it. This island is at war. No private flying is permitted and every airport is guarded by the military, who check your clearance before take-off. If it doesn't match, they shoot."

"Then help us get clearance."

Spencer smiled tolerantly and troubled himself to rise. "That would be impossible. Meanwhile as long as you insist on staying in Taipei I would like to offer such amenities as we have. If you will leave the names of the other captains with my secretary I will arrange guest cards for you at our officers' club. It's part of the Assistance Program and quite comfortable."

"Don't bother. None of us would know how to repay your warm hospitality."

Horn turned his back and walked out of the office. So far, he thought, there have been nothing but dead ends to this business. By the law of averages it was time for a change.

Passing the clerk, he said good morning in a tone which

he hoped would not betray his mood. He ignored the elevator and chose the adjoining stairs.

Once in the bustle of the street, his anger evaporated.

He paused by a merchant who had set up shop on the sidewalk. His wares were a variety of small birds in bamboo cages and Horn stood entranced for several minutes. How far behind in aeronautical knowledge were the most expert of men! Even these little prisoners knew secrets men had yet to discover. The power versus speed and maneuverability of a tiny hummingbird taunted any aircraft designer. No man had ever learned to fly soundlessly as any owl can do, and the most efficient aircraft, a sailplane, has three times the skin friction of an ordinary black buzzard.

He walked on, lost in comparisons. Perhaps someday man would know as much about slotted wingtips, vortex generators, leading edge flaps, and noise suppression as the birds. Perhaps then he would understand why certain devoted and skillful men, who were themselves half bird, occasionally failed in their imitation.

The courthouse was of Victorian architecture and Horn thought its aroma of woe was as fixed as that of any other structure where people and their troubles gathered before officialdom.

Considerable remodeling of the interior was in noisy progress and he was obliged to weave his way around scaffolding, stacks of lumber, and cement mixing troughs until he found a young man who obligingly escorted him to the office of Prosecutor E. K. Han.

The office was small with a reception counter traversing its width. A trio of clerks hammered spasmodically at their ancient typewriters, springing into action in chorus and then stopping together as if on cue. During the periods of silence they simply stared at their machines. Horn thought they must be required to look busy only at intervals.

Han proved to be a sallow man with a long-suffering look. "I am honored to meet a visitor from so far."

A jackhammer pounding in the hallway nearly obliterated his words. He waited patiently until only the three typewriters behind him competed with his voice. "I apologize you must view such a noisy place. Taiwan is growing so fast. This old building is too small. We must make new accommodations."

For new clerks to type and file away ever-increasing troubles, Horn thought. All to be accomplished without the slightest regard for what an official form might do to the humans involved.

"I am a friend of Captain Malloy's. Naturally I am interested in his case."

"Are you an attorney?"

Horn handed him his card. "No. Simply a friend."

"I understand. Is he recovering nicely?"

"I would hardly call it nicely. What you said to and about him doesn't help."

"I only do my duty, and his case is one of many assigned to me. Many persons lost their loved ones because of his negligence. Wives lost their husbands, children their fathers —the chain goes on indefinitely. As many as three generations were directly affected. Some retribution must be made as in any other crime."

"Crime? You're talking about revenge. How is it going to help anyone if Malloy goes to prison?"

The jackhammer chattered again and while Han waited for it to cease he carefully examined his polished fingernails. When relative quiet returned to the hallway he said patiently, "Captain, I am the prosecutor not one of the judges. If you desire to plead for your friend or offer something new in this matter I suggest you write them a letter clearly stating your facts. Be sure to make it in triplicate."

Horn wondered if there was some way he might persuade this man to rise above himself. He may have been aware of the emotional effect the repeated display of gory photographs might have had on Alex and the judges, but how could he understand how it might cloud the technical responses from the man held responsible? In his eyes undoubtedly the trial had not been unfair.

"Can you tell me when the judges might hand down their verdict?"

Han looked over his shoulder at a calendar on the wall. He twiddled a pencil between his delicate fingers and pursed his lips. There was a righteousness about him which angered Horn. Everything in his world has its place, he thought, and therefore the view is never altered. If the pillars of his beliefs showed the slightest crack he would be utterly lost. Suddenly Horn's anger melted into pity, for here obviously was just another bureaucrat. Given other influences in his life, he might have known some kind of glory.

"Let me see . . . this is Thursday the seventh? I recall the judges promised me a decision on the eleventh. That would be Monday—"

"That doesn't give me enough time to write and deliver a proper letter. Could I go see them—maybe ask for a postponement? Please, I would appreciate your help."

Perhaps, he thought, just perhaps, E. K. Han was not as tough as his conduct in court indicated. Somewhere in that overburdened façade he might rouse a moment of compassion.

Han only shrugged his shoulders. "Unless you have some very special evidence with absolute proof the judges would be obliged to refuse granting an interview. They themselves would be then violating the law. But who knows? They may be lenient, or I may have failed in my duty. Your friend may get off quite free."

"Do you think there is a chance he might?"

"No." Han smiled, bowed ever so slightly, and returned to his desk.

Moller packed very slowly. He found petty excuses for delay and spent long periods at the window staring down upon the parade of people arriving for luncheon at the Grand Hotel.

He had not seen any of the others since he had left their company the evening before. He knew the avoidance was deliberate on his part and he supposed the others were relieved at his absence. A chance encounter in the lobby would have been most embarrassing for all concerned, he reasoned. Since he had declared against them, or at least their project, it would have been most difficult to carry on any further exchange of opinion. And now that he had given the whole subject of Alex Malloy a most painful re-examination he tried to rid himself of the notion that perhaps he had judged too hastily.

Yes. It was going to be a very long time until his homeward bound flight took off at eight tonight. He would have lunch sent to his room, which would occupy the next hour, but then how would he pass the balance of the afternoon? He could taxi down to the city and buy gifts for his wife and mother, browse a bit, and there would still be hours left. Willie Moller, he thought, you must have courage to be the realist. Malloy erred. That is fact. All the wishful thinking in the world cannot reverse the terrible consequences.

He found it easier to think of a gift for his mother. Thanks to her small landholdings in Schleswig and his father's savings, his early life had not been at all harsh. He had received a better education than most German boys. There had been nine years of Latin, six of French, and six of Greek, all before he had turned eighteen. Caesar in Gaul, most of the Greek philosophers. Rather a strange foundation for a youth who knew what he wanted to do from the day the family settled down in Zeppelinheim. The *Graf Zeppelin* and the *Hindenburg* were operating regular voyages to North and South America, and the senior Moller was helping in the creation of the new *Graf II*. When he had applied for an apprentice position on the newest Zeppelin he had not even bothered to tell his parents.

Then the incredible happened and the *Hindenburg* blew up in New Jersey. Dr. Hugo Eckener risked his life and career by publicly stating that if the Zeppelins had not been forced to wear the damned swastika on their tail fins the Americans would have provided the Zeppelin company with helium and the explosion would never have happened. Dr. Eckener was the Mollers' God, and it was he who declared that the future of German gas bags was extremely dark. Instead he offered to recommend young Moller to Lufthansa, where he would be much better off flying airplanes.

Even though his power was fading, word from the great Eckener could accomplish miracles. In less than a month Moller was off to the civil airline school in Munich. The cost was high, 170 marks a month, but the course was the most complete in the world.

Moller sighed. Even today there was no more comprehensive school of flight. He had been required to learn navigation in all its forms, and qualify as a radio operator. A

"C" rating in gliders was mandatory, and students were required to make at least one ascension in a balloon. Long hours in the air were spent solely on aerobatics, then there was further training on old and current types of aircraft both land and sea. They flew Junkers and Dorniers; planes with two, three, and four engines; aircraft on floats and flying boats; the big Fokkers as well as the Blohm and Voss. If it flew in or out of Germany it was part of the syllabus. Finally, so they would better match and understand the sea in their flying, they were sent off on the huge square-rigger *Passat* for six months.

Moller went into the bathroom and wet a hand towel. He took it to the closet and carefully brushed the lint from his blazer. The brass buttons were souvenirs of the *Passat*, and now he wondered whatever had happened to Helmut Grubbe, her captain. How tough and yet how kind a man! There had been that night off the Azores when the ship was caught in a full gale. Moller was ordered aloft to the upper topsail yard, more than thirty meters above the deck. Suddenly he had found that he could not move. While the other cadets climbed into the howling night he had remained paralyzed, in spite of the third mate's yelling. For young Moller there was no sound but the terrible moaning of the wind.

Out of the darkness had come Helmut Grubbe. He had taken Moller's hand and said, "Come. We do it together."

Then they had climbed the shrouds side by side, a lowly cadet and a great captain. Halfway to the yard the victory was won.

"I can do it alone now."

Someone had said Grubbe was living in Lübeck now, only a short walk from his old command, which would never sail again. What would he think now of his former cadet? "Am I hesitating again while others do the job?"

After the *Passat* voyage came the achievement of a "C" license rating and assignment to active service with Lufthansa. New tutors took over young Moller, among them the huge Rudy Mayr and Preuschoff, his flight engineer. The two veterans had made many special flights together —a special expedition to Spitsbergen, the first flights to South America and New York in diesel-powered seaplanes. Moller went to his flight bag and felt deep within the side pocket. Yes, it was there. His fingers felt the hairbrush which Mayr and Preuschoff had presented to him on the day he had finally qualified as captain. All of the jokes about his premature baldness suddenly became tokens of affection and even respect. For the great men of Lufthansa had fixed a plaque to the brush and had it engraved, "For the bald eagle of Bavaria. Well done!"

During the years since, the brush had never touched his head, but it had flown with him everywhere even through a war when his cargo had been iron instead of people. What would Rudy Mayr think now? And Preuschoff? Would they still consider his work well done?

Verdammt! The trouble with all Germans and particularly Bavarians was their easy surrender to the sentimental. It invariably got them into irretrievable trouble, and to follow Horn blindly into this Malloy affair would be the height of sentimentality. Our old friend right or wrong—my fatherland and God combined can do no wrong. A hauntingly familiar ring to that attitude and the smell of useless exposure to danger. It takes more courage to face the truth than to discover convenient excuses. And certainly more sense. And yet?

We are a nation of rationalizers, he thought. It is a disastrous habit. We of all people should know.

But was it rationalizing to believe Alex Malloy? Suppose he really did see an outer marker light even though he was in the wrong geographic location. It would not illuminate by itself. And if the direction finder needle swung around as he claimed, it would not behave so just because it was tired pointing in one direction. So?

Moller closed the latches on his flight bag with a gesture of finality. It was no good, this continual vacillation. Sometime during the past few years Malloy had crumbled professionally. Indeed, his rather fringe airline, one of the outlaws really, had no comprehensive training program. And without constant refreshment in technique these days a man could easily decay. There was no middle course in the flying business; you remained current and right on top of everything or you fell behind.

He placed his flight bag near the door and debated putting on his blazer. No, it was much too hot, certainly for his shopping expedition.

He reached into the breast pocket of the blazer and took out his passport, which he transferred to the flight bag along with the return portion of his ticket to Frankfurt. He made a meticulous business of it because he found the action soothed him. If only he could find some absorbing manual diversion, then he might stop thinking about Lew Horn and the look on his face when he said, "Now here's the exit." Damn the man! Why did he insist on fighting a hopeless cause?

Moller glanced at his watch. It was twelve thirty, a time stamped forever on his thoughts. It had been at twelve thirty on a brilliant summer day that his Focke-Wulf 190 had been shot down into the Bay of Biscay. Miraculously, his descent had been sighted by a Luftwaffe patrol boat and he was in the water less than twenty minutes.

A few years previously he had been even luckier. The incident had sometimes prompted him to wonder if the hairbrush actually was possessed of special powers.

Twelve thirty was the time of day he customarily landed at Tempelhof after flying the round-robin Berlin-Vienna-Milan-Zurich-Berlin schedule. The flight was normally made in a Junkers 52, a faithful old cow of an aircraft which could be landed in any small pasture if the need arose, and all fifteen passengers could walk away without a scratch. It was very slow and stable, but had one dangerous fault. The ailerons were separated from the main body of the wing by about ten centimeters, which made a fine place for ice accumulation. In certain conditions the ailerons could be rendered ineffective, or worse their actual airfoil reversed, and the only solution was to land immediately. Which was not always possible, even in a Junkers 52.

Every man who flew a Junkers knew about its treachery in ice, and wise pilots avoided it with all the cunning they could muster. And still many had been killed just because of it. Nearly among them had been the Bald Eagle of Bavaria.

Moller returned to the window and stood looking down at the arriving cars. He caressed his head thoughtfully as he remembered that certain noontime on the way home to Berlin from Zurich.

The time of day was evidenced only on the instrument panel clock. Beyond the windows of the Junkers there was the heavy winter muck only northern Europe seemed able to create.

Until noon the flight had been routine except that Hugo the flight engineer was catching a cold and sneezed so frequently he could barely attend to his duties.

"I wish you would keep your germs to yourself."

"Do you want me to go back to the cabin?"

"No, I may need you. But after we land go straight home to bed and stay there no matter how much Lufthansa says they need you. People die from what is happening to you."

Only a few minutes later that had been something he wished he had never said.

Life was almost too good then, before the war. Lufthansa pilots flew 150 hours a month, which was a great deal but quite endurable, and the pay was satisfying. If a pilot chose to fly the mail the pay was even higher, but then so was the risk. Mail flights were *never* cancelled because of weather.

Approximately 150 kilometers from Tempelhof the overcast had become even darker and the turbulence more pronounced. Moller had to decide whether to turn back at once or wait and see if it was only a local condition? Hugo's sneezing distracted him and by the time he made up his mind it was too late. In only a few minutes the Junkers had taken on a heavy load of rime ice. It was a late model with the big 750 horsepower BMW engines, so Moller had at least reason to hope they could stay in the air.

"Full throttles! To hell with the rule book. Give me everything!

The Junkers was made of corrugated metal, and as the globs of ice flew off the propellers it was like being bombarded with shrapnel. Luckily there were only six passengers, all of whom, Hugo reported, were praying devoutly.

"I wish I had made it in zeppelins. They never left the hangar in such weather."

Hugo suddenly ceased his sneezing. Perhaps he was too frightened.

"Verify with Berlin the Baké is working." Hugo touched his wireless key.

The Baké was a good approach system designed something like a track. It extended from the perimeter of Tempelhof and emitted a steady tone if the aircraft was directly on course. If it was off to the left an "A" signal was heard and off to the right a "B."

Berlin acknowledged the Baké was normal, but there were more immediate problems. In spite of full power the Junkers began to sink slowly beneath the accumulated load of ice. It trembled in incipient stalls, and each recovery meant a loss of more altitude.

Hugo, a Catholic, had taken out his beads.

"If you are going to do that get back in the cabin."

Hugo seemed not to have heard. He was waiting to die and there was no Captain Helmut Grubbe of the *Passat* to rescue him.

When relying on the Baké system, a pilot flew his aircraft over the aerodrome, reversed course, and descended according to the elapsed time, which was watched very carefully. At Tempelhof the initial fly-over was unnecessary. A recent improvement to the system transmitted a series of slow dashes when the aircraft was approximately three kilometers from the aerodrome perimeter. The pilot knew the moment had come for final descent.

In theory, Moller thought, it was much like the present-day outer marker system at Taipei, although no lights were involved.

On that memorable noonday there were only two hundred meters of altitude left to lose and twenty kilometers still to go for Tempelhof. Fortunately the land all around Berlin is very flat.

"Advise we are in heavy ice and unable maintain altitude."

"My head is splitting!"

How could Hugo care when the engines themselves might soon fly apart? Moller had thought.

Ten kilometers to go and altitude was down to less than one hundred meters. Nothing outside. The strong and unmistakable stink of fear inside.

There was an additional feature added to the new Baké system. Twenty seconds' flying from the perimeter of Tempelhof a series of fast dits interrupted the regular on-course sound. At last it was audible, faintly at first, then rapidly increasing in volume. To the desperate Moller it sounded like Beethoven.

Fifty meters and still nothing outside. An agonizing wait of ten seconds and then a slow reduction in power. There were no runways at Tempelhof, which was a blessing. Suddenly the brown winter grass rose rapidly from below, intersected by a series of white lines. An instant later the Junkers' gear struck the ground. It was a terrible landing, but the Junkers was an extremely stout aircraft and the passengers were convinced Captain Moller was the finest pilot in the world.

Moller smiled. One passenger had sent him a case of French champagne. It was an undeserved tribute. Pure luck had brought them home, a fact which was doubly emphasized twenty minutes later. After that graceless landing a second Lufthansa Junkers, also bound for Tempelhof, crashed only twenty kilometers short of the aerodrome. And the pilot's messages were uncomfortably similar: "Heavy ice. . . . Having trouble holding altitude."

Moller remembered how he had broken the news to his then bride of three months. He had wanted her to believe his profession was as safe as any other. "Poor fellow, there must have been a quick change in the weather. I had no trouble at all."

He had not burdened himself with going to see the wreckage. Since it was above freezing on the ground the ice would have melted and he would only see a pile of corrugated metal scattered about a hole in the ground.

Moller went to the telephone and ordered two ham sandwiches with a bottle of beer. Yes, Taiwan Pilsener would be all right. Strange, he thought, I really do not give a damn about those long gone days. It was another life. My concern is to forget the past. It is meaningless to the real world.

Is it? Then what about the discoveries made by the technical people who stayed so tenaciously with the crash of that second Junkers?

They were very clever. They knew the pilot was a very experienced man and they decided that if Moller could make it to Tempelhof, certainly the other man could. They studied his radio messages, discussing and analyzing each word and comparing transmission times against the final instant of impact as recorded on the instrument panel clock. And finally they decided that such a very good pilot did not crash involuntarily, but flew into the ground because he *thought* he was landing at Tempelhof. The aircraft had hit the ground in a near landing attitude, even bounced once, and it had come down on a railroad enbankment which marked its instant disintegration. The landing might have been acceptable if the terrain had been unobstructed.

The floorman arrived with Moller's sandwiches and beer. He paid the man in cash and included a more than ample tip.

I must be ashamed of myself and am trying to compensate, he thought. Why couldn't there be an earlier plane out of Taipei?

He found the sandwiches tasteless and the beer insipid. And he grunted angrily at his self-imposed confinement. Only a single floor below there was magnificent Chinese food available. But then the others might be there.

Before the war the Lorenze factory which made the Baké approach system was located on the south side of Tempelhof aerodrome. The basic system was used throughout Europe and each installation was carefully tested before being sent from the factory. After endless rounds of inquiries the Lufthansa technicians discovered that on the very afternoon the second Junkers flew into the ground a new system was being operated on the test bench. Transmissions were not continuous, but spaced at intervals. Normally signals transmitted under such circumstances would be so brief and erroneous they would not confuse anyone even if clearly received beyond the shielded test room. Then little by little more facts were revealed.

The more he reflected on the Junkers that had followed his own, the more Moller was impressed with the variety of disguises an impending disaster could assume. And how many lies people told if they feared some failure of their own might become known. On that day it began with an overflowing WC.

No one would ever know which employee originated the malfunction, and certainly there was no volunteering of information. It was established that at approximately ten A.M. the test mechanics observed a considerable flow of water emerging from the adjoining area which included the employees' lavatories. Investigation revealed an overflowing bowl and a most unpleasant mess of paper and excrement, which the highly trained mechanics at once voted was none of their business. They summoned the janitor, who was a long time arriving.

Meanwhile a Baké system destined for immediate delivery to Milan was in the very final stages of testing. The electrical work could not be safely accomplished with four centimeters of water on the floor, so the project was moved to the supervisor's commodious office on the second level. It was assumed the area was also shielded, a misconception which the supervisor himself would have denied if he had not been called to Stuttgart to attend the funeral of his father.

The tests were brief, and probably the resulting emissions would not have confused anyone except a pilot under great stress. Harassed and not a little frightened, the pilot of the second Junkers was glad to hear anything that might sound like home sweet home. He was on the correct frequency, but receiving the wrong signals. It was interesting to learn that not one of the Lorenze mechanics saw fit to mention their special excursion until the matter of the overflowing WC became known.

Moller munched unhappily on his last sandwich. Could something like the Lorenze affair have happened to Alex? Not a chance in a thousand! In those days there was only the one system to fix an aircraft's approach position. Alex had several systems working for him, and besides it was doubtful if electrical equipment capable of emitting confusing signals was manufactured in Taiwan. And then there were the flights before and after Alex's, operating normally —the exact opposite of the Tempelhof situation.

Moller finished his beer, belched, and once again verified the time. Twelve forty-five. How very slowly the minutes pass, he thought, when you are overloaded with hours.

9

Exactly at noon they met for lunch at the Central Theater Restaurant on Chungshan Road.

"I warned you," Sylvia said. "This is the noisiest place in Taipei."

"But it was easy for me to find." Horn smiled. "And I can use some distraction. It's been a full morning."

As she studied the menu she explained the merits of Szechwan food.

He complained he could not hear her.

"Then move here beside me. We live on noise. No Chinese restaurant is considered fit to eat in unless the decibel level is very high."

"In this case I highly approve."

He took the chair at her side. When she had ordered for both of them he told her of his interview with Spencer and then of his surprise call upon Marshall, the lawyer who had tried to defend Alex Malloy. He had been polite and seemed pleased that an outsider would take an interest in what he had done.

"He has been in Taiwan only a year," she said. "I'm afraid he had very much to learn. But I think he is honest."

"I can't reconcile his attitude with Spencer's, who in a sense was paying his fee. Marshall did everything he could to help me. He showed me a transcript of the testimony and let me take all the notes I wanted. I'm not too sure how some of it fits into the total picture."

Horn brought out his sketch pad and apologized for his scribbling. "Here the prosecutor asks Alex if he is sure his direction finder was tuned to the proper frequency for the Taipei outer marker. That's a logical question.

"Alex replies, 'Yes, I'm sure of it. Three hundred and thirty-five kilocycles.'

"Then the prosecutor asks, and I think he must have had some professional prompting on this one, 'Did your direction finder remain on that frequency until you struck the ground?'

"Alex replies, 'As far as I know. Certainly I did not change it.' "

Horn paused and studied her face. He was not surprised to find her bewildered. He patted her shoulder, an involuntary gesture which he instantly regretted because it seemed patronizing.

"Bear with me. There is a thin chance this brief exchange may eventually reveal much more than is first apparent. At least it indicates Alex had his wits about him just prior to the crash."

He quickly drew a diagram on his sketch pad.

"In a Boeing 727 there are two toggle switches which are located almost directly in front of the captain. Those switches have caused some confusion in the past. The two switches are for each direction finder, and each switch has two positions—up for VOR use and down for marker beacon use. Never mind the difference now; they are both just navigational facilities sending useful signals from the ground. The important point is that if those switches are inadvertently left in the wrong position the direction finder will give an erroneous reading no matter what frequency is selected. Alex was asked, and again I am certain the prosecutor had professional prompting, if he thought those switches might have been in the wrong position at the time of his approach. Are you still with me?"

"Right on your wing, Captain."

"Here is Alex's reply which is certainly very positive. He said, 'Of course not. I personally treat those switches like the trigger of a gun held at my head. We refer to them as the Kamikaze switches. I know they were in the right position because I make a habit of checking them before starting any approach.' "

Horn stared at his notes and shook his head unhappily.

"Maybe . . . Now that I look at it here, somehow it doesn't seem so significant. But I keep tying this on to what was heard on the cockpit voice recorder. Someone in that cockpit said, 'Something's wrong!' Then boom, that was it. Alex doesn't seem to remember saying it, but if it was him then those two little words might indicate he could not accept his direction finder bearings with his altitude, and he hit the ground just as he was in the process of making a correction.

"Do you still believe him then?"

"It isn't getting any easier, but if everything he has said is linked together and accepted as the absolute truth, we are at last making progress. Are you free this afternoon?"

"I have permission to visit Alex at six."

"You'll make it. Under the circumstances I don't think he'd mind if I borrowed you until then."

It pleased him to see her smiling.

After lunch she drove him to the office of T. S. Lee, engineering inspector for the Chinese CAA. A deputy who spoke only Chinese informed Sylvia his superior was in Hong Kong and would not return for a month. Then as Horn listened and sensed her rising anger, he saw a remarkable change in the deputy's manner. He became the bearer of obviously important news as he turned away toward an inner office.

Sylvia said, "I think he is going to discover that his boss has suddenly returned from Hong Kong."

"How did you manage that?"

"I casually mentioned my family name. It happens to be the same name as a very powerful family who are close to the Generalissimo. We are not really related except perhaps ten generations back, but our new friend doesn't care to risk offending me."

"He looks like a turtle."

"You can be sure he is not going to let you examine any records until he talks to his boss."

Soon the deputy returned. He was smiling and obsequious as he indicated they should follow him. He led them to a long hallway, then turned into a windowless room and waved his hand proudly at the rows of metal files. He took down two large canvas books and spread them on a table.

"He says this log is for the glide slope equipment and this one for the outer marker system. They are current until three days ago, and entries are made from the daily records only twice a week. If we wait until tomorrow we can see everything right up to the last inspection."

Horn was disappointed. The entries were in Chinese, although there were occasional notations written in English.

Sylvia carefully turned the pages and explained that all of the entries in the glide slope log signified "normal" before the night of Alex's crash. Immediately afterward she repeated a number of notations which Horn recognized as adjustments and repairs.

"Maybe I'm translating poorly. It sounds like gobbledygook to me."

"No. It makes sense. It's possible they took on a new manager who cracked the whip more than the other man. But I wonder why there was so much sudden activity, when two ships made it in before and after Alex and reported nothing wrong."

She pointed to the lists of times and a column of initials along the edge of each page, then questioned the deputy.

"He says these are the initials of the engineers who did the work or made routine tests according to date and hour. He says they are always extremely vigilant."

"How come this gentleman will only talk—"

Horn left his question hanging for he saw a sudden warning in Sylvia's eyes as she deliberately interrupted him. "Perhaps this other book will be more interesting?"

She pushed it hard toward him and he knew he had made a mistake in assuming the deputy understood only Chinese. Bless you, he thought. I must somewhere find your twin sister.

As she carefully translated the entries on the outer marker system he soon realized the activity was the opposite of the record in the first book. Now there were repeated entries before the date of Malloy's crash. The engineers were obviously having trouble until approximately a week after the crash, then they had apparently solved the problem. Thereafter the entries were regularly timed and always reported the system operating normally.

"Is there any notation about a new part being installed?"

Sylvia re-examined the pages then queried the deputy.

"He says, no. All replacement parts are identified by category and serial number. Discarded parts are also recorded. There is nothing in the log to indicate anything except normal maintenance."

"Tell our friend we appreciate his help."

Later, in the car enroute to the plateau, she looked at him inquiringly. "Why are you so sad?"

"I am not in the least sad. It's the way I look when I'm stumped. I can't decide if going out to the outer marker installation is a waste of time, or have we stumbled on the Yin and the Yang—"

She laughed and asked how he had known about such things.

"Johnnie Kan runs the best Chinese restaurant in San Francisco and he's a good friend of mine. I remember him telling me how Yin and Yang balance each other in the pattern of life, and I think it is more than interesting how the maintenance work on the glide slope system began so suddenly after Alex's crash and then practically at the same time work stopped on the outer marker system. I'm no electronics expert, but it seems to me the work records are all out of balance. And something else is bothering me—"

"Yes?"

"Has anyone told you today that you're very beautiful?"

"You and my grandfather are two of a kind."

A soldier armed with a submachine gun stood in the middle of the road. He held up his hand and Sylvia brought the car to a stop. Satisfied, the soldier approached the window and bent down to examine their faces. He shook his head and told Sylvia she must turn around.

In the distance, at the border of a tea farm, Horn could see a small building. According to his chart it should contain the Taipei outer marker system. He noticed now that it was surrounded by a wire fence topped with barbed wire.

"Ask him if we can drive another hundred yards or so. I want a closer look at that little building."

While she questioned the soldier Horn noticed three more soldiers at the very end of the road. Beyond them, sitting in a jeep, were three other soldiers. They were looking toward a small gully a few feet away. For a moment he thought there had probably been an accident.

"This man insists we turn around. This is always happening in Taiwan. It's a nuisance. Every so often the Army decides to practice their maneuvers on the main roads and traffic is tied up for hours."

"Ask him if I can get out of the car. Just for a minute."

The soldier nodded agreement. Horn was not sure why he wanted to look beyond the crest on the opposite side of the road. The urge, he thought, was really a hunger to view something tangible which was actually involved in Alex's crash. Everything else seemed to have disappeared or remained theoretical speculation. It was just a building, as he had known it would be, and it was located exactly where the chart specified. There was nothing magical or even mysterious about it. Inside he knew there was only a relatively simple electronic device which faithfuly transmitted useful signals. Undoubtedly this system was of the same low power as others in the world and its only claim to fame, he thought wryly, was that on a certain dirty night it had betrayed those who relied upon it for their lives—or had it? And according to the maintenance records its reputation had sometimes been suspect. Why then should it become so virtuous almost immediately *after* Alex's crash? It was becoming hard to believe the damned thing was only a machine.

He crossed the road and looked down into a gently sloping valley. It was lush with tea trees and on the far side of the valley he decided there must be a school. He could hear the shrill voices of children at play.

He turned his attention to the soldiers in the jeep and decided they were a lucky detail. They sat comfortably in the shade while some hundred yards away in the valley a half platoon of their comrades seemed to be engaged in some sort of construction project. They moved slowly in the blazing sun confining their efforts to a small area about the size of a tennis court. Most of them were stripped to the waist. A bulldozer frequently interfered with their work on a high fence and from the way each man immediately retreated to the shade of a tree he presumed they were grateful for the interruption. He watched their endeavors for a while, then, strangely puzzled, returned to the car.

Sylvia turned the car around and started back for Taipei. They rode in silence until she asked him if he was satisfied with what he had seen.

"No."

"There wasn't much. Just that little building. Why should it be important?"

"I guess it isn't, really. In some ways I'm more confused than ever. Why would those soldiers be up there?"

"They are everywhere in Taiwan. We're so used to seeing them they have become part of the landscape. We really live in a fortress. Sometimes I think every hill has a cannon hidden inside. I suppose it's all necessary, but I'd much prefer to live in a land not so entirely military."

"The first day we arrived and came to this area we convinced ourselves we were being followed. Would that be possible?"

"Oh, yes. Strangers are always interesting if they depart from the usual tourist routes."

"Who would be doing the following?"

"Possibly two agencies. One might be Military Intelligence—really quite necessary under the circumstances I suppose—and the other might be the Central Intelligence Department. They are not nearly so numerous as they used to be."

"Why would they follow us, either one?"

She shrugged her shoulders and glanced in the rearview mirror. "Were you sure?"

"No. But suddenly there were two men out by the rice paddy. Of course they could have been bird watchers with those binoculars and we just happened to be in their line of sight."

"Did they have a car?"

"Yes. It looked like a late model Ford."

She glanced again at the rearview mirror. "Maybe your guess was right. We have a similar combination behind us right now."

Horn resisted the temptation to look back. "How long have they been there?"

"Since we turned around. Of course they could be just two businessmen—"

"Out for a look at the birds again? Let's turn off and go out to the rice paddy. If they tag along, maybe—just maybe—things are coming together."

The route to the rice paddy was circuitous and it was nearly four o'clock before they arrived. Somewhere enroute, Sylvia was not sure of the place, they had lost their escort. Horn was disappointed. It seemed that every time he was about to fit a piece into the puzzle it changed shape. He tried to convince himself that being followed by two men in a Ford was merely a coincidence.

They walked together along the dike. As they approached the bamboo grove he instinctively reached for her hand and held it until they stopped beneath the trees. The air was stagnant and the only sound was the strangely melancholy call of the birds echoing across the glassy water. She asked him why he wanted to return to such an oppressive place.

"It seems like my day for hunches. I just want to have another look around, half hoping I might find one little piece of an airplane. It is inconceivable to me that such a thorough clean-up job was done. Do you know who did it?"

"I suppose the Army."

"Why the Army?"

She seemed uncertain and shrugged her shoulders. "Usually they are called out for disasters, to keep order I guess."

"It seems to me the Army is into everything. What I want to know is where did the wreckage go? Where is the tail engine, for example? It must have been in perfect condition, worth several hundred thousand dollars."

He took her hand again and they began to walk slowly around the dike which surrounded the paddy. He kept his eyes on the ground.

"If you see a piece of metal, yell."

"If we found something would it really make a difference?"

"Yes and no. I think it might be much more significant if we fail to find anything at all. When an airplane breaks up like that there should be hundreds, maybe thousands of pieces scattered all over the area."

"We are a very frugal people. Any object that could possibly have any use would be picked up, if only for a souvenir. And much of it might be under the water."

"Still . . ."

She squeezed his hand very gently. "I admire your determination, Horn."

They made a complete circuit of the paddy, then duplicated their stately patrol around the perimeter of the adjoining paddy. They found nothing except a child's rubber ball. It appeared old and so rotten-skinned that Horn was certain it could not have come from the airplane. When they returned to the bamboo grove they paused to look back at the paddy. And Horn noticed that although they were halted she had not withdrawn her hand from his.

"I thought I would hate this place," she said softly. "But I find it strangely peaceful."

He turned to look down at her for a moment. His free hand rose as if to draw her to him, then he saw only rebuke in her eyes. He dropped his hand.

"I almost—"

"Yes. I am not blind."

"Do you know what time it is in New York?" he asked suddenly.

"What made you think of that?"

"It's four o'clock in the morning. Too early to call a man named Brewster." He took her arm and propelled her toward the car.

"Who is Brewster?"

"A wise old owl. I saw something this afternoon I can't seem to put out of my mind. Maybe Brewster can find out for me why Chinese soldiers are such meticulous housekeepers and why they tear down what looks like brand new fencing."

Neither Chatsworth nor Diderot had expected anything like their reception at the Ministry of Communications. After identifying themselves, there was a short period of initial confusion, but soon they were escorted directly to the office of T. L. Seng, Deputy Chief, Air Transport Section, CAA. He proved to be a large and confident man, probably an asthmatic, Chatsworth thought, as he listened to his heavy breathing.

"Of course. I had rather expected you."

He immediately told Chatsworth that he had been to school in England. "Gresham's in Holt, Norfolk. I would have liked to stay there much longer. Unfortunately for my personal desires my country needed me—what is left of it that is, which matches what is left of me."

Seng laughed rather too easily and often, Chatsworth decided, but at least his welcome seemed genuine. He apologized for the Taiwan heat and offered them fans from a selection on his desk. He chose a fan for himself and breathed heavily of the air he stirred before his face. When he seemed to have refreshed himself he wiped at his damp cheeks and asked directly if they might have something new to offer in the Malloy matter.

"It's a shame. I dislike seeing a man condemned, and we've gone to great lengths trying to find something that might make Malloy look a little better, at least get him off with a loss of license or something of the sort. We haven't had much luck. The deeper we investigated the worse things seemed."

Seng shook his jowls unhappily and ordered his clerks to bring the Malloy files. "I want you to see everything. There are no secrets here. Our only desire is to guarantee civil air safety throughout the Taiwan airspace. We have much to learn, and opinions of men like yourselves are greatly valued by all of us in this section. If you see something that strikes you as inaccurate or even suspect, I beg you to call my attention to it."

Four hours passed while they examined the detailed sketch of the crash site, the approach path diagrams in relation to the localizer, the glide path diagrams, side elevations of the crash scene, sketches, photographs, the analysis of the local weather, and the communications log between flight three and Taipei Approach Control and the tower. They examined the flight data recorder read-out which gave the altitudes, headings, airspeeds, and even the g loads of flight three minute by minute all the way from Manila to the instant of impact. Seng ordered an assistant to bring in the voice tapes and they listened in fascination to the voices of Alex, Leonard Wu, and Flight Engineer Tseu, voices, they both decided, that offered no hint whatever of impending tragedy until the very last seconds.

They leafed through stacks of reports, the statements of each surviving passenger and crew member, the minutes of various technical meetings, and the full report of a special panel of experts sent from Seattle by the Boeing company. There appeared to be no question of any fault with the aircraft, an opinion Alex himself had verified.

"Take your time," Seng urged. "If you have any particular questions I can't answer I'll be glad to call in one of our staff who can."

Occasionally, as if to demonstrate his open attitude, Seng would leave them alone with the files: "There is a matter I must attend to . . ."

During one of his absences Diderot wondered why they had been expected. "Horn has not been here?"

Chatsworth made a face. He did not like even the possibility of intrigue. It was so un-British, and after all this was not a bloody film.

"I doubt it would make much difference. Perhaps these chaps have been following us about, but it's their country and they may consider us rude guests. Unfortunately I am also about convinced Willie Moller might be right. Somehow much of this material didn't find its way into the report we've seen. I find it devastating."

Later, when they had declared they were satisfied, Seng expressed his regret. "I was hoping you would notice something we had failed to do. In such a complicated matter one never knows how some small thing—" He made a delicate circular gesture with his thumb and forefinger, then fanned himself in thoughtful silence until he appeared to reach a momentous decision. He rose and ambled across the office to a separate steel file. He opened it and fingered the upright folders almost, Chatsworth decided, as if he were caressing them.

"Actually, I have been guilty of holding something back, but only pending any opinion you might wish to offer. I wanted to avoid creating any prejudice in your minds. Apparently the time has come to inform you further."

He slipped out a thin folder and returned to his chair. He took a moment to regain his breath while waving the fan very slowly beneath his nostrils. "Here is the confidential file on the Malloy case which we saw no need to publish along with what you have read. Although we are rather proud of our thoroughness, the technical aspects of the crash so obviously place the guilt we felt these discoveries were unnecessary. Some of these items might be regarded as mere gossip. We do not consider any of it really pertinent."

Seng waved his fan over the folder as if to clear the air above it. "When I left you a while ago I consulted with my superior, and we are agreed you should at least be aware of the contents herein."

He cleared his throat carefully and began to read. " During the past twelve months Captain A. Malloy of Far Eastern Airlines has been reported four times as descending below the minimums allowed for the subject airports. Specifically on January eleventh at Hong Kong and again April twenty-second at Hong Kong. Official ceiling and visibility on both occasions were below authorized minimums, yet the indicated flights commanded by Captain Malloy arrived on or near schedule. Next, on March ninth at Manila and finally on August third during a heavy rainstorm at Tokyo. Violations were filed at both Tokyo and Hong Kong, but for unexplained reasons not at Manila. In reply to all charges Captain Malloy stated the weather observations were incorrect and not according to his own estimates. Attached are official weather reports covering the periods involved.' "

Seng blew out his cheeks and pressed his lips into a rosette. "Be assured we are fully aware that local weather viewed from the flight deck may vary considerably from official observations made from the ground, and therefore these violations may be open to argument. However, some men are known as 'weather busters,' and perhaps this shows a trend."

Seng smiled at the folder then carefully wet his thumb and forefinger. He turned a page and smoothed its surface. "This item may not be pertinent, but you may wish to consider it. Captain Malloy's last physical proved him to be in excellent health. However, his visual acuity was registered at twenty-forty in both eyes without glasses, and a waiver was attached to his certificate requiring him to wear glasses when in command of an aircraft. During a clean-up of the debris after the crash Captain Malloy's glasses were found in his flight kit."

"Twenty-forty is not too bad," Chatsworth said. "Normal for most of us senior pilots, and quite acceptable for flight. The usual waiver specifies only that glasses must be *in possession* of the pilot."

"I stand corrected, Captain. That is precisely the wording here in Chinese. The English translation from which I am reading took considerable liberty. However—"

"However," Chatsworth thought, seemed to be Seng's favorite English word.

"For what it may be worth, here is a recital by a stewardess, Emma Chi, taken three days after the accident. She suffered only superficial bruises and was apparently in good mental condition in spite of the experience. She relates that on the night before the subject flight, Captain Malloy had taken her and another stewardess, Jackie Lo, to dinner in Manila. She alleges she saw Captain Malloy consume several whiskey and sodas during the course of the evening. When asked if he appeared intoxicated she replied that she could not understand how he could be anything else."

"Ungrateful little tramp," Diderot said.

"I quite agree," Seng replied with a solemn wave of his fan.

Chatsworth pulled fiercely at his goatee. Why were the low of caste so quick to pounce on the fallen mighty? The world was full of jackals, females as well as males.

"Unless his tolerance has changed greatly, several whiskeys would hardly render our friend intoxicated, much less incapable on the following night. I would wager the stewardess is a teetotaler who mentally multiplies the number of drinks she sees a man take and after she thinks about it a while the most innocent gathering becomes a debauch."

Seng tipped his head back and laughed. The effort brought beads of perspiration to his face and he fanned himself and wiped his handkerchief around his neck while he stated his full agreement. "Of course Malloy was pushing the twenty-four-hour drinking rule a bit, but we realistically acknowledge it is common to all airlines and rarely abused. This really should be struck from the file and I shall do so now."

He pulled the page from the folder, crumpled it ceremoniously and tossed it at his wastebasket. "And here is another item which possibly deserves the same treatment. Passenger Manuel Esposito of the Philippine Export Company stated that he saw Captain Malloy behaving most eccentrically as he boarded the aircraft. When asked what he meant by eccentrically he replied, 'He was singing softly to himself as he walked out to the airplane like he was trying to keep his spirits up.' It may interest you to know that although Mr. Esposito escaped without the slightest physical injury he is suing Far Eastern Airlines for one million dollars Taiwan for mental anguish suffered as a result of the crash."

Seng's smile faded and his thick lips drooped as he continued. "I wish we could dismiss all of this file as easily. Please listen carefully to this voluntary statement by First Officer H. E. Hsi, a senior co-pilot with Far Eastern and a highly respected gentleman. On a recent flight with Captain Malloy, specifically on September tenth, from Tokyo to Taipei, he distinctly remembers Malloy saying, 'I never trust that damn Taipei approach system. It's crazy and will get a man in deep trouble. So I always sneak in the back door.' "

Seng paused and allowed the contrasting silence to emphasize the importance of his reading. Finally he resumed. "First Officer Hsi said that after that flight he resolved to find some excuse to avoid flying again with Captain Malloy if and when assigned."

Seng closed the folder and tapped it gently with the edge of his fan. He focused his eyes on the high ceiling, waiting. The only sound in the room was his heavy breathing. "Well?"

Again there was silence until at last Chatsworth sighed. "Right. I think we will say good afternoon."

The sun was a steaming ball on the horizon when they hailed a taxi and directed the driver to the Grand Hotel. They rode in silence, staring at the sun, deliberately avoiding each other's eyes.

Finally Diderot asked if his companion had ever been to the Congo, where he had spent so much of his youth. This evening, he explained, the sun reminded him of Brazzaville, where the older Diderot had sent his family when he decided Hitler must certainly conquer France.

"I was always scheming to get across the river to Léopoldville, where there were so many young Belgians. When the war was over Papa was not pleased that I became Belgianized, and he has never quite accepted the fact that I voluntarily chose to fly for Sabena rather than Air France. He says Belgians eat too much. They fall asleep at the table. He says early to bed and early to rise and you will meet no interesting people."

The attempt to lighten their mood was an obvious failure.

Chatsworth made a low humming sound to signify he had been listening, although he did not turn his head. He knew they were avoiding discussion of the inevitable.

"I was once part of a BOAC team flying down to a dreadful place called Banana at the mouth of the Congo. We were surveying sites and laying moorings for flying boats and operated mainly between Banana, Léopoldville, and Lagos. We spent some time in Stanleyville also, where we were rather appropriately quartered in the maternity hospital. One might say we fathered those routes."

Diderot tried to chuckle, but the effort produced only a dry sound. He could not keep the results of their recent meeting out of his mind. He rolled down the window of the car and blinked at the red orb of the sun. "It's going to land right on Quemoy Island, where I understand these Chinese are still shooting at the mainland."

"What is going to land?"

"The sun."

"Oh? Yes. Of course." Chatsworth's voice drifted away and he rubbed at his eyes. He yawned and apologized for his rudeness, saying he was having more difficulty accommodating himself to time changes every year. "In a way I shall be relieved when it's all over."

"You mean this business with Alex?"

"No. I meant flying the line, but we might as well face up to the other matter."

He borrowed one of Diderot's cigarettes and after it was lit he puffed at it uncertainly. "First smoke I've had in four years. Subconscious demonstration of my inner surrender I suppose."

"Then we agree?"

"There seems to be no other answer."

"That statement about sneaking in the back door. Zut! It sounded like Alex."

"What are we going to tell Lew Horn? He's such an idealist. But I suppose he's accustomed to bumps. He's given his heart to this. We're deserting him, and yet I'm damned if I know what else we can do."

"I have reason to believe he will find at least some consolation."

"What do you mean by that?"

Diderot crushed his cigarette in the ashtray. For a moment he was standing at his window again looking down at the hotel portico and a delicate hand projecting from a car window. "Nothing," he said. "Nothing."

10

It was nearly six o'clock before Sylvia stopped at the American Embassy. Horn opened the car door, then looked back at her. They had said little during the drive back to Taipei, and now he wondered if she had sensed his growing desperation. "Is there anything you should tell me about Alex?" he asked. "How was his general health before the crash?"

"He was . . . weary."

"Why?"

"He had been flying mostly night trips which were off his regular schedule. One of the other captains has a son who was in trouble back in the States. That left Spencer short one captain."

"He didn't bother to mention that. Do you think Alex might have been so tired he couldn't think straight?"

He saw immediate resentment in her eyes. "No. Certainly not."

"I'm sorry. I had to ask. Where are you going when you leave the sanitarium?"

"Home."

"Don't. Come to the hotel. If I'm not there wait for me. I may need your local knowledge. Now beat it. You're late." He leaned across the seat, kissed her impulsively on the cheek, and was gone.

A marine guard led him through the deserted building to the office of Sam Fry. Horn found him to be as tall as himself and about the same age. He thought he looked like a young De Gaulle.

When asked if he always worked after everyone else had

157

left for the day, Fry explained it was the only time he could get any paperwork done.

"Right now I'm preparing a review on the 'Economic Impact of the Growing Taiwanese Ship-scrapping Industry in Relation to the Continuance of American Assistance Funds' for the next bi-annual. How do you like that for a swinging title?"

"It won't sell."

"Correct. Even with free copies distributed throughout the halls of our dear government, no one will read it. I lie awake nights trying to think of some way I can put some sex into the scrap iron business. Enough of my troubles. I take it this is not a social call."

"I have some questions and I need help in a hurry."

Fry shook his head. "I am a lowly underling in the State Department. After eight years I am an FSO-six, and if I live long enough and keep my nose clean I may make FSO-three. Thus my authorized power is approximately that of a flea."

"Just tell me who originally started the criminal prosecution in the Malloy case. Who put the pressure on? The whole idea just didn't come out of the blue. Who is the real villain?"

"I haven't the faintest—"

"Then make a faint guess. Never in aviation history have so many governmental agencies, or whatever you want to call them, been so solidly lined up against one man. I'm not sure what it is, but something smells. I think Malloy has been elected the scapegoat for something or possibly someone. Why?"

"Aren't you possibly imagining things?"

"Am I also imagining that I am being followed? Why?"

Fry smiled tolerantly. "Because of the endless war with the mainland, the military rules the daily life of every person on this island. This is a police state no matter how you look at it. If you are actually being followed don't worry about it. Either your behavior is unusual enough to be interesting or more likely these men on your trail just haven't enough to do. They have to look busy to keep their rice bowl full and they won't harm you."

"Does the military tell the CAA what to do?"

"Probably. Anything concerned with the airspace over

Taiwan is the military's baby. You can be sure of that."

"Okay. How about the judges? Can the military demand any kind of verdict they want?"

"I would doubt it. Of course, if they really were upset about something—What are you trying to suggest?"

"Nothing yet. Tell me where I can beg, borrow, or steal an airplane. I'll settle for anything that will get off the ground."

"Come on now, Captain Horn. I'm only the vice-consul, which is equivalent to clerk of the water cooler, and they don't even give me the key to that. Which reminds me that I am thirsty. It is now six thirty, and if it wasn't for you I'd just be snuggling up to the bar at the club for my first drink."

Horn leaned forward. The determination in his eyes caused Fry to involuntarily push his chair back a few inches.

"I have always heard that an American who seeks help from his official representatives abroad is wasting breath and time. Unlike the British Foreign Office, which will turn a country upside down to help their own people—"

"Now just a damn minute. If you want to air your views on this outfit, speak to the bosses. I'll try to set up an appointment with the ambassador."

"I do not want to talk to the ambassador or listen to him. I want action, and the more I listen to you the more convinced I am you are not a company man. Therefore I keep telling myself you might actually help me find an airplane."

"I don't know anything about flying machines. Perhaps you will remember they terrify me."

"Never mind. How can I get my hands on one, legal or illegal?"

"What for? You can't really believe I'd help you go into the smuggling business."

"Now you're starting to sound like the establishment. It doesn't suit you. I'll give you a number, you call my airline in New York and check my character. Meanwhile I want an airplane because I want to do some local flying and particularly refly Malloy's final ten minutes. I'm not positive, but I think the results could be important."

Fry closed his eyes and tipped far back in his leather

chair. He turned his head until he could see the American flag standing in the corner, and Horn heard him say softly, "What have I done to deserve this?" Then suddenly his body became rigid. He blinked repeatedly at the ceiling. "Wait a minute! Oh, no. My first boss in the foreign service told me never, repeat *never*, to become personally involved in the troubles of an individual citizen. It's the sure road to a post in Patagonia. But . . ."

Fry slowly eased himself down to a level position. He seemed to brood unhappily and for a moment Horn thought he would be dismissed.

"By some stretching of protocol and a little bending of interoffice memos there might be a rationale here. I'm vague on the details, but about three years ago an American named Keim came to Taiwan and bought an airplane, an old one. He was some kind of collector, and I do remember the transaction would be duty free because it could be classified as an antique purchase. The paperwork was all done, I remember that. Just about the time Keim was ready to leave he had a heart attack, in your very hotel lobby incidentally. I personally arranged for shipping his remains home, but that's all I did. About six months later I heard that the lawyers for Keim's estate had asked our commercial section to help sell the airplane to the highest bidder. It proved to be a headache because there were no bidders, and there was a lot of accusatory correspondence sent this way."

"What kind of an airplane was it?"

"I can't remember. Name some."

"Douglas? Lockheed?"

Fry waved his hand as if he might pull the name he wanted out of the air. "It was a German something or other."

"Focke-Wulf? Junkers?"

"Junkers! That's it! It should be still out at Ishan. That's about thirty-five miles from here."

Horn was already on his feet. "You just sold an airplane for five hundred dollars—subject to inspection."

"Only the commercial section is authorized—"

"My check will be here in the morning. You're in charge of permission to fly it. We won't need that until at least noon."

"Do you have any conception of what you are asking? If the Chinese authorities do not consider that airplane an essential item of defense, then probably we can arrange for an export permit, given two or three weeks. Flying it is another matter."

"You're about to say it's not in your department. Rise to the occasion and put it in your department. You must have friends who can chop down the red tape. What's your home phone? I'll call you from Ishan." He held out his sketch pad.

As Fry reluctantly marked down a telephone number he shook his head. "I have a sour taste in my mouth. It always comes to me when I know I have done something foolish. And I am cautioning myself never to fly your airline during my next stateside leave. I like my captains gray-haired, square-jawed, athletic teetotalers, faithful churchgoers, and above all, utterly sane."

Once he settled back in the taxi, Horn's energies seemed to melt away with his confidence. He closed his eyes and tried to sleep. Soon all of his doubts came charging out of the darkness and everything he had done seemed futile. Was he just going through the motions expected of a friend who was trying to help a friend? Certainly his powerful desire to vindicate Alex had propelled him toward *some* solution, but how much actual fact was involved? Now was the time to communicate with Brewster. He might offer an answer, but what if he viewed the theory as half baked, or even impossible? Then what good was a Junkers airplane, if indeed the thing was flyable?

It was just eight o'clock. In New York it would be only seven in the morning. Too early. He must wait another hour and a half before Brewster would be in his office.

He tried to open his eyes and found he was unable. God, he was weary! In the last forty-eight hours he had not known more than four of sleep and now there promised to be another full night of activity.

He was painting a New England winter landscape when he realized someone was shaking him gently. He awakened with a start, recognized the hotel doorman, and told him he would need a large hire car and driver in exactly two hours. Refreshed after only a few minutes' sleep, he mounted the main entrance stairs two at a time. Whether for good or bad, he thought that at last he had a program.

Chatsworth, Diderot, and van Grootes were waiting for him in the lobby. He ignored their morose appearance. Life was once again full of zest.

"Where's Willie Moller?"

"He said to tell you goodbye and he wished you good luck." Van Grootes checked his watch. "Thirty minutes from now he'll be bound home."

"He can't do that. We need the son of a bitch. What airline?"

"Japan Air—"

"We'll have to stop him. Meanwhile pack a toothbrush, razor, and an extra pair of socks. We're going away for a day or so. A hire car will pick us up in two hours. Meet you at the entrance and save your questions until then."

He left them abruptly. As he strode across the lobby Chatsworth called after him. "Lew, you have to slow down and listen. We have—"

Horn would not have heard him if Chatsworth had shouted, for his mind was whirling with what must be done, and the assignment of details was in itself a challenge. As he approached the main desk, he asked the clerk to call Japan Air Lines for him. He smiled thoughtfully. It seemed that regardless of geography and situation his life always returned to normal. Even now at the very start there were two necessary revisions to his flight plan.

When the clerk handed him the telephone he asked to speak with the Japan Air Lines station manager. In his most formal manner he warned him that passenger Moller, first initial W, should be removed from their departing flight and detained until the police arrived. An oversight perhaps, but the fact remained that he had departed without paying his hotel bill.

Satisfied with the response, he quickly recrossed the lobby. Threading his way through a noisy wedding party, he was suddenly brought to a halt by van Grootes.

"Lew. Calm down, will you? We've gone over this whole thing a hundred times. We gave Alex every break we could and always reached the same answer."

He shook his massive head and Horn saw his face turn red in his acute discomfort. "The only honest answer is that the weather where Alex hit on the plateau happened to be different than it was at the airport itself. He didn't know exactly where he was, and he was trying to sneak in. We don't blame the poor fellow for inventing excuses—"

"Are you trying to tell me you're all quitting?"

Van Grootes hesitated. He tried unsuccessfully to meet Horn's accusing eyes. "You're all tensed up and it's understandable that you should believe Alex completely. Of course we don't go along with the criminal charge, but—"

"But what?"

"You can't ask us to whitewash a man just because he happens to be an old friend."

"God damn it, I'm not asking you to whitewash anyone! I only ask you to give me a chance to change your minds. I'll explain on the way to pick up Willie Moller. See you in an hour and fifty-one minutes."

Without waiting for a confirmation, he moved quickly away and half ran up the broad lobby stairs. By the time he reached his hallway he was running. Once in his room he telephoned Sylvia. He waited impatiently through a series of empty clicks and rings, then called the sanitarium. Minutes passed until an English-speaking nurse came to the telephone. Would you please go to Room Eight and tell Mrs. Malloy to come to the Taipei Airport in two hours. She should bring an overnight bag, her husband's flight kit, a flash camera, at least four flashlights, and a battery-powered tape recorder.

He hung up the phone and pressed the button for a room boy. When he arrived he ordered a pot of coffee, a T-bone steak, and a triple serving of ginger ice cream. Immediately.

While he was waiting he wrote out a check for five hundred dollars in payment for one airplane and sealed it in an envelope marked for the attention of Uncle Sam Fry at the American Embassy.

Glancing frequently at his watch, he packed his airline carry-on bag with his toilet kit, an extra shirt, shorts, and socks. As an afterthought he slipped in his sketch pad.

As he moved about the room the bed became an ever-increasing attraction. He longed to stretch out for just a few minutes! But once down he knew he would be lost until morning. Desperate for distraction, he sat down at the desk and wrote a postcard to the woman who kept Orville Wright. He had forgotten to tell her to give him a thimbleful of whiskey if he seemed out of sorts. Scotch, if she pleased. Orville's depression deepened if he drank bourbon.

At last his steak arrived and he fell upon it hungrily. When he had finished he decided it was late enough to chance the call to New York. Minutes later he smiled at Brewster's familiar growl.

"I thought you were in Corsica?"

"I never did go for the mamselles. I suppose you can guess what I'm up to here?"

"There's no guessing. I'm certain. You're a born trouble maker."

"I need help. Who is our best electronic genius in the radio department?"

"Max Werner. He's the nuttiest of them all, which I guess makes him a genius. You know how radio people are."

"Can you get him on your conference phone. I have to talk with him right now."

"Jesus, it's only eight in the morning here. People who come to work at this hour in the radio department are not the genius types."

"Try. Alex's life may depend on something I have to know."

While Brewster was trying to set up the conference call he asked if Malloy had been hung as yet. Horn told him briefly of his shock at seeing Alex and named those who had come to Taiwan with him. Then Brewster introduced Max Werner, who answered cryptically. He explained that he had been working all night on a communications problem and would appreciate not being asked any trick questions at such an hour.

"What kind of source on the ground would affect the automatic direction finder in a Boeing 727 other than the normal transmitters?"

"None. These days most ADF's are a very sophisticated instrument with very tight frequency tolerances. Of course you still have to tune the correct frequency."

"Naturally. Assuming that's done, what else?"

"Oh . . . possibly a particular thunderstorm with lots of fire in it—"

"No, no. Man-made."

"I would have to know much more about the degree of fluctuation, the overall condition of the components involved . . . and the source of spurious signals. You're asking me something that isn't just all that—"

Horn sighed and found that he was squeezing the telephone fiercely as if he might extract what he wanted to hear. Why was it always so difficult to draw a straight answer from the black box people?

"All I wanted to know is what kind of signals transmitted from the ground might affect the needle of an ADF and also illuminate an outer marker light?"

"None."

"None? What do you mean by that? An ADF is basically a radio receiver isn't it?"

"Of course, but it won't lock on to an off-frequency signal unless someone accidentally selects that frequency and thinks he has the right one. And with the present equipment in a 727 that's highly unlikely."

Horn renewed his vow not to lead the expert into suggesting what he wanted to hear. Confirmation of his suspicions would have to be voluntary no matter how long they talked.

"What you are saying then is that nothing, absolutely nothing on the ground, can cause an ADF needle to give an erroneous course indication or reverse itself . . . or the outer marker light to come on?"

"Now wait a minute. You are putting words into my mouth."

"That's exactly what I am trying not to do."

"I didn't say *absolutely* nothing. There might be certain installations which under certain conditions just might—"

"Like what kind of installations for Christ's sake?"

No sect of humans in the world, Horn thought, could try a man's patience like black box people.

"Well, say a hydroelectric plant . . . perhaps in the near proximity of a heavy industry factory, or its power source—Where did you say you're calling from?"

"Taipei."

"That's an island in the Pacific isn't it? How I envy you. Bet you're getting lots of beach time. It's freezing here."

"You must be thinking of Saipan, and never mind the weather report on my nickel. There is nothing else in your experience that could cause the effects I've described?"

There was a moment's silence, and Horn wondered if the connection had been broken. He decided it would not make a great deal of difference since what he had so longed to hear had not been offered. Now should he stubbornly chase down his theory or abandon the whole project?

He was about to apologize for his shortness when he heard the voice again, hesitant and slightly deprecatory.

"Well, of course there is one far-out possibility which would not apply to your present location at all. I mean it simply could not apply to a little two-bit atoll where we fought the Japs, not unless there is something going on out there *Newsweek* hasn't mentioned. I put a lot of stock in *Newsweek*. They really keep you up on foreign affairs."

Horn groaned. He hoped Brewster was still on the line.

"Boss, will you please tell Mr. Werner where I really am?"

He listened impatiently while Brewster described the situation. Afterward there was again a long and tantalizing silence. It was broken by the eerie sound of Werner muttering to himself. A telephone rang somewhere in the background, then Werner "a-hemmed" several times.

Finally he said, "Perhaps in your situation the possibility I mentioned is not so far out after all. Would there be a guided missile site in the area? Specifically, the American Nike missile? They aren't very large you know, or very modern, and their electronics have given trouble before. If a Nike were being tested, it could quite possibly affect an ADF and even the outer marker light."

Horn resisted a temptation to cheer.

"Are you sure?"

"Affirmative. We call it anomalous dispersion. The degree of influence would depend upon the distance from the site itself. That's one of the reasons the underground silos in most nations have been installed way out in the boonies. One of those things can spoil a guy's television reception too. Damned annoying when your favorite program is on. I remember when we drove our camper to Montana about two years ago and we were watching *Bonanza*. All of a sudden the picture went wild. My wife hit the ceiling."

"Mr. Werner, I hope your wife didn't hurt herself. And I thank you from the bottom of my heart!"

He hung up and started for the door. Dragon one, throat slit and bleeding badly, he thought. Now there were two left, and they would have to be conquered one at a time.

As Horn passed through the crowded lobby, tourists turned their heads and followed his progress. For in spite of the myriad other distractions at this most active of hours, they found something irresistibly intriguing about a tall young American, strangely wild of eye, marching at full tilt and whistling with such total concentration.

11

THE CODE OF CRIMINAL PROCEDURE

Article 154: The facts of an offense shall be established by evidence. The facts of an offense shall not be presumed in the absence of evidence.

I, K. C. Hsieh, having heard the evidence presented before me in Taipei District Court on Docket #302, do find the following:

1. A crash of Far Eastern Airways flight 3 occurred on October 5, 1963, Captain Alex Malloy commanding. 14 passengers killed and 46 injured.

2. Evidence presented to the court by Prosecutor E. K. Han was based on various testimonies and displays prepared by the Minister of Communications.

3. The evidence clearly demonstrates how Captain Malloy did fly his machine into the earth. The defendant himself states he did not even look out the window.

4. Accordingly I find the defendant guilty of criminal negligence as charged.

Recommended: 5 years P.S. (Penal Servitude).
Fine: Taiwan $10,000. Revocation of license and Chinese visa.

It was nearly midnight before they entered the town of Ishan and after several false detours found their way along the narrow secondary road which a policeman insisted led to the airport.

For Horn the evening had been trying and his exhaustion was nearly total. Nothing had gone as he had foreseen. The hire car he had requested was half an hour late picking them up at the hotel and his once proud delegation was in an obstinate mood.

"This is madness," Chatsworth protested. "Absolute bloody madness."

Van Grootes had heaved his bulk into the car, but only after making it clear that he had no intention of participating actively in Horn's scheme. He was going along only because it was better than sitting in his room waiting for the next flight out for Hong Kong.

"Never mind, I'll find my own way back here tomorrow. At least I will watch and maybe talk you out of it. Maybe I can even keep you from killing yourself."

"Don't you ever sleep?" Diderot asked. "Why not go to bed tonight, and things will look different tomorrow. Even if what you claim was true, it is impossible to do anything about it tonight."

"Preposterous!" Chatsworth kept repeating. "A one-in-a-million chance which I simply cannot buy."

At Taipei Airport the reunion with Moller had been difficult. Horn sensed all had not gone as smoothly as he had hoped when it took so long to locate him. After numerous inquiries they found Moller had been confined to a bonded storeroom where he was kept under surveillance by a policeman. A sliding steel grill separated the room from the main concourse, and Moller's presence among the bonded stores and dutiable baggage caused considerable curiosity among the airport employees, most of whom found excuses to take a look at the thoroughly angry Caucasian who, it was said, had tried to fly away without paying his hotel bill.

Moller stiffened when he saw the delegation, and the look in his eyes was such that Horn decided against any light remark about the retaining of a sense of humor. Arranging Moller's release was time-consuming, costly, and laced with misunderstandings until Sylvia arrived to ease the language barrier. Even then more than an hour passed before Japan Air Lines agreed to return Moller's ticket, and the chief of the airport police had been satisfied an honest mistake had been made and accepted fifty dollars' squeeze to officially drop all charges. It was then some time before the man who had the key to the bonded room could be located.

Moller's exit was solemn. He marched directly to Horn, seized him by the arms, and accused him of being solely responsible for his inconvenience. He was so furious, Horn noted, that he even ignored Sylvia.

"What kind of a son of a bitch are you would do a thing like this to a man?"

When the German finally paused for breath Horn took his arm.

"Now come on. Stop behaving like an *Obergruppen-führer*. Things have changed and we need you."

It was as if Horn had been confined and Moller forgiven his transgressions. Finally, with Sylvia's help, Horn managed to persuade him into the hire car with the others. There he was greeted with sympathetic silence. Horn told Sylvia to follow them in her car and immediately ordered the driver to start for Ishan.

While they careened through the night Horn tried desperately to create enthusiasm for his plan. He had deliberately postponed telling them what kind of an aircraft he had found. It was much easier to describe his telephone call to New York and concentrate on its significance.

"Alex has been telling the truth all along. Don't you see? Everything jells now. The soldiers I saw tearing down that fence were removing a missile site. It happened to be in just the right place, and Alex receiving emissions from it at just the wrong time. Probably very few individuals are aware of this coincidence and those who know would like to forget it. That site will never operate again, but there must be many others. Can't you agree—"

"No." Van Grootes grumbled. "Even if it were true, how come all other aircraft had no trouble?"

"There is a long list of discrepancies, but nothing was done because nothing happened. The sites are probably activated for only a few minutes, then the system is shut down. In a whole twenty-four-hour period that site was operating at the wrong minutes for Alex, and my hunch is other sites will still be activated at the same time of day."

"Your hunch? Damn it all, man, we just can't go flying around on a hunch. The investigation teams must have—"

"They did not investigate anything along this line. And certainly no one would suggest it. I am convinced a few key military men are doing the best they can to cover the whole affair for the so-called good of the services."

"Wouldn't Alex know about it? He must have been told where the missile sites are," Diderot said.

"Maybe he did. But would he know what the testing of one might do to his electronics? Before this night, did *you?*"

Moller, still testy, grumbled that there had been some mention of peculiar signals noted by Lufthansa pilots over West Germany, but they had been thought to be of Russian origin and therefore nothing could be done about it. After a few months the signals had ceased and the matter forgotten.

"Every piece of armament on this island is American," Horn told them. "Which means the Chinese installed Nikes when they were available. One of them gave Alex a bad night and we are going to prove it."

"Just how do you propose to do that?" Chatsworth asked.

"That may be somewhat of a problem." Horn's voice fell away as a host of new doubts rose out of the night. He was suddenly appalled at how far he had gone without pausing for review. Very well, how *were* they going to prove his theory? There were far too many assumptions involved, he thought. He had simply assumed the Junkers was in airworthy condition and would be equipped with an automatic direction finder. He had assumed the excavation he had seen actually *was* a missile site, and now he assumed the Chinese Army would obligingly test their systems at a time convenient to prove his argument. Perhaps most heedless of all his assumptions was that Sam Fry would be able to obtain permission from the Chinese Air Force for several survey flights.

He heard Chatsworth saying, "You haven't told us what kind of aircraft you found. I daresay you've made certain it is available."

"It's available."

Why these sudden misgivings? Why hadn't he checked further before cranking up all this energy? There had been the pressure of time before the judges' decision, of course, and a certain amount of overeagerness because of Sylvia. Glancing through the rear window, he saw the lights of her car still following. How much of his impulsive action had been simply a show for her, an instinctive desire to make something happen? You have been strutting around her like a cock pheasant, he warned himself. And now the moment of truth.

"The only aircraft available in Taiwan happens to be a Junkers 52," he said as casually as he could manage. The stunned silence did not surprise him.

"An Iron Annie?" Moller groaned.

"Did you expect a jet-powered pumpkin coach? Now you know why you're needed."

Moller was shaking his head as if he were in a trance. "Twenty years . . . twenty-five years ago I am flying Junkers. At one time with Lufthansa we had over seventy Junkers Fifty-twos."

Horn was relieved when Diderot said evenly that he saw nothing basically wrong with a Junkers. During the early years after the war his father had flown them for Air France, and many French lines in Africa had used 52s. "I think there are still some flying in Bolivia and Colombia."

Their mood was easing, Horn assured himself. He had hardly expected enthusiasm, but at least there had been no condemnation. He debated confessing his only acquaintance with a Junkers was the memory of an old photograph in his collection. No, he decided, there were enough uncertainties. A Junkers was after all just another flying machine, somewhat like the old tri-motor Ford except for its low wing. Both aircraft had become legendary, but also obsolete. He found himself hoping the stories about their durability matching their cast-iron appearance were true.

During the balance of the journey to Ishan he told them in greater detail of his afternoon with Sylvia and his conviction that the maintenance records meshed exactly with everything else he had discovered. As he talked he watched their faces in the dim light, trying to assess their willingness to continue.

"I'm sure you didn't come all this way to let me finish things alone."

They remained silent, rocking half asleep to the motion of the car, and even in their eyes he could find no answer.

There were no lights of any kind to illuminate the airport, which apparently was inactive. Even the guardhouse at the entry road was deserted. There was a small tarmac of concrete threaded with wide cracks and potholes and an air of abandonment about the darkness beyond the car lights. When a pair of grazing water buffalo passed through the beams not one of the delegation saw reason to comment.

They maintained a disapproving silence as the driver turned about, retraced his course, and moments later nearly drove into a canal.

"The man is hopelessly lost," van Grootes said.

Horn looked back to make sure Sylvia was following. He was wondering if there might be more than one field at Ishan when the driver grunted and brought his lights to bear upon a dilapidated T-hangar at the edge of the canal. As they approached they saw it partially sheltered a Junkers 52, and Moller gasped. "We are digging up my maiden aunt. I would know her anywhere."

Their voices were unnaturally muted as they left the car and cautiously walked toward the hangar.

"A real Iron Annie," Moller whispered.

Horn was shocked. He had not been prepared for such a mass of corrugated metal, so grimly Teutonic and ponderous in every line. The plane rested askew, one wing lower than the other, and in the pallid car lights it looked like a cadaver.

Horn found it difficult to keep from groaning aloud. He should have known what five hundred dollars would buy. Along the canal that ran behind the hangar a chorus of bullfrogs seemed to be mocking him. He was so dismayed at the haggard relic looming above him he was hardly aware that Sylvia had come to his side until he heard her say, "It looks like some prehistoric monster."

"I'm afraid it is."

He passed the beam of his flashlight along the nose and saw that the propeller was missing from the right engine.

"American engines," Moller muttered. "Good. I was afraid they would be BMW's and we would have a hell of a time finding parts. Those engines are Vasps."

"Wasps, Willie."

Had there been a suggestion of partnership in Moller's voice? Did he actually believe this ghost could be made to fly?

"All right. Pratt and Vitney then."

"Why are we all whispering?" Diderot asked.

Chatsworth cleared his throat delicately.

"I daresay archeologist Carter felt the same conspiratory urge when he discovered the tomb of Tutankhamen."

They moved slowly around to the side of the Junkers. Suddenly something rushed at them from the darkness. Van Grootes caught the glare of its eyes in the beam of his flashlight. It proved to be a pig.

As they moved beneath the torn hangar roof they entered a wall of powerful odors.

"It's shit," Moller whispered.

Moving around the left wingtip, Horn was relieved to see that the tail assembly seemed to be intact. He shuddered. The leading edge of the vertical fin was badly dented, as if some vandal had taken a club to it. His flashlight followed the faded outlines of the letters C.N.A.C. painted in blue along the fuselage. Then it had flown on the mainland at one time, a unit of China National's fleet. That would have been before World War Two.

Horn's light swept along the fuselage and came to rest on the black maw where the cabin door had once been. He saw something moving within the cabin. A rooster appeared in the door and fluttered angrily to the ground. Immediately afterward a naked man appeared in the door. He blinked, shielded his eyes from the lights, and spat at the ground. He said something in Chinese which Horn thought was probably not a welcome.

"Turn the light on your face," Sylvia suggested.

Horn complied and the effect was immediate. The man let out a prolonged yell. There was a great rustling within the Junkers followed by human chattering and the muffled cluckings of fowl.

A woman appeared behind the man, stared into the light beams, and then withdrew. Her body was immediately replaced by a cluster of several small children. They seemed bewildered. One child pointed at the lights and another began sobbing. Almost immediately they were pulled back out of sight.

The man let himself down from the doorway and stood uncertainly while he tried to identify the intruders. Horn was struck by his belligerent pose and the dignity he managed without benefit of clothing. About him were all the petty treasures of his family, a few pots, several rice bowls, and a crude formation of mud and stone which was apparently a cooking oven. Smoke rising from its fire had stained the side of the Junkers. Near the man Horn saw a wooden water bucket, a small pile of faggots, and one wheel of a bicycle. A line of ragged garments hung from the aileron and a litter of swine was asleep beneath the wing.

Suddenly the man seemed to have reached a decision. He slipped beneath the fuselage and after a moment emerged bearing a heavy stick. He began to breathe very rapidly as he approached the sources of light.

Horn spoke softly to Sylvia. "Does it look to you like we're going to have an argument about squatter's rights?"

"I am sure we would do better to come back in the morning."

Horn hesitated. Even his cursory inspection had convinced him the Junkers was in no shape to fly, but how far gone was it? If it would take a week to make it airworthy then the whole plan must be abandoned, but if the functional elements belied its appearance they should start at once.

As the man continued his menacing approach Horn saw that he was quite small. His head would not have come to Horn's shoulders and his scrawny body seemed mostly sinew and bone. Yet Horn knew that a man fighting for his home can acquire phenomenal strength.

Grasping Sylvia's arm, he pulled her backward several steps. "Tell him we're sorry to disturb his sleep. We'll be back in the morning."

He continued the retreat as Sylvia relayed his words. The man halted, but maintained his belligerent stance.

Retreating around the wing, Horn was impressed with his unswerving defiance. What was it like to rise in complete darkness and stand as naked as the most primeval of humans before strangers who must appear twice your size? Suddenly it occurred to him that in a way he did understand, since the odds on what they were trying to do for Alex were about the same. And he found to his surprise that as they hurried away from the hangar Sylvia was clinging tightly to him.

Every room in Ishan's only hotel was occupied. It was one of the many matters, Horn thought unhappily, that he had neglected to consider in his eagerness to launch his plan. It was now past two A.M., and the time change from Europe was still relentlessly with all of them. While Sylvia engaged in a seemingly endless dialogue with the sleepy hotel clerk, the others collapsed in the hotel's motheaten chairs and wondered if they would be more comfortable sleeping in the car. Chatsworth fell asleep at once even as he was vowing he would return to Taipei by the first available transportation and continue without further delay to England.

Horn refused to close his eyes. It was afternoon back in Paris and his body should behave accordingly. And yet he could not remember how long it had been since he had known a full night's sleep.

As if from a great distance he heard Sylvia's voice and realized suddenly that he had been napping even as he stood beside her.

"This man says you can each have a room at the Fat Sparrow. It is a place just three doors down the street. It may not be too quiet, but he insists it's clean."

"Let's go then. Tomorrow is almost here."

"I will be unable to stay at the same place."

"Why? You can't make that long drive back to Taipei."

"I have a cousin, Sue. She is good family and lives just outside Ishan. Don't worry. She will welcome me. I'll meet you here in the morning. Say the time."

Horn glanced at his watch. They should be under way by dawn he decided and then changed his mind. No, by God, they would rest well for a change.

"Make it seven."

Horn saw something new in her smile, a mischievous quality which puzzled him.

"What are you grinning at?"

"I am wondering what they will think of you rising at that hour in the Fat Sparrow."

Sylvia's words came back to Horn when he sat beside her the following morning. All through their first greeting and while they waited for the others to appear Horn was determined to keep his composure. He knew she was waiting for some visible reaction, but they had all agreed to behave as if their night had been normal.

"Sleep well?" she asked finally.

"Very."

"Rooms clean?"

"Immaculate."

"I'm pleased. You look rested."

"Thank you. The staff was most considerate."

As they drove the few miles to the airport he said nothing more. Let her wonder, he mused. Any woman who would send five exhausted men to a whorehouse for the night deserved to suffer.

They parked Sylvia's car and the hire car more than a hundred yards from the T-hangar. Then at Sylvia's suggestion Horn allowed her to approach the structure alone, her armament six hundred Taiwan dollars, which she assured him was undoubtedly more than the peasant had seen in his lifetime.

They watched as she walked calmly toward the hangar from which a column of blue smoke curled lazily into the brilliant sky. Horn heard a child screaming, then a dog began to bark. Where had the dog been last night? He saw the man appear and confront Sylvia. Soon they vanished within the shadows of the hangar.

"I assume she's all right," Horn said nervously.

Chatsworth pulled at his goatee and shook his head. "I wish to go on record right now that I have not the slightest intention of flying in that contraption. I have not spent almost a lifetime in the air just to terminate it in a futile attempt to prove something that may or may not be so."

He fixed his pale blue eyes on Horn and continued with heavy sincerity. "With all respect and in spite of my great affection for Alex and yourself, I beg you to abandon this wildass scheme before it is too late. If someone is hurt—or worse—you will never forgive yourself. Neither, I daresay, would Alex."

Horn reached out and placed his hand on Chatsworth's shoulder. Shaking him gently, he smiled as confidently as he could manage. "Now, think how lonely you'll be here on the ground."

"I am returning to England on the first available flight. I do owe some loyalty to BOAC and I hardly think they would consider it sound judgment for one of their senior captains to be involved in such an escapade. I can see the headlines now. Surely you must recognize there is always the odd chance something could go very wrong."

Horn turned to van Grootes. The huge Dutchman was brooding at the distant hangar as if his mottled nose detected a highly suspicious odor. His heavy-lidded hound eyes focused upon Horn only an instant when he was asked his intentions.

"I'll wait and see. The whole idea is crazy, but maybe it is not too dangerous if the Junkers is sound. I'll go along if we can fix it."

"We can fix it," Moller stated flatly.

Diderot said he was still trying to convince himself that trying to revive the Junkers might not be some kind of sacrilege which might bring them bad luck. "It's like an old elephant that limped off to some lonely place so it could die. Now we come along and say, Get up and go again."

Horn saw Sylvia appear and raise her hand in the signal they had agreed upon. All was well. Now here in the cruel daylight the facts would soon be known.

As pigs and children weaved between them Sylvia explained that the now smiling man who had confronted them the night before farmed a small area on the other side of the canal. He had come north from the southeast coast of Taiwan three years previously and had been told he could use the Junkers as his home. No one apparently cared and now he hoped he would at least be allowed to live in the T-hangar.

"He can have everything back as soon as we're finished."

Once he understood that his home was safe, the man offered his entire family in addition to his water buffalo to assist in pushing the Junkers from beneath the hangar. The task required more than an hour.

When at last the Junkers rested gaunt and strangely alive in the sun, Horn was appalled at its overall appearance. It was like looking at a bedraggled old hag suffering from innumerable diseases, and his gloom nearly overcame his resolve as they discovered new areas of the rust pox which covered both wings and fuselage. They scratched at the more evil-looking pustules of corrosion and except for

Horn were unanimous in their opinion that the wing roots were probably in similar condition.

When they climbed inside the cabin they found that very little remained of the original interior except the bare metal of the fuselage. The sleeping pads of the family were scattered across the flooring and there was a small store of unmarked tin cans just behind the cockpit door. Now the heat of the day began to pound on the metal, and even though a light breeze whispered through the broken windows the interior was pungent with the many functions of human residence.

They moved glumly forward toward the cockpit and Moller said it was like coming home. He seemed in a trance as he automatically slipped into the left seat. Horn stood beside him alternately impressed and discouraged. The Junkers was built like no aircraft he had ever seen— apparently with some Teutonic notion they should long survive their crews. The control yokes were massive, with wooden three-quarter-circle wheels he thought would seem more appropriate on a battleship. The rudder pedals were gauged for the boots of giants, and the series of valves which Moller said controlled the fuel supply to the three engines might have been taken from a city reservoir. On the right side of the cockpit Horn saw a spool of antenna wire which still retained a hint of luster, the only item in the entire aircraft which seemed unaffected by the passage of years.

"How long do you think, Willie, since she's flown?"

Moller shrugged his shoulders and sighed. He frowned at the scratched and clouded windows which had turned a smoky turquoise from age and sun.

"I forget," he said softly. "The visibility is better than from a modern jet. We go backwards sometimes I think."

As he scratched at the accumulations of guano on the control pedestal they heard a clucking beyond the rudder pedals. Bending down, they discovered three chickens had made the dark area their roost. Their presence suddenly triggered a collapse in Horn's resolve. Chatsworth was right. This was no longer an aircraft but a forlorn and dangerous relic which should be pronounced dead. Alex would have long rotted in his cell before they could make it fly.

"You're the doctor, Willie. What do you think?" Horn was surprised at his own funereal tone.

Moller pointed at the automatic direction finder, which was still in place on the central console forward of the three throttles. "Well, if that thing still works—"

"It doesn't make much difference, if we can't get it up in the air. I can't see this old rust bucket actually leaving the ground without a complete overhaul. I apologize for stirring up the whole—"

He was astounded at Moller's interruption. "Oh, she don't look so bad. A Junkers will fly any time you give her a good enough kick in the ass. Of course we check everything—controls, cables, fuel and oil lines, and so on."

Horn wondered if Moller's sudden reunion with his past had unbalanced his judgment? He actually seemed optimistic.

"Then of course we must do something about that bad tire and find the propeller for the right engine."

Moller looked at Horn and smiled. And Horn thought that for the rest of his life he would never again try to predict anyone else's behavior. Of all the delegation, Moller had seemed the least enthusiastic. In every instance he had insisted on sober fact. Now?

Horn knew a sudden sense of exhilaration. There were still men in the world who stood ready to take the long chance.

"All right, *Kapitan*. The first flight is scheduled for tonight. You show us how."

12

Moller's sudden determination had an immediate effect upon the others and Horn seized upon their new willingness to unite them in common effort. Even Chatsworth offered to help, although he still repeated his vow not to fly in the Junkers. Horn put him in charge of procuring fuel, fresh oil, tools, and a new battery. He asked Sylvia to drive him into Ishan and act as his translator.

There were a few tools in the hire car, enough to convince them Moller was not exaggerating when he claimed their task might be impossible on any other aircraft. As they began to remove the inspection plates from the wings and the cowlings from the engines, they found simplicity of design everywhere rather than the usual aeronautical complication. Their hopes rose steadily.

Within an hour they had determined that all of the major airframe fittings were sound, the engine mounts still solid, and the landing gear Ohio struts almost like new. Several control cable fairleads were jammed with rust, but the wires were apparently serviceable. The ugly corrosion which had at first given them such a shock was confined to the outer skin.

When Chatsworth returned with additional tools Sylvia explained that they had been able to rent them rather than make an outright purchase. The same garage was bringing new oil to the airport, but fuel was apparently unavailable in Ishan.

"Details," Horn said lightly. Not since the entire expedition to Taiwan began had he been so elated. They were all working together in a way he would never have thought possible. As soon as the additional tools arrived they began

183

removing the spark plugs from the engines, setting them out in rows, and separating those they considered unserviceable.

Diderot took it upon himself to remove the left aileron, which had apparently suffered in a collision with something since the Junkers' last flight. It was badly out of shape and there was a jagged tear along the trailing edge.

"If we can find some tin cans we can fix it," Diderot insisted.

Van Grootes concerned himself with the cockpit controls, most of which were frozen in position and needed both oil and understanding gentleness to avoid fracturing some remote connection.

When Chatsworth returned he went at once to the direction finder. "I've had experience with this sort of thing," he explained. "Not a bloody wireless genius, mind you, or a true black box artist. But something as simple as this . . . I should think I could make the necessary repairs. It's the whole key, isn't it? Then let's get on with it."

Moller was everywhere, perspiring mightily, cursing and clucking about the Junkers with fatherly devotion. All of the exhaust stack brackets on the left engine were corroded away. Most of the ignition harness shielding was green with verdigris and would have to be dried out. At least two of the clouded cockpit windows had to be removed and ordinary window glass substituted.

"If we are going to fly at night, then we will be blind enough, I think. We won't bother trying to make instruments work."

There was the frustrating problem of the main gear tire. They considered various methods they might attempt to hoist the twelve-thousand-pound Junkers high enough so they could remove the tire. Somewhere they would have to find heavy duty jacks to accomplish the lift.

Equally serious was the need of a propeller for the right engine. A search of the T-hangar and its environs had been unsuccessful. By pantomime and much pointing at the remaining two propellers Horn and Moller finally managed to transmit their need to the farmer. Once he understood their inquiry he did his utmost to please. Plucking at their sleeves, he persuaded them to follow him along the narrow footbridge which crossed the canal. There in the field he proudly displayed a crude plow he had fashioned from a propeller blade. He had lashed it with rawhide to a V-shaped yoke which was pulled through rice paddies by his buffalo. The blade was hopelessly dented and twisted beyond repair and the farmer's comprehension seemed totally lost when they tried to ask where the second blade might be.

"We can't let a little thing like a propeller knock us out of business," Horn insisted. "We'll have to find some way to make do."

"How?" Moller was disheartened. It was all too apparent that he had lost his energy, and Horn was determined to revive his spirits.

"We still have two propellers, Willie. Why not take one from the center engine and put it on the right? The center engine can just go along for the ride."

"You are insane."

"Won't a Junkers get off the ground with just the two wing engines? It will be nearly empty—"

"Who knows? Not with me flying it."

"Then I will. You check me out on the ground."

Horn shook his head as if unable to believe his own words. What was he *saying?* Maybe the others were right in questioning his sanity. He halted a moment to study the Junkers. What an ugly beast! But it *would* take off on only two engines. It would if the man flying it had convinced himself it was possible. There would be no time or space at the end of the field for final misgivings. It would be either up and away or a big noise and a pile of junk.

News of the unusual activity at the T-hangar spread quickly about the surrounding countryside. By noon a considerable crowd had gathered, including two policemen who interrogated Sylvia at great length and then settled themselves in the shade of the wing and went to sleep. The majority of the visitors were in a festive mood and were delighted with the spectacle. Sylvia reported there was a lively business developing as some of the more knowing spectators began to make book on whether or not the Caucasians would kill themselves.

As the sun torched on the hot metal it became painful to

pick up a tool or touch any part of the Junkers. In the cabin and cockpit the air was so stifling van Grootes complained he could no longer tolerate it.

Horn had become increasingly suspicious of his own thinking. Either the heat had affected his brain or he had suddenly developed a talent for viewing hallucinations as reality. Improvisation bred more of the same, he decided, so it was inevitable that an enterprise begun with overtones of fantasy should continue in the same vein. There was indeed an illusory aura about so many people milling around a huge flying machine born in another era and looking like a legendary great auk rusting in the sun.

"No one in this world," he murmured, "would ever believe what my eyes declare is actually happening."

Very well then. Like Merlin the Magician he would cause more events to transpire. He called to Sylvia and told her his latest needs. Was there a construction project in the area where hydraulic jacks could be found powerful enough to lift the Junkers? Would she make immediate inquiries?

He watched her as she entered the noisy crowd as calmly as if she were descending for a swim in the sea. He saw the crowd part for her until she stopped before an elderly bearded man. As they talked, their gestures became increasingly animated and their voices were carried to Horn on the breeze. He was immensely pleased with the spectacle, for the same breeze ruffled Sylvia's ebony hair and toyed fitfully with her long blue skirt. Fascinated, Horn reaffirmed his opinion that there was no more provocative airspace in the world than the waist-high slit in a Chinese dress.

It did not strike him as unusual that when Sylvia returned she simply nodded her head and asked him to be patient, all would be well.

"My grandfather always said, 'I heard' is not as good as 'I saw.' "

In this wild and wonderful atmosphere anything was possible, Horn decided. All we need, he mused, is a propeller tree handy on the landscape and a Standard Oil fuel truck willing to take a credit card.

They watched as the old man faced the crowd, raised his hands for attention, and took command with practiced ease. He harangued them with ever-increasing fervor and then dispatched several men to the canal. When they had departed he ordered nearly fifty men and women to station themselves beneath the Junkers' wings and fuselage. To hold their positions many were obliged to bend nearly double while others had to reach above their heads to touch the surface. There was a constant interplay of laughing and shouting and all seemed hopeless confusion until the old man began leading them in a chant. As the sing-song gathered volume Horn wiped his eyes in disbelief. For the rhythmic chorus seemed to lend strength to those beneath the Junkers. Without appearing to greatly exert themselves, they caused it to rise like a gigantic float in a parade.

When the landing gear was barely clear of the ground the entire assembly of people and plane moved ponderously back into the shade of the T-hangar. The men who had been sent to the canal returned exactly on cue, each man struggling under the weight of a sandbag removed from the dike. The old man directed them to pile the sacks beneath the Junkers' belly, and finally with a downward wave of his hand, laughing and shouting along with his people, he had them lower the Junkers gently upon its new support. His calculations had been so precise there was barely an inch to spare beneath the left wheel, and the entire operation had required no more than three minutes.

Horn shouted his admiration and pounded his hands in applause. In his exuberance he seized Sylvia, lifted her high off the ground, and swung her twice around in a circle.

The spectacle of a tall Caucasian swinging a Chinese girl around in the wind like a little blue doll triggered a spontaneous reaction from the crowd. They pointed and screeched with glee and pounded one another and slapped their hands in echo of Horn's applause. Sheepishly, he set her down.

"Sorry. I was sort of carried away."

"If you threw me in the canal they would move heaven and earth for you."

"Let's save that for an encore. We still need several miracles."

The tire casing was serviceable, but the tube was so rotten Horn could pull it apart with his fingertips. It was a serious setback, since the tire was of prewar German manufacture and of an odd size. Van Grootes suggested they might buy a wheel off a truck and try installing the entire assembly even if the match with the opposite wheel was imperfect. "We might have to shim the axle if it's too small or cut the wheel to make it fit."

They decided it would make little difference except in appearance if one wheel was slightly larger than the other. Moller alone disagreed. If a take-off was to be made on only two engines, both would have to develop maximum power from the start. With the smaller wheel creating a torque in its direction, power on the opposite engine would have to be reduced until minimum control speed was reached. It was ironic, Horn thought, that such a basically simple element as an ordinary pneumatic tire could create such a problem.

Their examination and discussion of the tire was well attended by the crowd. Now having apparently decided they were part of the common effort, they crowded tightly around the foreigners, listening and whispering among themselves as they waited patiently for the next interesting event. Horn felt a gentle tapping on his shoulder and turned to look into the eyes of the bearded old man. He was squatting on his haunches. Now he spit between his bare feet and pointed at the wheel and repeated a request in Chinese. Or, Horn thought, it sounded like a request.

He called to Sylvia, whose face appeared on the fringe of faces encircling them.

"The old man says let him take the tire. He will fix it like they always do."

Horn nodded his agreement and at once three men stepped forward, hoisted the heavy tire on their shoulders, and started in the general direction of Ishan. Horn tried unsuccessfully to rid himself of a new uneasiness. Fuel could eventually be found, and with luck perhaps even a suitable propeller. But as he watched, three men he had never seen before were rapidly disappearing with what was undoubtedly one of the two available Junkers tires in the entire Orient.

By mid-afternoon Horn reluctantly admitted the Junkers would never leave the ground that night. Yet much had been accomplished. Moller and van Grootes, after examining the engines as thoroughly as they could without completely stripping them, were of the opinion they could be made to function providing sixteen new spark plugs could be found.

After puzzling over the circuitry for the better part of the day, Chatsworth declared that the automatic direction finder appeared to react normally.

"It's a bit sneaky, but I think that's low voltage. When the generators are putting out, it shouldn't be so sluggish."

Then he very quietly reaffirmed his opinions. "Much as I admire your perseverance, I simply cannot justify risking what is left of my career on a project in which I have so little faith. To say nothing of my precious neck. You may label me an old maid and I shall weep with remorse—but I am *not* making an ascent in that Hun battlewagon. Never."

Horn saw no point in arguing with him. Chatsworth was right and his objections were based on long years of keeping his brain, limbs, and organs in one functional unit. It was becoming increasingly obvious that what he proposed *was* going to be a tricky business and diametrically opposed to the flying philosophy of most line pilots. Horn smiled inwardly. If Brewster knew the true situation he would have been horrified.

He reviewed his plan, which he realized needed tightening here and there, with a powerful additive of pure luck to make it produce results. If the Junkers could be made *operational*—and he was prepared to stretch the meaning of the term until something gave—they could fly in shifts of two men for five hours. Since there was no way to determine when the Chinese might test their missile systems, coverage of the most likely hours should be continuous. To do so, he calculated, would demand the Junkers to be airborne at least eighteen hours a day. The hours between midnight and six in the morning might reasonably be considered the most unlikely time-space, so that period should be used for the inevitable servicing of the Junkers.

"What we really need is three aircraft and six crews," van Grootes argued. "Otherwise when do we sleep?"

"Tonight in the Fat Sparrow. Enjoy it, because it'll be your last until we lock on to a signal or the Junkers falls apart."

Diderot, soaked in his own perspiration, his face, arms,

and hands smeared with grease, sank down on the grass and said he didn't care what he did next as long as he had a shower. Then he lit a cigarette and frowned at the Junkers as if reproaching it for his discomfort. Watching him, Horn thought secretly that Diderot might well share the strange notion which seemed to have taken over his imagination. As if it were a resurrected pterodactyl, the damned Junkers had become a living creature.

Sylvia drove Horn into town at three. She engaged in another lengthy conversation with the hotel clerk, who shook his head almost continuously. Finally she explained to Horn there were still no rooms available. While she returned to her car she slipped on her white gloves and said she would visit Alex at six and return to Ishan in the morning.

"Is there anything I can bring you?"

"Yes. Ask Alex to send his blessing."

"Anything else?"

For a moment he allowed himself to reflect on his multitude of needs, but he found their nature so overwhelming he immediately retreated. "Bring yourself."

Their eyes met and he told her without saying a word how much she meant to him. It seemed incredible, he thought, how this one compact little person, still so crisp and bandbox neat, somehow managed to remain altogether enchanting.

He glanced behind him at the entrance to the Fat Sparrow. "I'm glad you can't find rooms anywhere else. A defeat now and then is the only thing that can keep you from being impossible."

She chuckled, told him to behave himself, and abruptly drove away. Watching after her, his sense of loss was almost instantly repaired. For just as her car turned at the street intersection he saw a white-gloved hand quivering in a quick little wave. He preferred to think there was a great deal to be read into the gesture. It was pure feminine instinct demonstrated while she must have been looking straight ahead. She *knew* he would be looking after her.

The only telephone in the Fat Sparrow was on the wall in the madame's ground-floor room. She was a voluble woman who filtered her perpetual stream of words through fences of gold-capped teeth. She understood just enough English to advise Horn that if he would pay for the call in advance she would be pleased to seek the number he wanted. After considerable shouting into the instrument she held it out to him.

"Is this my friend Uncle Sam?"

"I assume this is Captain Horn."

"Correct. I need hlep."

"That statement has a familiar ring. How did you come into my life? Are you by any chance one of the spooks from CIA? If not, will you please go home? I remember when this was a quiet post. Instead of serving our government I have spent the entire day in your behalf and I am pleased to report that your export documents for the aircraft have been processed. Also, by methods which I do not care to disclose on the telephone, I have obtained Chinese Air Force authorization for two test flights over nonrestricted areas. Now I am speculating on how hard the Chinese are going to put the squeeze on me the next time they want something."

"Well done, Sam. You should be moved up to ambassador. When I do get home I'll speak to the Secretary of State."

"Please don't! It says right in the regulation, volume three sub-part B, foreign service officers are not to ask favors or in any way risk obligation to officials of the host country. I am now wondering what will happen to me if anything goes wrong. And I am staring at your favorite flag and wondering at its power to lure men who should know better into trouble. Reassure me. This is a good airplane, isn't it?"

"Wonderful. Of course it's not the sort you see every day."

"What do you mean by that?"

"A few items are missing and that's where you come in."

"No, no. I am exiting from this entire affair. What is missing?"

"One propeller for a Pratt and Whitney Wasp engine. You'll have to find one."

"Oh, sure, a propeller. Even in my loathing for all flying machines I am aware that is a very necessary item."

"You'll have to find one and have it here by tomorrow morning."

"My dear sir, I am not in the aviation business."

"*Think!* Do you have any friends stationed here in the U.S. Air Force?"

"Of course I know our air attaché—"

"He'll know. Put the bit on him immediately and tell him we also need nine R.B. fourteen E. spark plugs for the same engines. Did you receive my check?"

"Yes, but—"

"I am very much impressed with the resourcefulness of our foreign service and particularly certain personnel. Would you like to call me back in an hour and tell me when the parts will arrive?"

"Certainly not. I am severing all relations with your scheme. If anything happens I never heard of you. You don't seem to realize that I have already far exceeded . . ."

Since the number on the telephone was in Chinese characters, Horn turned to ask the madame for a translation. She eagerly obliged. Wresting the instrument from him, she directed a torrent of Chinese into the mouthpiece. After a moment she nodded her head, smiled at Horn, and held out the telephone. She covered her mouth with her hand and giggled while he listened.

"Do I understand you've taken up residence in the Fat Sparrow?"

"It's comfortable."

"It's also notorious. You could not have chosen a worse place. Here you are asking favors of the Chinese government. Perhaps you are not aware that the Generalissimo and Madame Chiang are very strait-laced people, and most officials imitate them or pretend to. If they find out the kind of company you are keeping your project will atutomatically cease to exist."

"The officials probably own the place. Just don't tell anyone where we are."

"*You* are the one who said you were being followed."

Horn heard a click and realized the call had been terminated. He stood holding the silent phone, wondering if he should reinstate the call. Finally he decided against it. There was a certain type of man who could be pressed too hard.

"Madame," he said, bowing to the gold teeth, "if a telephone call comes for a Captain Horn I will be in Room Twelve. Do not hesitate to disturb me."

As she giggled her understanding he departed with what he hoped was reasonable dignity.

● ●

Chatsworth could not remember ever having been so at odds with himself. "Dear God," he murmured. "If my Daphne could only see me now!"

Surveying his surroundings, he knew that it was not in his wife's nature to approve of the crib of a room in which he had been installed. He rolled uneasily on the much used mattress which was supported by a netting of frayed sisal bound to a wooden frame. His mind boggled when he estimated the total number of copulations which must have taken place within such functional surroundings. In addition to the bed there was a wooden washstand equipped with a bowl, pitcher, and a towel. There was a single chair and nothing more to distract the eye except the bare light bulb of very low wattage which dangled from the ceiling. In spite of the faint aroma of perfume and disinfectant the room was, he thought, like a monk's cell, a place for concentration upon a single subject regardless of its nature. It was precisely that impressive value about the room which now so troubled him that he found it impossible to sleep.

It was not that they presently resided in a brothel. He had not been to one in years, and any temptation which might have persisted after observing the staff left him shaken with the realization they were all younger than his daughter. After all, he thought, one's morals hadn't changed so much since flying out to Singapore in De Havilland 86s, rather it seemed that one developed an annoying need for preliminary by-play. Alas, William Oliver Chatsworth, you are no longer a rutting stag.

As he stared at the amber light a ditty returned to his memory, one that he had chanted long ago in his local pub, never considering it might one day apply to his own image. He wished he could recall more of it.

"You are old, Father William," the young man said.
"And your hair has become very white;

And yet you incessantly stand on your head—
Do you think at your age that is right?"

Yes, yes, and then it went,

"In my youth," Father William replied to his son,
"I feared it might injure the brain;
But now that I'm perfectly sure I have none,
Why, I do it again and again . . ."

And that, he mused, reflected exactly his present situation. What in heaven's name was Captain William Oliver Chatsworth doing lying quite naked except for his shorts in a second-class whorehouse, waiting for the night to pass so he could attempt suicide on the following morning? Indeed, what would BOAC have to say and what might happen to his pension if the name of a most senior line captain was questionably exposed? And who could do it better than the English newspapers?

"BOAC Master Pilot Star Boarder in Taiwan House of Ill Repute!"

Imagine such a story appearing in proximity to one of the company's expensive advertisements—the guard change at Buckingham Palace sort of background, with the usual patronizing BOAC crew posed all smiling beside an embarrassed Grenadier Guard.

Air France might understand, but not the British Overseas Airways Corporation. Even more pertinent, BOAC was administered by businessmen not, like the airlines of some other nations, by operational people. Certainly they would not have the slightest sympathy or understanding for a man with nearly thirty thousand hours in his logbooks who would debate for one instant the advisability of flying an aircraft which was obviously a disaster.

And yet . . . he thought.

Horn was so blindly wrapped up in his theory he had lost touch with reality. The original project in which Chatsworth had agreed to participate had at least made some sense, but it was now lost in a storm of activity which held little promise except danger. The idea had been that if five highly qualified and respected airline captains of different nationalities could present undeniable evidence in Alex

Malloy's favor, then he would be exonerated. Now, he thought, we bicker and are disappointed in each other. And yet . . .

He wished he had something to read. Then perhaps he might more quickly find sleep and even forget the unpleasantness that followed their evening meal in Ishan's best restaurant, an establishment that might well have been in Soho. Of course they had all been edgy and short of temper and perhaps a little drunk from drowning their weariness in beer.

Moller had looked him in the eye and said, "So? You're going to run out on us. I am not surprised."

"I seem to recall that only last night it was you who had to be pulled off an outbound airplane."

"All you limeys are alike, brave as lions when all goes well."

The remark had triggered an instant reaction which Chatsworth now found he regretted. He had very ceremoniously, as if following some ancient rite, thrown his beer in Moller's face and called him a bloody Hun. As a consequence it had required the combined efforts of Horn and van Grootes to separate and calm them.

After they had reluctantly shaken hands, and while the fuzz on Moller's neck was still bristling, Horn revived the contest, probably without intending anything of the sort.

"You will see. We may fly slow, but we'll fly until I run out of money for fuel. Then I'll ask for contributions from the rest of you."

"I will *not* see. None of us came over here to be killed."

Alas, that had been petulant and quite unnecessary. The hurt on Horn's face had been all too obvious. It was not the sort of thing one joked about and he knew it. Then, confound the man, he should also realize that the hazard involved was responsible for the change in the delegation's mood. They were no longer accustomed to hazard except in theory. Flying jets had become such a routine business one was simply appointed chairman of the board pro tem. Now most captains embarked on a flight without the slightest expectation that anything unforeseen would happen. And year after year nothing unforeseen did happen. Much as one might mourn the passing of glamour and mystique in flying, it was all to the better that since the advent of jets, emergencies were usually confined to practice sessions.

Chatsworth watched a fly circle the light bulb and then land on the ceiling. And like all other airmen in the world he marveled at the fly's ability to conceal his maneuver. Did he land on the ceiling out of the top of a loop or execute a half roll from a climb?

Why, he demanded of himself, does my wretched conscience deny me sleep?

The honest answer was all too simple. Because, old boy, you *are* running out on Lew Horn and his crew.

In spite of their better judgments they have indicated they will probably carry on with Horn, an attitude which is perhaps better understood, he decided, if one reflected on their careers. If they had each not originally displayed an affinity for challenge they would never have become pilots in the first place. Now, here for the first time in years, was a chance to recapture the élan of earlier flying days. Eager to pick up the glove, Moller had reverted to the Luftwaffe; van Grootes was once more flying that hairy run between London and Lisbon circa 1941; and Diderot, who was so young he missed the more dashing days of flying completely, was now trying to discover what he missed. And God alone knew to what swashbuckling period Horn had regressed.

There was the rub. In their preoccupation with themselves they had nearly forgotten about Alex. He was at best a vague and symbolic figure somewhere in the background, serving merely as justification to accept a challenge.

"Not for me." . . . "Count me out." . . . "Not on your bloody life."

How many times this past day had he so expressed his sentiments? Men did not change—or did they? To what soft garden of conservatism had the former Chatsworth withdrawn? Where was the dashing mustachioed character who had flown to the Congo in a "C" class flying boat— "the canoe that goes for up," as the natives called it? Where was the jaunty soul who flew so casually to Khartoum, Takoradi, Gura in Eritrea—nice place that—and Rutba Wells in Iraq? Atlantas out to Malaysia and Gaza. Armstrong-Whitworth Ensigns. Yorks to Cairo in 1944, all in a day's work for a vital man who still believed the sun would never set on the empire. Yes, where was the man who laughed through ten thousand miles of sky with a load of bloody elephants in a plodding old York, that same aerial gypsy who knew Vancouver, Baghdad, Colombo, Toronto, Belfast, Sydney, Bermuda, Lisbon, and Delhi sometimes better than the way to his cottage in Berks?

Yet the original Chatsworth had not quite perished. What the others did not know was that just before evening he had slipped away by himself and paced off the field. His resulting estimate of the total available take-off run in the Junkers came to slightly less than two thousand feet. Then there was the irrigation canal, beyond it a rice paddy, and fortunately no obstructions, wires, hills, or even trees for two or three miles. According to Moller the normal take-off run for a loaded Junkers with all three engines performing could be as short as one thousand feet. With only two engines and the further handicap of Taiwan heat to rob what lift remained in those ancient wings, was there an even chance the old bucket would sail over the canal?

If there was, then William Oliver Chatsworth, unless you have indeed become an old maid, you can hardly afford to miss the party. What was that prayer of Kipling's?

"My brother kneels, so saith Kabir, to stone and brass in heathen-wise . . . but in my brother's voice I hear my own unanswered agonies."

13

Van Grootes awakened from a confused dream and switched on his light. He rarely dreamed and the few he could remember never involved flying. He stared at the Chinese magazine which some previous occupant of the room had left on the chair and wondered drowsily if Orientals read while fornicating.

His dream had taken him back to Amsterdam's Schiphol aerodrome in the late thirties. All had been familiar as he was making an approach in nearly zero visibility. Sometimes in real life it had been necessary, since even if parts of Amsterdam might be visible, Schiphol itself would be solid with fog.

In the dream, just as it had once really been, he was flying a Fokker and had caught sight of Olympic stadium, which was close to the final approach course. He continued the descent and sure enough out of the fog came the familiar V-shaped red neon symbol which marked the perimeter of the aerodrome. Immediately afterward, though he was still unable to see the ground, he spied the loom of a second V-shaped signal, this time of green neon. It was then customary to cut power, haul back on the controls, and simply wait for the wheels to brush the grass. He had done exactly that many times and thus far the dream had been totally realistic. Then suddenly the Fokker became a Junkers 52. It was laden with ice and he had crashed right on the aerodrome.

The bed creaked ominously as van Grootes rolled his great bulk to the wall and switched off the light. Dreams were silly and meaningless, but should he tell Horn of his true feelings about the Junkers? It was very doubtful if it would leave the ground without all three engines turning. There was just too much built-in head wind, too many parts flying in loose formation. The huge off-set ailerons were fine as long as ice could be avoided, but they did contribute greatly to the overall drag of what was basically an aerodynamic monstrosity.

Now, lying thoughtfully in the dark, he remembered that before the war the Germans had a custom of naming their Junkers in honor of Lufthansa pilots who had been killed. Their names were lettered beneath the cockpit windows and there had been plenty to go around.

Yes, he thought, courage was a very good quality and not so rare in men as some believed. Yet like all good things, courage possessed the hidden power to destroy, and when that ability was taunted the consequences were often labeled fool-hardiness.

Van Grootes had great difficulty falling asleep again.

Étienne Diderot was the last to go to his room. He lingered in the Fat Sparrow's tiny bar because he believed he was too excited for sleep in spite of his continuous yawning. He had convinced himself that the cause was his anticipation of the morning to come.

Sometime during the hot day at the T-hangar Diderot had become so exhilarated it was like those first days when his father had taught him to fly in a Morane. The zest for life had suddenly returned because an irrepressible American was attempting a nearly impossible aeronautical feat and badly needed his help. He wondered if Horn had any idea how very much that meant to the son of Julien Diderot?

He wanted to celebrate rather than sleep, so he told the madame he was lonely. When he offered to buy her a brandy she displayed her gold teeth, clapped her hands officiously, and moments later he was surrounded by three girls. He was immediately attracted to the smallest because she laughed easily, a quality he had rarely discovered in French or Belgian women. She declined a brandy but asked for a lime squash.

Later in his room she smoothed the bed and then stood expectantly as if awaiting further orders. Diderot was perplexed. He sat down and studied her for a moment, wishing she understood French. He became vaguely uncomfortable because the moment he had closed the door she had ceased laughing and behaved more like his slave than a companion. He longed to tell her how important it was that she share this special occasion with him.

She approached him uncertainly, stood before him a moment, then slowly unzipped her long Chinese dress. When it was fully open she reached out tenderly and pressed his face against her flesh. She held him tightly until a little cry escaped her, then she sank to her knees before him and tugged anxiously at his pants.

Soon they were lying side by side and while her delicate fingers caressed him most gently he heard her breathing quicken as if the urgings within her must soon reach a climax. He told her in French that she was a very convincing actress, but her obvious lack of comprehension left him disappointed.

She toyed with him, too impatiently, he thought. How could he explain to her that the whole of this day had inspired him in a way he had never known and the prospect of tomorrow was even more satisfying. How could he make her understand that something very important had happend to Étienne Diderot, who would at last know something of true hazard? In a matter of minutes he would be liberated from routine and delivered from the womb of security. Tomorrow his envy of his father's whole generation would disappear, the sense of having been forever protected, of never even having the opportunity to risk his precious skin would dissolve. He wanted very much to tell this little Chinese girl that although he had been flying for seventeen years he had never faced a genuine emergency in the air and, curiously, not once had his life been threatened on the ground. Since Papa had sent him off to Africa so he could escape the rigors of his own land at war there had been something missing from his life, something mysterious which now had at last been identified. Unless his blood was milk a young man needed danger for fulfillment as surely as he needed the approval of his peers. The blind and often passionate drive toward hazard was as ancient as the first youth who voluntarily threw himself at the enemy in expectation of becoming a hero. That instead he so often became a martyr was merely the result of a need.

She rose to her knees and straddled him. Swaying rhythmically she brushed the nipples of her firm little breasts across his lips. And for a moment he felt a surge of enormous pleasure. Suddenly, throughout his lean body there was a tingling physical recognition of what had happened to the spirit of the man who occupied it. If a young man knew there was even the slightest chance he might be killed within a matter of hours or even days, he had always thought, the anticipation would be depressing. *Au contraire,* he thought, *c'est formidable!*

He looked up at the girl and she smiled. Yes, Papa would approve. This was the way to celebrate the sensation.

As if she partly understood, she paused to question his eyes. The apology in her manner was replaced almost immediately by mischief and she laughed softly. She eased backward until her buttocks rested on his lower legs, then bent her head, and while she teased his groin with her darting tongue she made low and sonorous little purrings to express her pleasure.

She wet her lips and began to polish his poignard just as he had hoped. He tried to think of nothing else and gave himself totally to her increasingly determined ministrations. Yet nothing rose within him and finally he pushed her away. He shook his head unbelievingly, for it was the first time in his life he had refused such an invitation.

The bed was a foot short for Horn's length and it sagged in the middle in such a way he could not long maintain a jackknife position. So he rose before dawn and bathed and shaved as best he could in the feeble light while he deliberately tried to avoid reviewing the problems he knew the day would bring.

The attempt was almost a total failure. He managed to dwell very briefly on the matter of his divorce and wondered, without really caring, if Barbara was still in Mexico City.

Orville Wright entered his thoughts briefly.

Probably, he decided, since we'll be living alone we'll become even better friends.

And why not? He would soon be back on his familiar flying schedule and he would much prefer coming home to a boisterous mynah bird rather than to some of the wives who greeted his fellow airmen.

As he dressed he resolved that the first thing he would do once he had returned to Long Island was give his little aerobatic plane a thorough wringing out. Inverted flight combined with two or three g's flushed the brain with new blood and stimulated a man's entire system. You looked up at the earth and down at the sky and at will, in seconds, reversed the entire situation. Petty problems fell into their proper perspective and the sweets of life were right there aloft.

Then, in spite of his determination, his mind turned to his delight in Sylvia and at once there was the specter of Alex Malloy again. He *must* be saved! He was more than a man in trouble. Alex was a living legend whose exploits were permanently woven into the international history of flight. Little memories would always be with him, oddments which reflected each era. During tri-motor Ford days passengers were furnished with gum to help relieve the pressure changes and cotton to stuff in their ears because of the engine noise. Food was served in a paper box by the co-pilot. When his early passengers had to relieve themselves they sheepishly entered a cubicle in the tail. There, through the open hole beneath the seat, they could regard the passing countryside until they had gathered nerve enough to expose their privates to the outside temperatures. When Alex was flying Fords, a contemporary of the Junkers, the engine instruments were not in the cockpit but side-mounted on the engine cowlings, and at night he depended on a flashlight to observe their readings. The health of the center engine was best known by watching its vibrations against the horizon and eye-measuring the amount of oil on the windshield. If only a light film dimmed the view, then the engine must be robust, but if the accumulated scum was such that the glass appeared opaque then the engine would bear watching. Fortunately Fords could be landed in a very small field.

Alex was terror conquered. He had seen it all, almost from the very beginning and stories about him had been retold by his co-pilots until they had become legend. Horn remembered how Alex had once flown into a vaporous mass which concealed a thunderstorm. As he ventured into the darkening maw his lumbering Ford was swallowed easily. He weaved his way through the towering cumulus, detouring smoothly from one inner mouth to another until he was caught in the very intestines of the thing. There the Ford was digested in a terrible series of spasms. One of the passengers said later it was like being thrown into a gigantic washing machine. The noise of the rain on the corrugated metal fuselage was like the tearing of heavy canvas, and when the rain became hail the pandemonium compounded itself. The bombardment became so violent the wild drumming of the engines seemed muted.

Finally they passed into the true bowels of the storm and the Ford's fifteen thousand pounds became as the weight of a butterfly. The turmoil became volcanic and the whole assembly of flying metal bent and twisted cruelly by alternate descending and ascending cascades of air. The odor of puke was drawn forward from the cabin.

Suddenly the Ford was overwhelmed in a downdraft and the rate of descent increased alarmingly. Alex had pushed the throttles full forward, and the resulting uproar from the protesting engines accented the garish flashes of lightning. The co-pilot, who would now be a veteran captain himself, said he suddenly became a little boy looking for a place to hide. Convinced they were doomed, he tried vainly to convince himself that Malloy sat on the right hand of God.

Then unbelievably, above all the mind-stunning sounds of tortured mechanisms and a ferocious sky, he had heard Alex singing. The co-pilot had turned to watch him struggling with the controls and managed a weak smile. He asked Alex if his singing was some form of prayer.

Alex replied above the cacophony of three out-of-sync engines mixed with the cannonades of the elements. "Praying? Hell no! I'm just singing to keep awake!"

In the era of DC-3s Alex would remember the "elephant's pecker." Those were the long flexible tubes which ducted hot air from the heating system to the windshield. If ice had rendered the glass opaque, then sometimes application of the elephant's pecker would melt a hole about the size of a silver dollar—sometimes. When it worked, visibility through the hole was enough to make a landing.

Alex was snow and rain and fog, the weathered statue of ten thousand winds. He was roll-your-own cigarettes and greasy hamburgers in those poor days when his kind tried to make a few dollars flying at county fairs. He was a monument to risk taken for granted and the sudden loss of comrades.

When the salad days arrived the hard-won cunning of the survivors was still in demand. Alex and his tribe knew the vagaries of the early radio beams and how they would sometimes betray a man. They passed naturally from the crude to the sophisticated in aeronautics, each contributing from his store of flying knowledge, exploring because their minds were adventuresome, testing new techniques and gear, in time forming a dedicated hierarchy. From them flowed a faithful stream of wisdom. Although they were fiercely independent there was rarely any holding back either of themselves or of what they knew. They believed the young apprentices who flew at their side should acquire certain habits if they would also survive.

Alex was leather jacket, helmet and goggles, transformed into scrambled eggs on his cap visor, brass buttons, and four gold stripes. He was the cocky booted youth paddling along at a thousand feet, content when headwinds did not exceed half his speed, who in time became the master airman cruising above thirty thousand feet at nearly the speed of sound. Most of the things he had done in his labor of love had contributed to the well-being of his fellow man; and now, deeply afraid for the first time in his life and nearly helpless, he should not be forgotten.

No! Horn vowed as he left the little room. I am in this to the finish, no matter what.

Horn's room was one of the eight cubicles on the third tier of the Fat Sparrow. The doors faced on a U-shaped balcony which hung precariously over a stone courtyard. Now he noticed a ladder at the end of the balcony which apparently led to the roof. While he breathed deeply and appreciatively of the cool morning air and watched the first hint of sun along the horizon, he decided to climb the ladder for a better view. When he gained the rooftop he stood entranced and for a time thought of nothing but the beauty of the dawn.

Vastly content, he watched the sunlight creep across the rooftops of the town, leaping from one peak to another in accelerating progression. Then with the roofs alight, the soft light slid to the open country beyond, capturing field after field until the morning ruled all to the farthest western hills.

Not until the sun was full above the horizon did his obsession return to him. Even on such a morning dragons were still snapping at his heels.

The only source of fuel for the Junkers was a Shell dealer on the outskirts of Ishan who had taken one look at the dilapidated bridge leading to the airfield and flatly refused to risk his tank truck crossing it. Now from his rooftop vantage Horn thought he saw a solution, although the amount of labor involved appalled him. There was an area where the road leading to the airfield ran closely parallel to the irrigation canal. If a barge could be hired and perhaps ten fifty-gallon drums found somewhere, fuel could be drawn from the truck while it remained on the road and transferred to the drums. The barge could then float the drums to the rear of the T-hangar. Next, if a hand pump could be found and enough muscle to turn it, the fuel would finally reach the Junkers.

Dismayed at the complications involved in what should have been a simple matter, he suddenly thought of Geoff and Dorothy in Paris. Only a week ago, greeting another morning from the windows of their apartment, it had certainly not occurred to him that he might soon be harassed by such logistics.

Next time, he thought, I am going to try something easy like building a pyramid.

Meanwhile he would throw the details and supervision of the fuel problem right back at Chatsworth. It would keep him out of mischief.

The smell of cooking rose from the street below and his hunger became demanding. He expected his breakfast would be rice and tea and if he was lucky perhaps a piece of fish.

He discovered the source of the cooking odor was a tiny cafe situated almost directly across the street from the Fat Sparrow. Entering, he saw there were three tables, a counter, and two male customers huddled over their rice bowls. The proprietor, wearing a lopsided chef's hat, smiled and waved him to the first table.

"How you want eggs? Sunny side?"

Horn blinked and shook his head. The day had just begun and he was right back in never-never land. "How did you guess?" he answered lamely.

"Have only instant coffee. Got bacon, but no toast."

"Okay. Whatever. Would you mind telling me where you—"

"I am cook in Oakland four years. Nice place Oakland, but I don't like."

"Why not?" Horn was not at all sure why he asked the question. It was really none of his business.

"Too many pigeons in Oakland."

"What's so bad about that?"

"I don't like pigeons."

Without the slightest change in his expression the proprietor swept around the end of the counter and addressed himself expertly to the cracking of two eggs.

As he watched in wonder, Horn resolved to ask Sylvia if there really was something inscrutable and very different about the Oriental mind. He had asked a question and received what the proprietor apparently considered a perfectly logical answer. The man could not be happy in the company of pigeons. Since removal of the pigeons from Oakland was not possible, the man moved. The more Horn thought about it the more he envied the proprietor. A man who allowed his life to be ruled by such naked logic would always be content.

As he ate, the proprietor stood opposite him. "You like Fat Sparrow? You enjoy?"

"How did you know I was there?"

"Everybody know you. Big American—make business in old airplane. Everybody know everything in Ishan."

Horn suddenly took an interest in the two other customers. Was he just imagining they resembled the two men who had watched them when they had originally surveyed the crash site? They appeared to be about the right age and they certainly seemed in no hurry to be off for a morning's work.

As he was sipping his second cup of coffee and listening to the proprietor's lengthy review of his menu in Oakland, a sleepy-eyed girl entered. She pointed at Horn and spoke anxiously to the proprietor.

"This girl say you hurry come telephone."

The Fat Sparrow's madame was obviously displeased with Horn. There was no display of the ore in her mouth or even a hint of a smile.

The voice in the telephone was Sam Fry's. "Have you ever seen a Chinese beheading sword? It is the instrument they are going to use on me if you deviate from the specifics of the letter I have just received from the Chinese government."

"Trust me, Uncle Sam. A head like yours must be kept in place."

Horn smiled at the death of a lurking fear. Sam Fry *had* called back. He thanked him and said he had known all along he would not desert the ship.

"I have not been given the opportunity. I did not fully appreciate the strange kinship which seems to exist among you flying people. While I admit it is rather touching, it is also inconvenient for those of us who prefer decent hours and a well-ordered life. Are you still there?"

"Very much so. I hang on your every word, especially if you mention spark plugs."

"Last evening at the club I foolishly related your needs to our attaché, Colonel Sorenson. He immediately took over the problem, which convinces me that he really hasn't enough to do here to keep him out of trouble. It seems that he has a friend who supervises an overhaul base in Tainan, which I'll have you know is more than one hundred and fifty miles from here. Several telephone calls were made, all at my personal expense. Item one. There is no propeller such as you require in all of Southeast Asia. That news was transmitted to me at two thirty-five this morning according to the clock at my once tranquil bedside. I am hoping that you will now abandon the whole enterprise and find some other way to prove your point."

"There is no other way, and I'm going through with it even if I have to steal an airplane from the Chinese. You're holding something back. I can tell from your voice."

"That is correct. Item two. I do have your spark plugs, which were delivered to my apartment at six fifteen this morning. With them is some sort of portable radio which the colonel says you absolutely must have so that you can communicate with the Chinese air traffic control. He urged me to warn you, and I quote, 'Failure to do so will most certainly result in him being shot out of the sky.' "

"My compliments to the colonel and my gratitude to you. Perhaps I should promise my undying gratitude."

"Now item three. You must have a copy of this letter from the Chinese government. I ask you to remember the tenderness of my neck when, hopefully, you commit it to memory. Now how do I get these items to you?"

Horn gave him Sylvia's number. She could bring everything to Ishan later in the morning. He repeated his thanks and said that on his return to Taipei he would reimburse him for his expense.

"Sometime today we're going to be open for business. I'll call you when we have the answers."

14

REPUBLIC OF CHINA

Mr. Samuel Fry
U.S. Embassy
Taipei

Pursuant to our conversations, the following directive has been received by this department from the Chinese Air Force and a copy numbered AA-427 is attached hereto. Since the directive is in Chinese I think it advisable to translate the principal specifications. Please take careful note of the following:

1. Under direct supervision of the CAA, authorization is granted for two (2) test flights of one (1) Junkers aircraft for the sole purpose of evaluating airworthiness of said aircraft. Under no circumstances should additional flights be attempted.

2. The primary flight will be from Ishan to Hsinchu via routes W-5 and W-4. Thence return direct Ishan (RS). Deviations for the purposes of flight evaluation only may be made within the Taipei control area after obtaining radio permission from Taipei Center.

3. Prohibited or restricted areas are to be avoided at all times.

4. The total authorized flight time for the two (2) flights will not exceed ten (10) hours.

5. Immediately upon completion of the secondary flight the aircraft will be surrendered to the appropriate Chinese authorities who will be notified at least two hours before the aircraft's landing. They will place the aircraft in bond preparatory to export and under no circumstances will any item be removed therefrom.

I must remind you that you will be held personally responsible for full compliance with this directive and it has been issued only because the purchaser is a U.S. citizen of established integrity. Any deviation whatsoever from this directive could result in immediate reaction by the Chinese Air Force and/or ground defense forces, with certain tragic consequences for the Junkers' crew.

My interest in your personal welfare compels me to warn you also that any such breach of faith would bring about the strongest official reprimands to your government.

Warmest regards,

T. Y. Loo
Chief of Section—Liaison
Executive Yuan

By noon Horn was satisfied the day would indeed match his forecast. The necessary tin for repairing the aileron had arrived in the form of eight oil cans, which Diderot cut to pattern and reinforced with a piece of the T-hangar roof.

Van Grootes volunteered to help him and by noon they had nearly finished the job. Although it was not a work of aeronautical beauty, none of them doubted it would function.

A Chinese man arrived on a bicycle cart which contained his welding equipment. At the time Horn had walked to the far end of the field trying to establish landmarks on each side of his intended take-off run which could be used to judge a "go"—"no-go" situation. He decided on a foot bridge which crossed the canal at a point three hundred feet from the extreme limit of the field. He reasoned that if the Junkers was not off the ground by then it was never going to fly. Whether or not he could stop before colliding with the dike was admittedly a bit of a gamble.

The usual crowd had gathered and now Horn had recognized the regulars. Had the whole community of Ishan knocked off work? The bearded old man arrived leading his faithfuls who carried the Junkers' heavy tire. Horn was dismayed to find it was so solidly packed with jute fibers he could make no impression with his probing fingers. After a moment his disapproval changed to admiration. Why not, he thought wryly. If there are too many pigeons, go else-where.

They had the tire on the Junkers in minutes and the old man vigorously refused any payment.

All of the Junkers' controls were now free, the oil changed in both wing engines and the screens removed and cleaned. All hose connections were tightened as much as they could be, considering the age of the material. All elec-trical leads were purged of corrosion, and the serviceable spark plugs were reinstalled. Now, except for the sixteen gaping holes where the new plugs would fit, the engines were pronounced nearly ready.

They had decided the bashed-in tail fin would not have any great effect upon the Junkers' flight characteristics, and since the rest of the plane was apparently built to last forever, there was little danger of structural failure. In an effort to reduce all possible drag, Moller had eliminated three radio masts, and to minimize the Junkers' take-off weight every removable fixture had been stripped from the cabin and cockpit. Horn estimated that the pile of junk re-moved weighed nearly five hundred pounds.

They had debated removing all accessories from the use-less center engine, but Chatsworth, who had more engi-neering knowledge than the others, held out firmly against such action.

"Without the weight of a propeller on the center engine the bloody beast is going to be tail heavy as it is. I strongly recommend we leave it be." They finally decided to wait until after the first flight when they would better judge the Junkers' stability.

Only Sylvia's absence spoiled Horn's mounting sense that all was going better than he had hoped. He glanced frequently at his watch and at the road leading from Tai-pei. At twelve thirty there was still no sign of her car.

He watched the man who had arrived on a bicycle as he completed the welding on the exhaust bracket. He was pleased, for the man seemed to know exactly what he was doing. Yet horn was vaguely troubled. There was some-thing strangely familiar about him. When he turned down his torch and tipped back his mask Horn recognized him. He caught his breath in wonderment. The welder was the

chef-proprietor who loathed pigeons. Immediately concerned, Horn checked the quality of the welds and found
each one most expertly done. Of course, he thought. In the
magic world of Ishan anything unusual was normal.

She had hoped that telling Alex about the Junkers and
what Horn intended to do with it would cheer him. She had
been disappointed. Now as she sped along the road to
Ishan the look in his eyes still haunted her.

"Sylvia," he had said solemnly, "there are all kinds of
things that can happen to an aircraft when it sits unused for
a long time."

He had paused and studied the evening sky through his
window. Finally he rolled his wheelchair close to her and
slipped his bandaged hands beneath hers. It seemed as if he
hoped the wordless moments that followed would speak for
him.

"There has been enough blood," he said at last in a
voice so empty of life she thought it was not at all like Alex
Malloy's. "If there were any more I doubt I could continue."

"But don't you trust Lew Horn? If he believes so completely, he must be very near the truth. He impresses me as
the sort of man who could make the world turn faster or
slower if he gave it a try."

Alex studied her eyes momentarily and she saw him grin
for the first time since the crash.

"By any chance," he said gently, "have you fallen a little
in love with him?"

She blushed and tried to smile. Then, looking him directly in the eye she nodded her head very slightly. And in
the next moment, she thought, her husband had once more
proved himself the very great man she had always held him
to be. For he smiled and raised her hands to his lips.

"I admire your taste. A lot of us have felt the same way
about him. He has that strange ability to inspire others beyond themselves." He looked away to the window and
spoke to the evening sky. "I've always believed that if a
man thinks too much about himself he's asking for trouble,
but the time has come when we must be more realistic. I'm
not sure just how to say this without offending you or
sounding like I feel sorry for myself, but I must try."

He paused and she was relieved to hear the power return to his voice. "If the verdict goes against me we'll be separated for a long time. I'm no longer a young man. If and when I do return I will definitely be an old man."

She started to interrupt, but he held up his hands in protest. "No, don't throw me off the track now. I have to face some truths. It's surprisingly easy, because I've had such a magnificent life and the years I've spent with you are more reward than any man deserves. What I am trying to say in a clumsy way is that I would be far more miserable if I knew one of the loveliest girls in the world was going to waste. I would feel much better about everything if such a woman rejoiced in her years of beauty remembering they can't last forever. Do you understand me?"

"Perfectly. But if you live to be a thousand you'll never understand a certain kind of woman. You're stuck. You are my husband and the love of my life forever."

She had sensed that her response had pleased him, but almost at once his attention seemed to drift away. "Our friend's talent for persuasion can be dangerous when he starts on himself. Now I'm afraid he has forgotten that an old airplane is just a collection of antiquated machinery and will not behave just as he would like. If that pile of scrap iron lets him down in the wrong place it can kill him just as easily as any other man—and whoever is with him. I'm having trouble enough living with myself now. If anything happened to him or the others . . ."

"He is convinced he can clear you."

"Somehow you've got to stop him. I'd rather risk prison."

For the balance of her visit they had talked about other things, but his last words to her had been "Somehow you must talk him out of it. I'll be waiting to hear."

Her next authorized visit would be in three days—Sunday. And on Monday the judges were scheduled to hand down their verdict. Alex's word might be the law by her choice, but how could she deter Lew Horn when she told him about her midnight telephone call.

She had been asleep for an hour when she realized the phone had been ringing persistently. Fearing something had happened at the sanitarium, she had rolled out of bed and in her haste neglected to turn on the light. She stumbled to the telephone in the living room and standing naked in the darkness listened in growing annoyance while a drunken man complained of her tardiness.

"Whassahell's matter with you, Sylvia? How can you sleep like that when I can't? Whassahell's matter with people in this world they sleep all the time?" The language was English, but she knew the voice belonged to a Chinese.

"Who is this?"

"Who the hell do you think?"

"I don't feel like playing games." She added that if he didn't speak their own language she would hang up.

"What I have to say will not fit. You are talking to Leonard Wu."

She held her breath. He seemed to be uncertain whether he wanted to continue. She heard him banging something, then he mumbled incoherently for a moment.

"Yes, Leonard. What can I do for you?"

"You're quite a dish, Sylvia, and you could do a lot of things for me. But your husband would not approve."

"Get to the point or I'm going to hang up."

"Well, you can tell your smart-ass American friend . . ."

There had been a long rattling sound and then the banging again. She thought it sounded like he had dropped the telephone and then had difficulty retrieving it. He must be very drunk.

"Yes, Leonard. Go on."

"How come you get mixed up with such a wise guy? Something going on between you two? You ought to be ashamed of yourself."

"Never mind the insults. What do you want me to tell him?"

"You say to that guy, well . . ."

Again the muffled background noises, but nothing more. She waited in silence hoping to avoid distracting him.

"You tell him I can't sleep much nights, because . . . because I have too much on my mind. And I have decided that I *must* have seen the outer marker light at the same time Alex did, even if I didn't hear the identifier signal. Otherwise I would have done or said something before he started down. Now wouldn't I? Get the message? You understand me, Sylvia? You heard whatthehell I said?"

"Yes. Why did you lie? Why didn't you say so when it would have meant so much?"

There was only the rattling sound again, and though she called his name several times she finally realized he would say nothing more.

Confused and apprehensive, she had reluctantly returned to her bed. *Now* would Alex want the Junkers' flights stopped when at last his co-pilot had confirmed the most important factor in his testimony? And would there be any stopping Lew Horn when he knew? And from drunks sometimes came other truths. Should she really feel ashamed because of the feeling she had for Lew Horn?

It had been dawn before she had found honest sleep, and it seemed like almost immediately afterward the telephone rang again. She opened one eye, surveyed the bedside clock, and discovered it was seven thirty.

She yawned all the way to the telephone. A man introduced himself as Sam Fry and asked her to stop by the American Embassy. "Captain Horn said you would be willing to take some things out to Ishan for him."

Captain Horn, she thought several hours later as the outskirts of Ishan rose out of the countryside. My dear husband has noticed how you have troubled my conscience, and since it is already in such a turmoil I might as well break my obedience vow. My grandfather once told me it is the bird which chooses the tree, not the tree the bird. So I shall not try to stop you . . . even if by some wild chance I could.

By mid-afternoon the sun had dissipated its authority in high multilayers of withered cirrus, and then later it became totally dissolved in a gigantic bastion of bloated cumulus beyond the western hills. When he bothered to glance at the sky Horn found the total effect ominous, but when the others suggested the possible approach of bad weather he insisted that at this time, when their very first essential was good ceilings and visibilities, God would not dare. Even so he sent Sylvia off to Ishan with instructions to obtain a detailed forecast. When she had gone he regarded the sky with suspicion, swore softly, and crossed his fingers. There in the western heavens might be the ultimate dragon.

Soon a cooling breeze swept inland from the ocean and his confidence was greatly reinforced. Both the lower temperature and the light wind would help the Junkers leave the ground.

The cooler air also seemed to revive the spirits of his delegation who had labored continuously through the hotter part of the day. Their activities had drawn a considerable increase in audience. When take-off time came Horn wondered how they could be kept out of the way.

As the light began to fade the fuel barge arrived and Horn was grateful for the spectators. There was not enough hose on the hand pump to reach from the barge to the Junkers, so once again the bearded old man led his faithful to the problem. Each full drum of fuel weighed over three hundred pounds and without proper equipment proved to be extremely difficult to handle. Working alongside the volunteers, laughing and grunting as they wrestled the drums off the barge, Horn guessed the heaviest man could not weigh more than a hundred pounds. All grit, he decided.

Pumping the fuel was accomplished by a hand crank fixed to the end of a pipe and inserted in each drum. At first each member of the delegation spelled each other at the strenuous task, but after the first drum was emptied the audience took over. They argued with one another as to whose turn was next, and the younger men contested the speed of their turns and the number they could endure without slowing.

It took less than an hour for the fueling and by that time Sylvia had returned with a weather forecast. As Horn read it he reminded himself that meteorologists the world over relished gloom, and if all they had predicted in his past had actually come true he should long since have begun gathering animals for the Ark.

He tried to smile at the assortment of phenomena which were prophesied for the next several days. A low pressure over the sea east of Japan was moving rapidly southwestward pushing a cold front which would pass through Bashi Channel and into the South China Sea. Ceilings would be lowering to one thousand feet, with visibilities decreasing to three miles and less in showers. Turbulence was expected preceding arrival of the front, intensity unknown.

Sylvia's concern was very obvious. "It's bad, isn't it?"

"Only if you believe in goblins."

"Maybe we should burn a different kind of joss."

"Let's just leave well enough alone."

A man becomes spoiled if everything goes his way, he thought, and certainly he had no complaint with the day's progress. One more drum of fuel and the Junkers would be as ready to fly as it ever would be until it had another propeller. Best of all was the emergence of a new and totally unforeseen problem. Now it seemed every member of the delegation was determined he would be the co-pilot on the first flight. Van Grootes claimed he should be selected because he had personally done so much work on the engines and would be the first to detect and understand any malfunction. Diderot made a similar protest and insisted that because of his youth he was not as weary as the others. Moller announced there could not possibly be any sensible choice but himself since he was the only one in the group who had actually flown a Junkers.

Chatsworth challenged him crisply. "And how much of that time was with only two engines? Considering the alterations we have made on this relic of the Third Reich it is going to fly like no other aircraft ever has."

It was precisely for that reason he argued, that in view of his weight, which was so very much less than any of the others, the co-pilot on the first flight should be himself.

To avoid a possible revival of the previous evening's bitterness Horn decided they should draw straws, "For the dubious privilege of helping me sweat."

Sylvia held the grass markers and Chatsworth won the longest. Horn was secretly pleased, for after all the work they had performed to remove weight from the Junkers the relatively diminutive Chatsworth would have been the logical choice.

While Horn and Chatsworth readied their charts, the tape recorder, flash camera, and reviewed their flight strategy, van Grootes and Diderot made a final fix on the navigation lights simply by taping small Japanese pocket flashlights where the former bulbs had been. Moller, grumbling over the need for a thorough test run on the engines, busied himself at draining a discouraging accumulation of muck from the fuel tanks. Except for a ban on smoking in the vicinity of the Junkers they all preferred to ignore the persistent leaks which dribbled fuel from the underside of the wings.

As evening came, Moller's continual fussing began to irritate the others. By suggesting they pull the engines through thirty times to ease their starting they managed to bleed off some of his nervous energy.

Equipped with sandwiches and coffee from the pigeon hater's cafe, Horn and Chatsworth entered the cockpit at early twilight. Moller had already familiarized them with the location and identity of the simple controls. He said he would personally like to start the engines this first time and Horn agreed. It was obvious that the Junkers had become Willie Moller's personal airplane, in fact it had become such a consuming passion with him Horn wondered why he had not insisted on flying it. Yet once he had resigned himself to remaining on the ground he ceased objecting.

"There is something I like about a Limey and a Yank flying a Kraut aircraft," he said. "It gives me hope."

As they slipped into their seats, Horn on the left and Chatsworth on the right, they reached automatically for their safety belts. Their hands halted in mid-air and they exchanged smiles of understanding. If ever there had been belts in the Junkers they had been long gone, presumably taken for more mundane uses.

Still panting from his exertions at pulling the propellers through, Moller came to stand between them. He apologized for smelling like a goat and rubbed his greasy hands on his pants. As if engaged in a conspiracy, he wiped at the sweat on his face and asked if they were ready.

Horn nodded and Moller reached for the left throttle. "Prime, if you please."

Horn worked the short wobble pump beside his seat, and although he knew it would not have the slightest effect he frowned at the left engine. Moller threw the starter switch and as if it had been stabbed in the left flank an animal-like groaning rose from the Junkers.

Horn held his breath as he watched the propeller revolve very slowly. He counted the passing of eight blades then the Junkers trembled in response to a minor explosion.

Blue smoke gushed from the left engine as the detonations followed each other more closely.

"It's firing!"

Moller pushed the left mixture control to the full rich position and Horn ceased his pumping. A long secondary tremor passed through the Junkers and they sighed together as the engine rumbled into steady life. Leaning over the control pedestal, Moller watched the oil pressure meter and tachometer until he was satisfied.

They turned their attention to the right engine and repeated the ceremony without success. The propeller turned fifteen blades in silence.

"It's flooded."

"No. It's not getting fuel."

Moller swore in German and looked out at the engine as if it had betrayed him. Chatsworth suggested they make another attempt with the mixture cut off and the throttle full open.

"It will never work," Moller sneered.

Yet after a moment he tried the combination and before they could believe their fortune a tongue of flame vomited from the air breather and the engine gave itself over to a series of violent spasms. In response the Junkers shivered all over, and Chatsworth said it was either in great pain or they were witnessing a true resurrection.

"Thank you, Mr. Pratt and Whitney," Horn muttered to himself.

Looking out, he saw Sylvia applaud vigorously and then blow him a kiss with both hands. For an instant the expression of pride and delight on her face made him forget how far he was from victory.

Moller had asked to accompany them to the end of the field where they had decided it was best to perform the engine run-up and what little was required on their homemade checklist. On Moller's advice they intended to use only ten degrees of flaps. And that, Horn thought, will be our total concession to modern aerodynamics. Even the landing gear was fixed and now he found strange pleasure in mentally comparing the twenty-minute pre-take-off checking in a jet with the simplicity of the Junkers.

When the engines had stabilized, Horn advanced the two outboard throttles slowly and the Junkers began to move.

Beyond the left wingtip he saw the Chinese waving and shouting encouragement. Diderot, smiling broadly, puffed out his chest and held a flat-handed French salute. Van Grootes, towering over everyone, clasped his hands above his head in the manner of a triumphant boxer and shook them vigorously. Between them Sylvia was jumping up and down clapping her hands joyfully.

He swallowed with difficulty and suddenly found it necessary to wipe at his eyes. Watching him, Chatsworth asked, "Are you quite all right?"

Horn nodded. If he lived to be an old man, which Brewster had always said was highly unlikely, he would never forget the complex emotions which had so suddenly captured him.

As all airmen taxied before nose wheels became standard, Horn steered the Junkers to the opposite end of the field by easy use of the opposite wing engines. At the limit of the field his intention was to turn the Junkers completely around to face the breeze and so utilize every available foot of space. At what he thought the proper position he advanced the right throttle and retarded the left, which should have resulted in a left turn, since the brakes were activated by retarding the throttles. The Junkers continued inexorably in a straight line, lurched slightly to the right, and finally eased to a halt in a position much too close to the canal dike. It would be impossible to swing the tail around.

"This is a mess," Chatsworth declared, but Moller pushed him aside and began struggling with the tail wheel locking mechanism. "I know I fixed the son of a bitch!"

Horn blamed himself for not testing the tail wheel lock release as he taxied down the field.

"We're stuck," he said flatly. "All dressed up and no place to go. We might as well shut down the engines."

"Wait!" Moller protested. He reached for the throttles, adjusted the engines to a fast idle, and immediately disappeared into the cabin. He jumped through the opening where the door had once been, then ran back toward the T-hangar waving at the crowd of Chinese. To Horn's dismay they began running to meet Moller, pausing only briefly while he made emphatic gestures. Then the horde ran shouting toward the Junkers.

Glancing at the turning propellers, Chatsworth said, "Dear God, I hope we don't decapitate the lot."

The crowd followed Moller to the Junkers' tail and moments later Horn felt it rise. He saw the nose engine slowly rotate around the horizon, hesitate momentarily as if seeking exact alignment, and finally halt pointed into the breeze. The tail descended and there was a slight jar as it contacted the ground. Looking back, Horn saw the Junkers' tail had been set down at the very edge of the dike. He hoped the hundred-odd smiling faces would understand his wave of gratitude.

Moller, dripping with perspiration, came to stand between them again. As he ran the engines to 1600 rpm Chatsworth checked the magnetos. Listening, sensing with all his airman's perceptions, Horn knew a moment of stunning apprehension as he compared the available power to the demands of the task. Against the puny sound of the Wasps this poor old Junkers seemed an enormous airplane. When Moller ran the engines to full power the vibrations compounded until massive shivers flowed through the Junkers. The poor thing is frightened silly, Horn thought, and so am I.

He glanced ahead. The field had suddenly shrunk to half what he had envisioned. Perhaps it was the dim light or perhaps it was the effect of the brooding hills which had now become a forbidding barricade along the western horizon.

He checked all the controls once again, half hoping he might find some last-minute fault. Even as he did so he realized he was stalling. He studied the field ahead and in his mind's eye saw the Junkers gathering speed. The tail should come up about there, say halfway to the end, then it should leave the ground just before the footbridges he had chosen as targets. He glanced at Chatsworth. "Ready?"

"My obituary is on file at the *Times*," Chatsworth said.

Horn looked back at Moller. "You might as well bail out while you can."

Moller smiled and placed his hands gently on their shoulders. *"Hals und Beinbruch."*

He turned back into the cabin. Horn made sure he actually let himself out the door opening. Then he took a deep breath and shoved the throttles forward to the limit.

Horn was appalled at the Junkers' sluggish response. While he had certainly not expected the acceleration of jet power, his instincts warned him that unless there was an immediate improvement failure was inevitable. He kept his eyes on the field ahead which still slipped very slowly beneath them.

"Have we got full power on both engines?"

"Everything. The lot."

Chatsworth's voice was so unruffled he was tempted to match his cool. He pursed his lips to whistle, but if any sound came from them he could not hear it. In his planning the field had attained a certain size. Now in direct contrast to the Junkers' placid progress it suffered a sudden shrinkage.

Horn resisted the urge to raise the tail prematurely. Shoving on the elevators at this speed would only slow acceleration. Speed? As they passed the halfway mark he estimated they had not yet achieved forty miles per hour.

He eased back a touch on the control yoke. Too soon. Iron Annie, he thought, you have approximately twenty seconds to prove yourself! A bump in the field would help, he thought, something to bounce them into the air at just the right moment.

They passed the T-hangar at fifty miles per hour, so slowly Horn recognized anxiety in the faces of van Grootes and Diderot. He caught a flash of Sylvia and seconds later the footbridges. He was able to ease the tail up a little and saw the airspeed touch sixty.

"Doesn't appear we're going to hack it!" Chatsworth shouted.

Horn agreed. They must abort now or smash into the dike. He reached for the throttles, intending to yank them back, which would automatically apply the brakes. Yet as the wings passed the footbridges he knew that very special sensation which was nearly impossible to achieve in jets. The seat of his pants told him the Junkers was ready to fly.

Now there was no choice. They could not possibly stop before the dike and the airspeed quivered between sixty and sixty-five. He withdrew his hand from the throttles and eased back on the yoke. Suddenly the rumbling ceased, the Junkers trembled uncertainly, and then all became smooth. The dike rushed toward them nearly at eye level and vanished beneath the wings. The canal and the open fields were no more than ten feet below.

"Airborne at eighteen fifty one," Chatsworth said as casually as if he expected some unseen crew member behind them would record the time.

"What did you say?"

Horn was totally occupied in trying to keep the Junkers alive and flying. Had Chatsworth seen or heard something which might now prevent their trying to climb? His voice had been lost in the wild howling of the engines.

Chatsworth leaned across to him and gauged his tone to penetrate the thundering racket which pounded through the open windows. "I said, 'May the skin of your ass never cover the head of a banjo.'"

As their speed increased to seventy and the ground slowly sank beneath their wings, Horn decided he had made an important discovery. It was impossible to whistle while holding his breath.

15

After nearly an hour Horn managed to nurse the Junkers to six thousand feet. The task proved both frustrating and totally absorbing. All his skill as an airman was in constant demand and it seemed the Junkers quickly resented any sagging of his attention. Now, even more than on the ground, it created the impression it was something more than a machine.

If he held the Junkers on the feather edge of its stalling speed it would continue its agonized climb. But the relationship was so tenuous that in spite of his wariness and rude warnings from the Junkers it had twice slipped away from him. The initial signal was a subtle shiver followed by a violent tremor which shook the Junkers' every bone. Then it would tumble toward the right wing and the nose would appear to rise almost to the vertical before Horn could labor it down. At such times he thought it behaved like a harpooned whale.

Recovery from the stall was slow and ponderous. The first time they had lost nearly a thousand feet before Horn had everything under control again. The problem was mainly visual, since the only instruments working were the altimeter and airspeed. They were alternately illuminated by Chatsworth's flashlight. The only fixed light in the cockpit was the faint luminescence encircling the azimuth of the American-made direction finder. Until the lights of Taipei came in sight Horn had no reference line to advise him when the wings were level or even of their angle of attack. There was only the black void of the countryside below, and in the vicinity of the mountains the low overcast obscured any dependable horizon.

It was a return to seat-of-the-pants flying, which both men recognized as mandatory and dangerous. During the worst of it they kept silent, as if the very act of speech would offend the laboring Junkers.

Once the loom of the Taipei city lights became visible their mood improved rapidly with the situation. Now Horn had a horizon. Watching it past the useless nose engine, he was able to hold a reasonably steady climb and finally ease into level flight. Even then the Junkers wallowed rather than flew, and Horn recognized the development of a unique emotion within himself. Almost since the beginning of manned flight, pilots had been known to regard certain of their aircraft with undeserved affection; often the more dangerous and difficult they were to fly the more unreasonable became the pilots' perverse devotion. Like the fathers of recalcitrant children they shrugged off the more obvious faults and claimed to see qualities which remained invisible to others. In the same way, he reflected, so many pilots seemed to marry shrews. Yes, he was already regarding the Junkers as a wounded bird entirely dependent upon him to keep it alive in a dark and hostile ocean of sky. If they survived the night and safety returned to earth he knew his affection for the Junkers might become incurable.

"Did you ever fly an overstuffed pelican?"

Chatsworth said something about his pucker factor parameters, but whether or not he considered the strain unbearable was lost in the roar of the slipstream and the drumming of the engines. Horn was immeasurably grateful for his stoic acceptance of his role as co-pilot. Although Chatsworth's total flight experience far exceeded his own he had not once offered an opinion as to how the Junkers might be better flown. Instead he had kept track of their position on Alex's charts and quietly reported on the health of the engines at regular intervals. Thus far the readings were encouraging. Temperatures and pressures were normal except for the right engine head temperature, which had climbed very slowly.

"Of course it could easily be the gauge."

"Of course."

Chatsworth seemed to understand without being told that the actual manhandling of the Junkers required nearly all of Horn's attention. He had tuned the automatic direction finder to the Taipei outer marker, fussed with it for several minutes to be certain he had tuned exactly to frequency, and then monitored the needle when he was not otherwise occupied. He had also established communication with Taipei Approach Control via the portable transceiver he held on his lap. They were cooperative and cleared the Junkers to cruise according to visual flight rules. Horn wondered how they would react if they were advised of his intention to carry out the clearance on two engines presently doing their best to keep a thirty-year-old three-engined aircraft aloft.

If all continued well he had calculated their endurance at five hours. Counting the time required for returning to Ishan, they should touch down just after midnight. With Sylvia serving as his interpreter, Moller should even now be making arrangements to set out flare pots along the perimeter of the field. The lights of her car plus those of the hire car should be ample for landing.

During the third hour the fuel consumed had lightened the load enough to reduce power and still maintain altitude. The very slow speed of the Junkers and the much lower noise level contributed to their sense of flying in a ghostly airship rather than in an airplane. They appeared to be suspended in space, immovable, while the lights of Taipei and its environs slid slowly beneath their wings. They established a pattern, flying west until they could make out the coastline, then southwest until they approached Hsinchu and finally east again to complete a huge triangle.

Chatsworth was navigating. "I'm keeping well away from the restricted areas."

"Good."

Occasionally they saw other aircraft, big airline jets inbound and outbound from the airport at Taipei. Horn always turned well away from their brilliantly illuminated images. The Junkers' lights were of much too low intensity to attract attention and he knew that even if they were seen the jet pilots were likely to be more confused than surprised if they tried to judge their speed against the plodding Junkers.

At half-hour intervals they alternated the tasks of flying and navigating. Both men were continuously aware of the direction finder needle and were certain they would have caught even a minor deviation. Yet ever since it had been tuned to the proper frequency it had pointed faithfully at the Taipei outer marker. No matter which way they turned or wherever their location within twenty miles of Taipei, the needle pointed the true bearing to the outer marker.

"Damned fine instrument," Chatsworth said.

It was of little comfort to them that Alex had been using two direction finders of more modern design and finer quality.

Now, without the slightest indication of spurious signals from the depths below, new doubts plagued Horn. The tape recorder and the flash camera which were primed to record and prove that combination of factors which he believed had betrayed Alex, now seemed to mock him. Was the risk involved plus the effort simply a waste, an ill-judged attempt to defend a man who was guilty as hell? There was time now with the Junkers behaving decently, once again to review such things.

"The needle is steady. We couldn't ask for better."

"Considering its age. Quite amazing."

"How is that right engine head temperature?"

"Climbed a bit. About five degrees in the past hour. I doubt it's anything to fret about."

"No."

Both of them knew the Junkers would not fly on one engine.

"We have another forty minutes to go before we start back for Ishan. That should give us twenty minutes' reserve."

"I'm sleepy. We should have brought some coffee."

"Even the Fat Sparrow will look good."

To combat his mounting discouragement Horn thought of Alex. How had he managed not to despair? Great news for you, old friend. Damned if we could pick up any interference with the outer marker. So maybe you were just seeing things. But don't you worry about a thing. I'll look after Sylvia while you're away. You can depend on your friend, good old true-blue Lew. There is something special between us, something bigger than we are, or have you heard that one before? Sorry the way things turned out my friend. *Non carborundum illegitimai.* Don't let the bastards grind you down.

Horn made a face in the darkness and asked Chatsworth to take over the controls for a few minutes.

"Weary?"

"No. Just full of piss and remorse."

He stood up and went back to the cabin. There, wavering slightly in rhythm with the Junkers' increasing oscillations, he urinated into the bucket they had brought along for the purpose. The front is moving in now, he thought unhappily. Turbulence, low ceilings, and rain were just what they needed.

When he had finished he stood in the darkness looking down at a necklace of lights which marked the western fringes of Taipei. How he longed for a shout from Chatsworth—"Come quick! Look! We're right on frequency and the needle is swinging ninety degrees to the right!" Or to the left. Who cared which way it was off as long as the bearing was false.

As the lights of the city slipped beneath the broken windows Horn's loathing for himself eased. There was still another flight to go and maybe van Grootes and Diderot would have better luck.

Shortly after midnight they flew over the field at Ishan and saw that Moller had pointed the lights of two cars in the direction of the wind. Nearly empty of fuel, the Junkers was now so easy to fly that Horn was certain his first night landing in this strange aircraft would be smooth and satisfying. He was soon disillusioned. He flew the Junkers into the ground, bounced several feet in the air and finally settled down on the grass with an embarrassing thud. Accustomed to jets, he realized he had held far too much speed and had been slow in flaring out.

"Apologies," he said quickly.

Taxiing back to the lights, the Junkers bucked as if it were passing along a corrugated road.

"I think we've pranged our homemade tire," Chatsworth said.

"Thank you for saying we."

There was no need to tell of their failure. As they dropped out of the Junkers' door they were met by van

Grootes, Diderot, and Moller. Beyond them Horn saw Sylvia waiting near her car. He avoided her eyes as he explained the first flight must be off the ground by seven in the morning. Van Grootes would be in command, Diderot the co-pilot. Watch the right engine head temperature, especially during the climb. Be alert for a half spin to the right and patient about recovery. Cruise at 1800 rpm, which would just keep them in the air. After the first three hours they could relax. And now for sleep.

Moller would remain with the Junkers for the rest of the night. He insisted he had just time to supervise the refueling, check the engines, and have the jute stuffing renewed in the tire.

"You make a flat wheel," he chided Horn. "Never mind. We make it round again."

Finally Horn went to Sylvia. "Thanks for your lights. There are some people who make good landings and then there are men like me."

"You look tired."

"I am . . . from making dents in this nice field."

It was unnecessary, he thought, to describe their hours over Taipei. He was sure she had known the instant she saw his face that nothing useful had been heard or seen. On the way into Ishan she told him that soon after his departure she had driven to her cousin's house, "thinking about you and about all you had done, and wondering if somehow I couldn't be of more help. I was preoccupied and driving very slowly. Then I noticed a car seemed to be following me. I speeded up a little and it did the same. When I turned into my cousin's lane it slowed almost to a stop and then went on. It was so dark I couldn't be sure, but I think it was your friends from the Central Intelligence Department."

"Then hear this order. You're not driving out to your cousin's place again tonight. Not alone. Not if we have to sleep in the Junkers."

"My cousin has moved a cot into the front hallway for you. There is only one bathroom for us all, but you will be comfortable."

"You're going to deny me the luxuries of the Fat Sparrow? How many people is . . . for us all?"

"Eleven counting you. There are seven children and that is a very good thing."

"What's so good about it?"

"They will keep us from chasing each other."

Horn shook his head in disbelief. At last fatigue and the frustrations of a very long day had caught up with him. He was hearing incongruous words expressed by the loveliest chauffeur he had ever seen.

"Just what did you say?"

"It's very simple. I detest hypocrisy. We have a very powerful attraction for each other and I was not born an angel. Women who are, or even pretend to be, bore me. Every time I am near you I desire you and my present loneliness only makes it more difficult to control. In different circumstances the chase would have been over long ago. Sooner or later one of us will surrender, and I'm old-fashioned enough and Oriental enough to believe that would be a tragedy. I also think it would be wrong to deny . . ." For the first time she hesitated. "Shall I say *enthusiasm* for each other? I am very proud to know you, Captain Horn, and even more proud to hear the things your eyes so often say to me. But I am convinced that if we are going to live with ourselves and keep even the sight of each other a joyful experience, we had also better keep a lot of people around us. Now here is the lane, here is my cousin's house."

Because of his long legs Horn always had difficulty extricating himself from low profile American cars. Now, stiff from his hours aloft and stunned by Sylvia's direct honesty, he took a long time emerging from the car. There were no lights in the lane and the darkened house was only a vague shape against the black sky.

He thought that he would have liked a few stars for decoration when he reached for Sylvia and pulled her gently toward him. He forced himself to be alert to any resistance in her body and found none.

He held her in silence, capturing the soft outline of her face in his memory and searching the deep shadows of her mouth and eyes. He thought to tell her how much she had been in his thoughts but changed his mind. What for? She had said it all and in such a straightforward fashion a misunderstanding was impossible.

"God bless you," he whispered. Then he took her face in his hands and bent down to the shadow of her lips. He felt her arms encircle his waist and hold him tightly against her. He remained motionless until he sensed her stiffening. Then very gently he pushed her away.

"See?" she said out of the darkness.

"Yes, I see. Thank you . . . forever."

A fine rain spewed out of the overcast, but it was carried on such a strong southwesterly wind that the Junkers left the ground as if all three engines were functioning. Those who witnessed the take-off from the shelter of the T-hangar —Horn and Sylvia, Chatsworth and a sleepy-eyed Moller —were relieved. The Junkers appeared to climb into the wind with relative ease and it soon disappeared through a pass in the western hills.

Moller, who had spent the night preparing the Junkers for its second flight, lay down in a corner of the T-hangar and fell instantly into a deep sleep. Horn regarded his prone figure with wonder and compassion. What kind of devotion had driven the man so hard? What could compel a four-striper to cheerfully accept his present predicament? He was utterly filthy. He was unshaven and smeared with black oil and grease. Only he knew when he had last eaten, and how he lay in a bed of mixed dirt and guano formerly occupied by chickens. As for reward, he had undoubtedly sacrificed a certain amount of Lufthansa flight pay during his absence from Frankfurt and like all the others was carrying his own expenses in Taipei.

Van Grootes and Diderot, he remembered, had conducted themselves with the same style. Now in very real hazard, which would continue for several hours, they too had found something in the cause of Alex Malloy to drive them beyond their years of habitual prudence. As for Chatsworth, who stood frowning at the metallic sky, he suddenly appeared very old for his fifty-four years. His defiant brace had given way to a slump and even his cheeks sagged like the wattles of the rooster which paraded smugly before him. The cynics were as wrong as ever, he decided. For there were still men who believed in each other. After nearly a lifetime of flying, Chatsworth had been willing to risk all he had won. For Alex alone? It seemed unlikely. It was something far more fundamental.

Horn crossed his fingers—since this would be the last authorized flight, a token gesture toward superstition could do no harm. They must find some excuse for the judges to change their opinions and still save face. Tomorrow was Sunday. On Monday the decision would be almost impossible to reverse. On this dirty ashen morning van Grootes and Diderot must discover the prize.

Weekdays from noon until two o'clock the officers' club was a raucous place, lurid with smoke in spite of the air conditioning, and pungent with an admixture of bourbon whiskey and the previous night's testimonial menu. All those Americans who were in one way or another connected with the Military Assistance Program (MAAG), or other Occidentals who managed to obtain admission cards, gathered at noon in common retreat from a culture the majority had no desire to understand. The more dedicated bar patrons stamped out their doubts in the heavy pounding of dice cups followed by shouts of dismay or triumph as the cubes rattled across the mahogany.

It was a familiar atmosphere to most members of the U.S. Embassy, including Vice-Consul Fry, who was thoughtfully chewing on a gumlike hamburger. While he masticated with increasing frustration, a man he vaguely recognized paused at his table. Like many others in the grill his hair was crewcut and he wore a linen suit—the standard uniform of those long accustomed to uniforms. He was smoking a cigar, which was also standard, and he rattled the ice in his glass importantly before he introduced himself. Fry noted with relief that he was quite sober. Somehow men who wore heavy military rings always made him uneasy.

"Sheldon Spencer. Far Eastern Airways."

"Oh, yes, of course." Fry debated the wisdom of inviting him to sit down and almost instantly decided in the negative.

"I have it on my note pad to call you," Spencer said easily.

"Well, well. You've saved a dime."

"I hoped you wouldn't be offended if I offered an un-asked-for opinion."

"I am offended almost every day by one thing or another, Mr. Spencer. That's part of my job."

"What I wanted to tell you is that you're sponsoring something which may reflect very badly on you personally —and even on our embassy."

"I'm not sure I'm entirely with you."

"Then I'll draw you a diagram. The investigation of air-craft accidents is a matter for highly trained experts trained in the latest technology and equipped with the finest tools. Well-meaning individuals, no matter what their other quali-fications, are very apt to obscure the facts and make life difficult for all who have patiently concerned themselves with discovery and prevention. In this case the totally un-called-for intrusion of others is complicated by the very real possibility they may lose their own lives, and if they happen to hit in the wrong place they could take a lot of in-nocent people with them."

"I assume you are referring to Captain Horn and his merry men? How did you know about them?"

"You of all people should know there are no secrets in Taipei, or the whole island for that matter. I don't know how merry your friends are at the moment, but as an ex-pert I can assure you they are damned dangerous to them-selves and to whoever happens to be underneath them at the wrong moment."

"I was not aware—"

"If I had thought you had been aware I would not now urge you to bail out. The aircraft they are flying should have been condemned long ago." Spencer took a long sip at his glass and then stretched his lips in a gesture Fry found difficult to interpret as a smile. "Enjoy your ham-burger. Damned if I know where the club buys them."

Returned to his office, Fry took two digestive pills. It was a pity, he thought, that all the wounds he had suffered as a young man in the service of his country were entirely abdominal and promised to remain scars upon his appetite forever. Then he saw a typed note on his desk and immedi-ately reached for a third pill.

"Message received through switchboard: 12:35 P.M.

'Call the Fat Sparrow immediately. Desperate. Horn.' "

Chewing anxiously on the pill, he made five circumlocutions of his office, touching the American flag gently each time as he passed it. Now just a damn minute! Who was this fellow Horn but a glorified bus driver, and what business was it of Samuel Fry, FSO-Six, to be seeking trouble? People of ambassadorial rank were entitled to and even expected to make absurd mistakes but not FSO Sixes God and the Secretary of State forbid!

If what that centurion in mufti, Spencer, had said was true then a certain vice-consul might soon be managing the motor pool in Santa Isabel, Equatorial Guinea, or stamping visas in Ouagadougou the capital of Upper Volta, should anything go awry with a certain flying machine of questionable integrity.

He halted at his telephone and regarded it with suspicion. If Horn was desperate then he was in trouble, which could mean the head of S. Fry was also hanging over a bucket.

He belched several times. There should be some special remedy for the incipient ulcers developed by juniors who were so foolish as to overstep their authority. If the ambassador knew, he would be displeased. No, livid!

He placed a call to the Fat Sparrow and eased into his leather chair. "Horn? Fry here. Now what?"

"We have had some problem with the right engine. Our morning's flight had to return after only an hour in the air. That blew our second authorized flight, so now we need clearance for a third. We should have everything fixed and ready to go by six tonight. Maybe earlier."

"I am no longer interested in your woes or your progress."

"What was that? This is not the best connection—"

"You always have a deaf ear handy. But you had better hear this. All communication between us must cease after you assure me you haven't killed anyone—as yet."

"Of course we haven't killed anyone and we're not about to. This whole operation is as safe as you once were in your mother's arms."

"Please be discreet enough to leave my mother out of this."

"We're trying to save the life of a fellow American and you're closing the door on us? No British diplomat would leave his people in the lurch."

"How many times must I remind you I am not a diplomat, but only a glorified file clerk. And you've read too much Kipling. British subjects of your ilk long ago taught Whitehall to mind their own business. I repeat—I will not, I cannot, do anything further. If the ambassador finds out what I have already done—"

"If you don't get us clearance for a third flight I'll tell him."

"As a personal accommodation I will be pleased to make reservations for all of you on the next plane out. Absolutely nothing more."

"Look, Uncle Sam, due to circumstances beyond our control we were forced to abort the second flight. It is only reasonable and fair that we be granted another try."

"My friends in the Chinese government are not interested in fair play. They are extremely pragmatic and interested only in what they can twist out of me in return for the slightest favor. This prune is now dry."

"I wish you would talk plain English, Sam. Or maybe you've been out here too long? I understand that happens to you people if you spend too much time at the same post? You become brainwashed, part of the native scenery, in your case an old China Hand. Maybe it's time you were sent home for a refresher, Sam. Wow, wait until you get reacquainted with those stateside prices—food, booze, apartments—especially in Washington. You're in for a real thrill, Sam."

"You are wasting wind."

"We're about the same size, but I'll tell you one thing, Sam. I certainly don't feel very safe going for a walk alone in Washington these days even for a breath of fresh air, that is, if you can find any. Come to think of it, as a patriotic citizen and substantial taxpayer, maybe I ought to write the ambassador a letter outlining my reactions to certain of his staff and the reasons therefor."

"He receives many nut letters. Yours would unquestionably go in that file."

"Well, it looks like that's a chance I'll have to take."

In spite of himself Fry was intrigued with the sudden

change in Horn's voice. He had just been told he would be shot at sunrise. The man was in the wrong profession. He might light a spark in the United Nations.

"Captain Horn? How many times have you been booked for blackmail?"

"All I'm asking is *one more chance!* Please, Uncle Sam. I promise to God if it doesn't work this time I'll give up the whole project. Please, there is one wonderful guy as American as yourself, sitting in a wheelchair and just about out of hope, who is waiting for you to do your bit. Jesus, all you have to do is pick up the telephone."

Fry had decided he had been wrong in his choice of a different career for Horn. The United Nations did not give Academy Awards.

"Come on, Uncle Sam. You've got blood in your veins. You're not just some ordinary government servant with his eye on a pension and nothing else. You've got guts you've never even bothered to use. Tell you what. You think about it for a little while. Remember, we'll be ready to go at six. I'll wait right here until you call back."

After the receiver clicked, Fry regarded the instrument as he had his luncheon hamburger. Then he replaced it and bowed his head in his hands.

16

According to the official report, Alex Malloy had flown into the ground at twenty-one minutes past eight. Since he had first considered the possibility of spurious signals from a missile site, Horn had wondered if the time of the crash might have some special significance. The two airliners which had landed before Malloy's flight had reported nothing abnormal. Both had touched down shortly before eight o'clock. Then later, at nine fifteen and nine forty-two, two other airliners had made instrument approaches without difficulty. Was there a chance then that the customary time chosen by the Army for testing might start at eight o'clock and terminate at nine or even eight thirty?

Although he repeatedly warned himself that speculation was dangerous, one possibility kept nagging at his thoughts. Unless the Chinese military mind was different from all others, the preference was to schedule duties and actions at even times, or at least try. The military liked things ticked off at twenty hundred hours precisely, not twenty hundred hours and eight minutes or sixteen minutes or anything so disorderly. Likewise, termination of any activity was usually prescribed. Twenty hours thirty, not twenty hours thirty-one, two, or three. If the even time syndrome was as fixed with the Chinese military as elsewhere, then it was very possible Alex Malloy's approach-time span had coincided with a test. How often those tests were initiated was undoubtedly a military secret, but the failure of the previous evening's flight to detect any spurious signal might prove it was not a nightly affair.

All pure conjecture, Horn thought unhappily. He found

some comfort in reminding himself that although the military might be predictable, human beings in general were certainly not. Two hours after he had pressed Sam Fry for a third clearance he had called back. And there had been a new ring in his voice, an almost defiant tone had replaced his diplomatic restraint.

"Your left-handed comments on my character, that business about having blood in my veins has subverted the real Fry. I spat out my pill and threw the rest away. Then I called my contact in the Executive Yuan. Permission granted for one more flight. Any chance of going with you?"

Horn turned his flashlight on the Junkers' instrument panel and aimed the blob of light at the clock. It was like Moller to wind the clock before the take-off, and it had proven remarkably accurate after such a long hiatus. The sweep second hand was just completing its staccato march to seven forty-five.

He switched off the light and glanced at Chatsworth, who was doing the actual flying. A cigarette drooped from his lips, the tip glowing occasionally as he inhaled. He had said he had not smoked in years but had developed a bad case of the wind up about this final flight and needed something to soothe his nerves.

"Aren't you afraid of setting your beard on fire?"

"I'll thank you to put it out if it ignites."

Horn looked down at the luminescent archipelago created by the lights of Taipei underneath a lower cloud deck. They were flying between layers. The lowest level was thin enough to be translucent and was so torn and fragmented by the wind that large sparkling islands of light were in the clear. The upper layer of cloud was solid, and the mass directly above the center of the city became a pale yellow which faded above the outlying districts. All of the horizon was clearly marked by a black void.

Horn estimated the altitude of the upper cloud at four thousand feet and he was careful to remain well below its under surface. The Junkers was unbelievably slow to maneuver, and a chance meeting with another aircraft was not in his plans.

He checked the time again. Only two minutes had passed. Could the missile testing routine have been the result of a duty-watch change? He had done his best to remember a brief conversation with a young Air Force lieutenant who had once been his passenger between New York and Rome. His job with SAC had been at a missile site in Montana and he had guardedly touched on his duties. It had sounded like a complicated and dreary business, and at the time Horn had not been much interested because it had seemed such a waste of a young man who was qualified to wear wings. Now all he seemed able to surely remember was that the lieutenant seemed to agree. He had been very eager about his new flying duty near Rome and hoped he had seen the last of fancy electronics.

If the systems were so fancy wouldn't it follow that the Chinese, so far from the source of supply, would hardly be able to make major changes in the short span of time since Alex's crash? Even if they recognized the need? Conjecture upon conjecture. If even some of it was true wouldn't Spencer, or the team of experts sent out from the States, have investigated and come up with factual answers?

He studied the lighted azimuth of the automatic direction finder. It was tuned to 335 kilocycles, the frequency of the Taipei outer marker. If he turned up the volume control he could hear the middle C tone of Morse signals, dot-dash-dot-dot followed by dash-dot-dash, the LK identifying letters of only that facility. When they had first reached the area he had tuned to other significant frequencies—just to make sure. At 400 kilocycles the needle had swung promptly and undeniably to Taoyuan, GM. At 510 kilocycles it had even offered a reasonably steady bearing on PO, which was Hsinchu, almost forty miles distant. As on the two previous flights, the ADF was performing faithfully.

Horn placed his hands across the lens of his flashlight and directed it toward the instrument panel on Chatsworth's side. He separated his fingers so that only a narrow beam of light illuminated the right engine oil temperature gauge. It had been rising slowly and now stood at one hundred degrees. If this had been a regular airline flight he knew they would have landed as soon as possible for an investigation, which was exactly what van Grootes had done on the morning patrol. Their examination of the engine was admittedly superficial, but they had found nothing significant. A complete tear-down, which might reveal the hidden fault, was out of the question. Ever since take-off from Ishan Horn had been trying to persuade himself the trouble must be in the gauge itself.

The sweep second hand on the clock tripped lightly past seven fifty-five.

"Going to be a long evening," Chatsworth sighed.

"Don't you know smoking will ruin your night vision?"

"Flying over this kind of terrain on two engines is not my notion of a holiday. What I can't see won't frighten me. I'm bloody terrified."

Horn smiled. It was characteristic of the bravest men he knew to exaggerate their fears. And any man who sat in the Junkers and disclaimed worry about a forced landing at night and the influence of pure luck on the outcome was either a liar or a fool.

They were well to the west of Taipei. Looking down, Horn thought he saw the shoreline through a hole in the lower deck of clouds. Or was it only a turn of the Keelung River? He was trying to establish their position more exactly when he heard Chatsworth say, "Hello!"

He turned to see him bent over the ADF and in the soft glow from the azimuth his eyes were anxious.

"The needle swung. I just happened to glance down at it and—" Chatsworth shook his head. "Now it's gone back to the bearing it held on the outer marker. But I swear—"

"Are you sure?"

"Absolutely. It swung round almost forty degrees." He tapped his finger on the azimuth scale. "Right there."

"How long did it hold?"

"I don't know. I wasn't watching. Only seconds after I noticed that it was holding an odd bearing it swung back where it belongs."

When Horn played his flashlight on the area chart he found his hands were quivering slightly. Chatsworth was not the kind to be seeing things. He tried to relate the strange bearing to what he estimated as their present position. If he had actually seen the shoreline in the darkness below, then the needle had swung toward something at least five miles from the outer marker, maybe more. *What* something? There were no thunderstorms visible in the area. Possibly a momentary change or loss of power in the outer marker system?

With most of the terrain below hidden in cloud and no navigational equipment in the Junkers to read the modern VHF stations, their position was at best an educated guess. And the strong wind could easily have carried them several miles off their dead-reckoning position. Only when actually over the lights of Taipei could they confirm their true position in relation to the outer marker. So the forty-degree variance was difficult to assess.

"You weren't by any chance turning when you saw the needle swing?"

"What sort of clods do you suppose BOAC employs?"

"Sorry. I'm just so damned frustrated. If it swung forty degrees to the left I think we should reverse course right now."

"Now?"

"Go."

As Chatsworth initiated a gentle turn toward the east Horn noted the time as three minutes past eight. He also became aware that the right engine oil temperature had climbed ten degrees.

As Chatsworth leveled out and settled on course toward the loom of Taipei a tremor passed through the Junkers. It was a stiff, iron-hard quivering which ceased as abruptly as it had begun. Horn's flashlight immediately sought the right engine oil temperature gauge. It had risen to the faded red mark which long ago someone had painted on the glass face. In silhouette against the light beam he saw Chatsworth shake his head, but he made no comment. What was there to say?

The Junkers plodded through the night at eighty miles an hour. Horn would have preferred to fly even slower if they could maintain altitude, but experimenting had proved it could not be done until most of the fuel load was burned away. Tonight he was determined to stay in the air until the very limit of their fuel endurance. When they finally decided to turn back for Ishan the west wind would be in their favor.

Looking down, Chatsworth said, "I hope that lower stuff doesn't slip between the hills in a few hours and cover Ishan. Our balls would be in a proper vise."

"You worry. I'm out of practice."

"Once in Beirut I placed a single wager on the red eleven and a minute later walked away with ninety-six Lebanese pounds. I quit because I was convinced chances like that do not occur twice, and I am beginning to feel the same way about this flight. The percentage is all on the side of the house. We'd have to be shot through with luck to catch the Chinese tinkering with their electronics just when we were eavesdropping."

Horn wished Chatsworth would not sound so reasonable. There was no arguing with his statement, no more than there was with the upward creep of the right engine oil temperature, which had now been joined by the pointer on the head temperature gauge. It was like visiting a friend stricken with cancer and avoiding the subject. Usually the inevitable was so near it did not merit discussion.

Off to the right, beyond the dark shadow of Chatsworth's torso, was the sea. Even if the Chinese had any sort of air-sea rescue service Horn was determined not to give them practice. Now, he thought, the urge for self-preservation is beginning to foam. Brewster had always claimed it was the best weapon a pilot could have, and if given time to save his life even the dullest of wits would find some way to escape.

To the east the mountains were not very lofty, but even three thousand feet could become an Everest if an aircraft must stay above it on one engine out of three. If things started coming apart the east would be the wrong way to turn.

Below, the Formosan countryside was relatively flat in the vicinity of the river delta, but rolling elsewhere. And there would be no friendly car lights to indicate a haven.

Landing anywhere near the city itself was not even to be contemplated.

There was one great and saving quality about the Junkers. In comparison with modern aircraft it could be landed very slowly. With a light load it could be brought to earth at slightly less than sixty miles per hour, according to Moller, and its fortresslike construction and high cockpit should give the crew a fair chance to walk away from the debris.

If, Horn thought. *If* everything worked just right, with

the stars in the heavens all in the right influence, and the pilot could see what he was doing.

Horn squirmed uncomfortably in his seat as another tremor shook the Junkers. It was like the erratic experimental pounding of a kettledrummer before a concert. After a moment it subsided. He was reluctantly debating the wisdom of turning for Ishan when he noticed the ADF needle swing. They had been flying directly for the Taipei outer marker with the needle steady and pointing straight over the nose. Now it was quite as steady, but cocked forty degrees to the right. And Chatsworth had not made the slightest course change.

Horn held his breath as he rechecked the frequency. The ADF was tuned exactly on 335 kilocycles. He was almost afraid to turn up the volume control and his hand shook ever so slightly as he reached for it. In his earphones he heard a low thrumming sound, powerful and persistent as if it came from the bowels of the earth. It completely obliterated the identifier "L-K."

"Tally-ho!" Horn breathed. Then he pounded Chatsworth's shoulder. "Good old union missile testers!"

Chatsworth watched the needle for a moment and said, "Amen."

"Pick up that course and hang on to it!"

Chatsworth banked the Junkers until the needle was once more pointing straight ahead. Horn marked the time on his chart alongside their approximate position. Eight twelve. The earlier transmission must have been a preliminary test while setting up the power.

Three minutes passed without the needle making the slightest deviation. And yet now they could see the plateau where the true outer marker was located. Their present heading would take them at least five miles to the west of it.

In his mind Horn began to visualize how any pilot, even an old fox like Alex Malloy, might have been tricked into a wrong heading. Once tuned to the correct frequency he would listen for the confirming Morse code identification, and hearing it be satisfied all was well. Then, because there were many other varieties of information he needed he would turn the volume off and continue according to the needle. Some time within the ensuing minutes the missile site would commence transmitting and suck the needle to an erroneous bearing. From the present position of the Junkers the angle of difference would be obvious and doubtless would have been caught. But on the final approach to Taipei from the west the needle would not have changed more than two or three degrees. The difference could easily be attributed to a cross wind.

Now there was enough reflected light from the city to outline a pair of low hills projecting from the lower cloud deck, and the black outline of a river was partially visible. It twisted between the occasional clusters of village lights and the black expanse of Formosa Strait. Horn drew a bold circle on the chart. They were approximately over an area marked as Tanshui. The river then must be the Hsintien.

He placed his hands on the controls, indicating he would take over the flying. He asked Chatsworth to call Taipei Approach Control, report their position and the reception of unknown signals on the outer marker frequency.

"And give them our altitude and course. We'll want it all on their tape for proof."

Their own tape recorder had been linked to Chatsworth's microphone. Now to make doubly sure their discovery would be preserved Horn reached to the floor beside him and switched it on.

"Do you want to tell them about our sick engine?"

Horn hesitated. Here was an age-old aerial temptation which men like Alex Malloy had long ago taught him to resist. When trouble arrived there was always a powerful urge to relate the situation to the handiest fellow human being who was himself free of trouble. To what purpose except for consolation or relief of loneliness? More often than not there was absolutely nothing anyone on the ground could do except distract with demands for further information, and in Horn's opinion the crew would better occupy their precious time doing what they could for themselves.

"No. Just keep feeding them reports on the signal."

As Chatsworth talked into his microphone Horn watched the needle with an increasing sense of triumph. It had held steadily on target for more than three minutes. Now it was beginning to quiver slightly, the normal indication they were very close to the source.

He glanced down at the terrain, now better seen in the

increasing loom of light. Portions of the coastline were unmistakable. He could make out lighter lines paralleling the coast which were the crests of seas.

He turned back to the soft glow of the ADF and studied the minute hunting movements of the needle. He became so lost in its behavior Chatsworth's voice seemed to be calling to him from another world.

"I think we are about to have a real problem."

He looked up. Chatsworth was tapping the right engine oil pressure gauge. "It's slipping down fast." His voice was calm but there was a distinct bite to it.

"Can you see anything out there? Any sign of fire?"

Chatsworth turned and looked out. "Can't see a bloody thing."

The Junkers did not have feathering propellers. If one engine was shut down the propeller would continue to windmill, setting up a heavy drag which would make it even more difficult to fly the plane.

Horn swore silently. He was in command, but Chatsworth was no ordinary co-pilot. He had more than a right to express an opinion and he deserved a full claim on his own safety.

"Want to head back for Taipei Airport? We could be on the ground in ten minutes?"

"We can't quit now. The hounds are just feathering!"

Horn was greatly relieved. God bless the English and William Oliver Chatsworth in particular. In the glow from the ADF he caught a momentary smile on his face. He saw him nod toward the right engine and shrug his shoulders.

"It hasn't jumped off the wing—as yet."

Horn alternately studied the needle and the breaks in the overcast below. The coastline was curving gradually and yet the needle held steady. His conviction weakened, for it was becoming obvious that if they failed to pass over the source within the next few minutes the transmitter could not be on the land. A wild possibility occurred to him. How much tragic coincidence could there have been if the original signal which deceived Alex had come from a missile equipped submarine, even one of American flag? He dismissed the notion as ridiculous. The same submarine would not be twice in the same area at the same time.

Anxiously, he watched the needle falter, swing slowly to

the left, then right, then hunt once more to the left and stop. It was pointing truly at the plateau which held the Taipei outer marker. He turned up the volume. There was the correct identifier, loud and clear, a distinct LK.

"Damn!" Chatsworth said. "Looks like they've packed up their testing."

A violent spasm shook the Junkers. It continued for several seconds. The beam of Horn's flashlight danced across the right engine instruments.

"Let's try reducing power on the right engine just enough to keep us in the air!"

Horn slowly retarded the right throttle and the vibrations eased. He suddenly realized he was perspiring very heavily. He fought down a compulsion to turn the Junkers away from the sea.

"Hello again. Our friends are back at work!"

Chatsworth was leaning over the ADF. The needle had swung away from the Taipei outer marker and once again pointed directly ahead.

Horn turned the volume up to the full position. The LK was obliterated by a hollow monotone.

"They're pumping out a signal we can't miss if they'll just keep it up."

In response to the reduced power on the right engine the Junkers had slowed to only seventy miles an hour and was commencing to tremble. Convinced it was about to stall, Horn shoved the nose down. They could spare a little altitude and still clear the hills on the way back to Ishan.

The lights of Taipei were some fifteen miles off the left wing and fading rapidly. A murky twilight enwrapped the coastline while ahead it melted into a void. Yet just below, a break in the cloud cover revealed a slight indentation and then a curve in the coast which crossed the Junkers' line of flight. Although most of the formation was hidden Horn was convinced he was looking at a small peninsula.

Chatsworth tapped his arm. He pointed at the ADF needle, which was slowly revolving.

"We're there! Whatever is transmitting must be right below. If that isn't a null I never saw one, and if I were flying in from the sea expecting the outer marker, I might start letting down right now."

Even as Alex must have done, Horn thought.

"Call Approach Control. Give them the time. Say we're over what looks like a small peninsula. Don't know the name. Meanwhile let's see if . . ."

Horn did not feel it necessary to finish his sentence. Now that his theory was proven he suddenly realized he had a very poor flying machine on his hands. As he banked warily around toward the lights of Taipei he saw that unless there was some marked improvement it would be impossible to make the airport, let alone slip through the mountains to Ishan. The Junkers was losing three hundred feet a minute and he dared not ease the nose up or it would certainly stall. The altimeter read two thousand feet and they were sinking.

Hoping for even a little more power, Horn advanced the right throttle slightly. At once the heavy vibration increased.

"I think we're about to break a master rod," he said as flatly as he could manage. He passed the chart to Chatsworth. "Have a look and tell me how high the terrain is in this area."

Screening his flashlight with his fingers, Chatsworth studied the chart. As calmly as if he were examining a page of the *Times* he took a pair of half glasses from his shirt pocket and slipped them on his nose.

"The contour lines show it must be quite lumpy below, but if we can hold on until we're further north things seem to flatten out. About five miles ahead is the Hsintien River. Unfortunately, in England our rivers are festooned with high tension wires. Progress, they say."

"Can you swim?"

"Rather. I was brought up near Brighton."

"Then if you hear a splash you'll know we made the river." Chatsworth would see, Horn thought, that Americans were also capable of understatement.

"Do you want to call Approach Control and declare a Mayday?"

"Go ahead. Tell them we'll try to make the river."

Horn reached down to the tape recorder, jerked off the reel and placed it in his shirt pocket. Then he buttoned the pocket.

17

At Ishan, van Grootes, Diderot, and Moller chose to remain in the vicinity of the T-hangar until the Junkers returned. Sylvia also elected to remain at the field, and her presence relieved the increasing tension as the cloud base lowered and the rain squalls became of longer duration.

"It's not going to be easy finding their way back if this continues," van Grootes said.

Diderot smoked continuously and stared angrily at the black sky. He talked at length in French with Sylvia, mainly about Alsatian wines.

Moller refused Sylvia's invitation to sleep in her car, saying he was too filthy, but he eagerly consumed two bottles of the Taiwanese beer she had brought from Ishan. Afterward he lay down in his guano-strewn corner, where in spite of his exhaustion he found it impossible to sleep.

The original inhabitant of the T-hangar returned. As if he realized his family could soon resume their residence, he settled them in the corner opposite Moller. He built a small fire and made tea.

"I don't know which way we should point the cars," van Grootes complained. He pointed his great nose at the sky and sniffed suspiciously. "The wind keeps swinging all around the compass."

There was no reply to his comment. The silence was only another in the long series which fell upon them. When the squalls arrived conversation was difficult because the rattle of rain on the hangar's metal roof dominated all sound.

For a while Sylvia tried to distract them by telling stories

about her grandfather. The attempt was soon abandoned.
They were obviously interested only in the glowering sky
and events within it.

In the MAAG officers' club Sam Fry accepted an invitation to make a fourth at bridge. He knew the other players
only in passing, something to do with pumping equipment
and oil storage depots, he thought, but he could not remember if they were building for the Chinese government
or selling to them. He played badly because he had consumed four vodka-tonics and had still failed to drive Lew
Horn from his thoughts. He had left word both at his
apartment and the Embassy where he could be found if a
call came.

In the main radar bunker of the Chinese Air Force,
Central Combat Air Command, Major Y. T. Leong,
Fourth Fighter Wing, watched the special screen which was
devoted to the observation and processing of civil aircraft
movements. Ordinarily the screen was of little interest to
him, because of its relative lack of activity and his disinter-
est in its displays. The peaceful passage of airliners was not
his affair as long as they remained on their procedural
tracks.

A single sergeant manned the post and communicated
with civil aviation authorities only upon direct request or in
a state of military emergency. Like his officers he was not
prone to communicate with civilians and saw no reason to
share the benefits of military equipment.

Tonight Major Leong spent some time before the civilian console. There was at last some variance in the vigil
kept by Leong and his fellow officers, the eternal waiting
for something "hot" to appear from the Chinese mainland.
Tonight he had been advised through channels that a very
slow aircraft designated as a Junkers 52 would be making a
special flight. He had never heard of such an aircraft, but
as long as it was duly authorized its movements became his
business only if it entered the restricted areas. So far its
"blip," which floated like an amoeba across the glowing
screen, had behaved itself. He speculated idly upon its ec-
centric track. Possibly they were testing some sort of tar-
get-towing device, since the flight was designated as "test"

and its speed was so incredibly slow. Or was it some new and top secret type of reconnaissance aircraft?

Leong watched with increasing interest as the blip passed directly over Missile Site Twenty-eight and then made an abrupt turn back toward the north. There was nothing illegal about the maneuver, since Site Twenty-eight was not designated on the charts as "restricted." Why tell the communist Chinese where the sites were located? The restricted areas so clearly marked on charts anyone could buy were kept deliberately barren of any sort of weaponry. When the enemies of Chiang decided to attack, it was hoped their hardware would fall upon open countryside.

Major Leong was disappointed because after watching the blip continue northward almost to the Hsintien River, it suddenly disappeared from the screen. For reasons best known to the pilots, they had obviously decided to fly very low. He was regretful because it had been an interesting diversion.

•   •

The Junkers throbbed in response to the heavy pulsations from the right engine. It floundered rather than flew, noisily descending toward the dark earth like a dying bird. Horn's leg ached from holding full left rudder to compensate for the rapidly diminishing power of the right engine. He asked Chatsworth to help him. If they once let the Junkers have its way Horn believed it would surely roll over on its right wing and begin a belly up descent from which there would be no recovery.

Their combined efforts on the left rudder pedal caused the Junkers to lunge and shudder in agony with every slight change in angle of attack.

Chatsworth leaned across to him. "They have just asked if we can make Taipei Airport. I told them if we could we would not be sending Maydays."

"Good." Horn was totally absorbed in the gloom beyond the center engine. "I think I see the river. Does it have a hill or a small mountain rising out of the far shore?"

Chatsworth checked the chart. "Nothing indicated."

"No. I guess I'm looking at some low cloud."

They watched in uncomfortable silence as the altimeter slipped below two thousand feet. Now the scud cloud, rumpled in the reflected lights from the higher overcast, stretched before them like a storm-tossed ocean. The clear areas between patches of cloud could no longer be seen and the mass appeared solid.

"I'm going to try stalling her right on down."

"You've no choice."

"I'll keep my eyes outside. You say my airspeed and altitude."

"Right. We're out of two thousand. Sixty-eight on the airspeed." Chatsworth cleared his throat apprehensively. "Can't say I enjoy this."

Horn understood. If the right engine blew entirely they would have to land immediately. And if the master rod let go in just the right way it could start a fire. Even now they were just managing to stretch the glide—a very final glide, he thought, at least for the Junkers. From their original higher altitude the lower deck of cloud had not appeared very thick so they should not be long in it, but how far was the river?

"Let's try for a little more poop from the right engine."

Chatsworth eased the throttle forward as Horn put down an urge to look out at the engine and beg its support. How very much depended on that assembly of metal parts, many of which were now at war with one another. He shook his head hopelessly. Eyeballing the fray would not have the slightest effect.

A violent hammering shook the very bones of the Junkers. Chatsworth immediately retarded the throttle.

"Forget it!"

"Right. I'm trying to."

"Say my altitude now?"

"Passing through fifteen hundred."

The Junkers was suddenly enveloped in heavy cloud. The windshields and the plexiglass roof seethed with moisture and the air became muggy. Without instruments to aid his blinded senses Horn pushed the nose down. He must avoid a complete stall, and the quicker they passed through the cloud the better.

"Say airspeed?"

"Seventy-five . . . seventy-seven."

"Altitude?"

"Out of one thousand."

"Jesus."

"What?"

"Nothing."

"You're out of nine hundred."

"*We* are."

The overcast was obviously bottomless, Horn thought. His stomach churned with the sort of fright he had not known in a very long time. An almost forgotten tingling sensation began creeping up the back of his neck and mounting to his scalp. Seventy-seven miles an hour was too fast to collide with the side of a hill or anything else. A blessing. Alex never knew what was coming. Out of nine hundred feet? Descending at about three hundred per minute? Then at the very best this flight must terminate in four minutes. Or less?

"She flies better down here."

"Bravo. You're out of eight hundred."

Horn was close to surrender when the Junkers slithered out of the overcast.

"I see the river! There are a few lights along the north shore!"

"Can we make it?"

"I—"

Horn decided to stifle his reply. It was something to do with luck, he thought. You did not announce the gift of a chance for life until you could breathe normally. Along with grateful prayers, congratulations were better postponed. Yet he had never beheld a more beautiful sight than the ribbon of lightness which ran between the darker shores. It appeared to be about two miles ahead. If he held every inch of altitude, they just might survive the distance.

"Five hundred feet . . . airspeed seventy. Four fifty . . . beautiful. . . . Watch it! You are down to sixty-eight on speed. Remember Jesus walked on water."

Horn yearned for landing lights and was instantly contrite for his greed. If he knew his business, even the feeble line of lights along the farther shore would be sufficient to establish the final glide.

"Two hundred feet . . . wizard work."

Horn dared not blink his eyes.

"I'll try holding her off as long as I can and let her settle in on three points!"

There was no further reason for the calling out of airspeed or altitude. Now Horn reverted to his seaplane training. As he slowly reduced power on the left engine he gradually brought the Junkers' nose up. Instead of looking directly ahead he yanked open his side window and watched the lights and the dark mass of the riverbank.

"Give me all the flaps she has!"

When the Junkers' wing appeared to be in landing attitude as measured against the lights, he held the control yoke steady. The final sounds of flight from the Junkers diminished to a low rumble.

Horn saw the blobs of light reflected in the water rise to meet the wing.

"Hang on!"

He pulled the master switch, heard the engines backfire, and felt the first brush of the wheels against the water. He heaved the control yoke full back to his stomach and closed his eyes.

The first impact was surprisingly gentle. Immediately afterward they were thrown forward against the instrument panel. Horn waited for the cascade of water as reported in every ditching he had ever read about. During the first seconds there was only a hissing sound.

The Junkers decelerated rapidly and seemed to rise on its nose. Then the water gushed through the open windows. Fighting for air, Horn pushed himself toward the ceiling. To his astonishment the rush of water ceased and he saw that its level was less than halfway up his window.

He called to Chatsworth in the darkness. "Are you all right?"

"Yes. Quite."

Beneath the surface of the water he saw the eerie glow of Chatsworth's flashlight. It rose on a luminescent ladder of bubbles and broke the surface. Its beam swept the cockpit, which was strangely askew, then passed to the cabin door, which was at an angle above them.

"By God," Chatsworth said, "I believe our wheels are on the bottom and we're standing on the nose engine!"

"Let's get the hell out of here!"

"After you."

Even as he sloshed about the cockpit seeking for a solid footing to push himself toward the cabin door, Horn wondered if he was not dreaming. For the effect of the tilted

Junkers was confusing and every move he made seemed to be the wrong one. When he finally managed to hoist himself through the door he realized Chatsworth would have an even more difficult time because of his shorter reach. He turned back, extended his hands, and dragged him upward.

They wriggled up the cabin floor, slipping backward frequently. When they came to the door they rested momentarily. Panting, Chatsworth played his light on the water, which appeared to be about ten feet below. The current was very strong and while they regained their strength they questioned the wisdom of leaving the Junkers. There was no evidence the landing had been witnessed from the shore, so rescue was certainly not imminent. But what was the effect of the tide in the river? If it was flooding would it raise the river level enough to cover the Junkers? And how deep was it now directly below the cabin door?

"And what," asked Chatsworth, "is that incredible stink?"

Horn laughed, most unnaturally, he thought. How sweet a recaptured life could be regardless of the trimmings. "I apologize for dunking you in a big city sewer."

"I'll find a way to thank you. Well done."

Horn lowered himself from the doorway and hung by his hands for a moment. Chatsworth's light revealed the water's surface still well below his feet.

"If it's above my head the current will carry me to the wing. I'll climb from there to the top of the fuselage and perch there for the night."

He let go his grip on the doorsill and dropped into the river. He disappeared momentarily then came up, shook his head, and snorted.

"Come on in, the water's fine. I'm standing on the bottom."

Chatsworth watched the water gurgling against Horn's shoulders and hesitated.

"I daresay it will be over my head."

"You can ride piggyback. Come on."

"How undignified," Chatsworth muttered as he dropped into the swirling river.

Stumbling toward the shore through the turbulent eddies and countercurrents, Horn fell down repeatedly. Each time Chatsworth was propelled forward and they became briefly disengaged. Then, choking and spitting, he would again mount Horn's back and, laughing, they would once more proceed. They were fully aware they were hysterical and cared not at all. Like drunkards homeward bound they shouted and murmured to the night at large, passing on to all that surrounded them, the twirling branches caught in whirlpools, the curious insects and night birds which fluttered past their fitful light, the chunks of garbage and foul excreta which nudged their bodies, to all of such things and even to the putrid river itself they uproariously announced their unbounded joy in once more knowing their lives were their own.

18

MEMORANDUM from the Honorable R. D. Chew, Judge, Taipei District Court.

1. At 09.00 this morning (a Sunday), the following individuals presented themselves at my residence. Since they claimed their mission was urgent I ordered them to be admitted.

2. Present were Captain Jan van Grootes of Amsterdam, Holland, Captain William Oliver Chatsworth of London, England, and Captain (first name missing) Moller of Frankfurt, Germany. They advised me that two other members of their delegation were at this same hour calling upon Judge H. G. Liang.

3. The above-named individuals presented hitherto unknown evidence pertinent to the case of Captain A. Malloy.

4. Having carefully considered this new evidence I have now concluded the charges against Captain Malloy should be dropped. There exists considerable history of even experienced aviators suffering from optical illusions during approach to landing, particularly at night and during rainy periods. It is my considered opinion that Captain Malloy was the victim of such an illusion, having been convinced he should land when actually he should not. Therefore he cannot knowingly have been negligent or careless in his duties and cannot be so convicted.

RECOMMEND: Dismissal.

TAIPEI DISTRICT COURT

Chambers of Judge H. G. Liang

Colonel S. T. Chengchih
Deputy Commander, Taipei Area
Chinese Air Force
Taipei, Taiwan

Colonel Chengchih:

This will confirm our telephone conversation of yesterday morning (Sunday) re the matter of a crash involving a Far Eastern Airways Boeing 727 and in particular the criminal trial resulting therefrom of one A. Malloy, a U.S. citizen who was commanding the aircraft.

It is my understanding that as an expert you declare that the cause of the crash was not due to any negligence on the part of Captain Malloy, but was undoubtedly due to a malfunction of the navigational equipment aboard the aircraft itself.

Since all such electronic equipment was destroyed in the crash, actual proof of neglect or negligence of any sort on the part of Captain Malloy would in your expert opinion, be impossible to prove.

It is my intention therefore to recommend immediate dismissal when the District Court convenes tomorrow morning.

Respectfully,
H. G. Liang, Judge

THE CODE OF CRIMINAL PROCEDURE

Article 154: The facts of an offense shall be established by evidence. The facts of an offense shall not be presumed in the absence of evidence.

I, D. P. Hsiao, Presiding Judge in Taipei District Court, having heard the case of the Chinese People vs. Captain A. Malloy, U.S. citizen, do find the following:

1. Defendant was duly licensed by the Chinese CAA, which is responsible for the qualifications of air person-

nel employed by companies operating with the approval of the Republic of China. (Chung Hwa Min Kuo.) The abilities of Defendant were therefore considered acceptable by the agency involved.

2. The charge of "criminal negligence" is therefore unsupportable, since it is not the official policy of the CAA to certify criminals, potential or otherwise. (Sec. 34-A 574: "No person convicted of a felony shall be licensed by the Civil Aeronautics Authority, etc.")

3. In spite of the efforts of the Prosecuting Attorney I am not convinced Defendant was guilty of negligence, since proof of such an action (or lack of action) must pre-suppose an irresistible suicidal mandate in Defendant. In all the exhibits offered I find no evidence of this, historical or otherwise.

4. If Defendant were found guilty as charged, then it must follow that the Civil Aeronautics Administration is an accessory and therefore vulnerable to the same charge.

RECOMMENDED: Dismiss.

ADDENDUM: A memorandum bearing the seal of this court should be addressed to the Minister of Communications with copies to Chief, Safety Section, CAA, Chief Engineering Inspector, CAA, and Facilities Chief, CAA, recommending an immediate review of performance and maintenance records concerned with the aviation approach equipment to Taipei Airport. It should be emphasized that any incident involving a foreign air carrier and chargeable to those devices owned and/or operated by the CAA, could be particularly embarrassing to our government.

19

October had come to Long Island again and Lew Horn had enjoyed four satisfying days of the month he considered the best of all. The light, the colors, and the crisp hint of the coming autumn best suited his familiar pleasures and the occasional loneliness he had known since his return from Taiwan. Now it was time to make another Atlantic crossing, his 768th according to his logbooks. He was not impressed with the number. Many veteran captains had logged over a thousand.

When he left on a flight a cleaning lady kept his apartment from becoming a bachelor's shambles, and she also fed Orville Wright.

These days, when he was not scheduled for training or a physical, Horn avoided the bustling immensity of Kennedy Airport. Brewster had been retired and had died within two months of the ceremony. He had been fishing off Florida, suffered a stroke, and had fallen overboard. Horn refused to believe the story. When he wanted to go, Brewster would have jumped. He had been replaced by a soulless man named Fisk to whom all pilots were merely numbers and who in Horn's opinion actually thought like the computers he worshiped.

Flying was changing so fast the awed old-timers who occasionally dropped by Operations hoping to find a familiar face were soon overwhelmed and hardly recognized they had ever been a part of it. Almost invariably they retreated to whatever refuge their pensions provided. Horn, who had yet many years before retirement, was glad Brewster was not around to witness the ruthless depersonalization.

During his time off between flights to Paris Horn indulged himself in more exciting pursuits. During most of the day he painted, and to his great pride a local gallery had sold eight of his skyscapes. They were asking for more. When the afternoon light failed he would drive to East Hampton, where he kept his aerobatic airplane. Then during the hour which led into twilight he would "stimulate his thoughts." He found the rush of blood to his brain and the balletlike rhythm of aerial maneuvers especially invigorating on October afternoons. The swirling color combined with the sensual joy of flying such a responsive craft never failed to inspire him, and when he landed at dusk, always refreshed and newly content, he would sometimes glance up at the sky and whisper his gratitude.

Horn regretted having missed most of this October day. He had slept through the afternoon in preparation for his regular night flight to Paris. When he awoke he showered and pulled on his uniform pants. Then he packed a small bag with enough clean linen to last four days in case he returned via Athens and Rome, and he added the two most recent copies of *New Yorker* magazine plus the Sunday *Times* for Dorothy and Geoff. Between the pages of the *Times* he placed a cowboy record for Rosalie, and after removing the classified section he managed to squeeze in his tweed sports coat and a pair of slacks.

He whistled softly as he checked through his black leather flight kit. It was a part of his preflight routine. There were his two volumes of Jeppesen brought up to date with the latest insertions. They contained enough charts to take him anywhere in the Western Hemisphere. There was the schedule of the line's Atlantic division flights for the month of October combined with his personal assignments—all compiled by computer and based on his bidding status. There was the company seniority list for flight personnel, with L. Horn standing in the approximate middle. It would not take too much of a cutback to put him back flying first officer. There was his red-bound ALPA contract, which all provident pilots carried against the possibility of a "guest" on the flight deck in the person of an FAA inspector. It was regrettable, Horn thought, that so many of them were ponderous with self-esteem and sometimes the red book became a pilot's only defense. Finally there was his flashlight and the roll of masking tape which was considered essential by many pilots. It served to hide and hence diminish the annoyance of inoperative instruments, of which there were invariably several on every aircraft. The tape was also handy for securing the pertinent meteorological chart to the windshield, not to compare its inaccuracies with the actual weather encountered, but to avoid the punishment of the direct early morning sun at twenty-nine thousand feet.

As he closed the kit and snapped the clasp he suddenly found himself thinking of others who might be doing the same thing.

Willie Moller, probably. He was flying the Rio, Buenos Aires run according to a postcard received from Montevideo. Van Grootes was on the New York run out of Amsterdam. He had telephoned one hot August night and suggested Horn might like to join him in taking two of his Dutch stewardesses to dinner. The party, which had commenced at Horn's apartment, was not a smashing success. The stewardesses were solely interested in finding a prospective husband, and when he had said he was not quite ready for a second performance they had pouted for the rest of the evening and spent most of their time gossiping in Dutch. But it had been a pleasant reunion with van Grootes, who said he was actually looking forward to retirement. "It is not the same," he insisted, and Horn had understood.

Only a few months after their return from Taiwan, Diderot had been killed, not in an airplane, but in a car. An infinitely sad letter from his father had told how a giant truck laden with potatoes had forced Étienne off the road during a rainstorm. "Fortunately his destruction against a stone wall was instantaneous. After a long lifetime of hazard without so much as once missing a breath," the older man had closed his letter, "it is such things I find difficult to comprehend."

Horn stopped whistling. Yes, it had seemed a strangely ignominious finale for such a dashing young man.

Chatsworth had retired and had been awarded an OBE. But apparently the peace of his cottage at Didcot soon palled on him. A testy postcard from Madeira advised that he had accepted employment as a commission agent for a Portuguese vintner. "Rather doggo pay, but then of course there's the lovely sun. Trading the heritage of my native heath for genteel poverty, acid stomach, and actinic rays, I expect to live a hundred years."

Alex and Sylvia were living outside San Francisco. At Christmastime they had invited him to their small farm where, they explained, they were raising ducks for the commercial market. Horn had been unable to accept because he was scheduled for a Paris flight on Christmas day. It was a trip he could have easily traded with one of the more junior captains, but he had decided against it. During the Malloy victory party, which had been celebrated at Taipei's Grand Hotel, Sylvia's grandfather had said something to him in Chinese. Sam Fry, who had been invited to join in the occasion, translated. "He says, 'What is whispered in the ear is heard miles away.' "

Sylvia's grandfather, as Horn had previously decided, was a very perceptive man.

He slipped into his uniform jacket, placed his cap squarely on his head, and picked up his bags. He turned out the light in the bedroom and went into the living room, which he preferred to think of as his studio.

After he was certain Orville Wright had sufficient water and food until the next day he pulled the cloth around the cage.

"Good night, old friend. Keep your beak clean, and if anyone calls tell them I've gone to lunch."

At the door he reached for the light switch, then paused. He looked back quizzically at the painting on his easel. It was of an Oriental girl sitting in a high-backed cane chair. She was in shadow and behind her a sun-baked plaster wall provided sharp contrast with her blue dress.

Horn made a face and shook his head. Haven't quite caught it yet, he thought. The dress should be more of a cobalt. And the face? Better to leave it blank for a while, then maybe it can tell me anything I want to hear.

ERNEST K. GANN began his flying career in his twenties as a daredevil stunt flier. He then became a commercial airline pilot and has logged almost nineteen years and a million and a half miles in the air. During World War II he flew missions for the Air Transport Command and was decorated with the Distinguished Flying Award. Mr. Gann now lives on his ranch on an island off the northwest coast of the United States and devotes his time to writing, painting, sailing and piloting his Cessna 310. His other works include THE HIGH AND THE MIGHTY, BLAZE OF NOON, BENJAMIN LAWLESS, SOLDIER OF FORTUNE, TWILIGHT FOR THE GODS, THE TROUBLE WITH LAZY ETHEL, FATE IS THE HUNTER and OF GOOD AND EVIL.

More **BALLANTINE** books
You will enjoy!

AMERICA'S #1
INVESTIGATIVE
REPORTER

JACK
ANDERSON

WITH GEORGE CLIFFORD

THE
ANDERSON
PAPERS

available at your local bookstore

the joy of sex . . .
from
PENTHOUSE / Ballantine

The Sensuous Couple, ROBERT CHARTHAM

The best-seller by Britain's foremost sexologist reveals the simple things every couple can do together to bring the greatest pleasure and enjoyment to each other.

$1.50

What Turns Women On, ROBERT CHARTHAM

These women in letters to a sympathetic and qualified friend have discussed in their own graphic and sometimes startling words, their more intimate desires. One thing becomes very clear—there is a lot more that turns women on than might have been expected.

$1.50

Super Marriage-Super Sex, H. FREEDMAN

A handbook for people who already know about sex—and want to learn more. A good sex relationship is basic to a good marriage, and it is clear that "good" means totally accepting.

$1.50

BESTSELLERS
from

BB

BALLANTINE BOOKS

RABBIT BOSS, Thomas Sanchez	$1.95
THE SENSUOUS COUPLE, Robert Chartham	$1.50
WHAT TURNS WOMEN ON, Robert Chartham	$1.50
THE SECRET TEAM: THE CIA AND ITS ALLIES, L. Fletcher Prouty	$1.95
THE ANDERSON PAPERS, Jack Anderson	$1.75
SWEET STREET, Jack Olsen	$1.50
THE TEACHINGS OF DON JUAN, Carlos Castaneda	$1.25
ENEMY AT THE GATES, William Craig	$1.95
SUPER MARRIAGE-SUPER SEX, H. Freedman	$1.50
REVOLUTIONARY SUICIDE, Huey Newton	$1.95
LONG SUMMER DAY, R. F. Delderfield	$1.50
BACK TO THE TOP OF THE WORLD, Hans Ruesch	$1.50
THE IPCRESS FILE, Len Deighton	$1.50
CITY POLICE, Jonathan Rubinstein	$1.95
POST OF HONOR, R. F. Delderfield	$1.50
THE UFO EXPERIENCE, J. Allen Hynek	$1.50

At your local bookstore, or

To order by mail, send price of book(s) plus 25¢ per order for handling to Ballantine Cash Sales, P.O. Box 505, Westminster, Maryland 21157. Please allow three weeks for delivery.